Fleur Blüm is a Melbourne-based writer, performer, and musician.

Her blog can be found at https://fleurblum.com/blog

Also by Fleur Blüm:

Sophie's Path: A choose your own romance adventure
Discovering the Franklins
My Mother's Secret

First edition 2021

Copyright © 2021 Fleur Blüm
ISBN 978-0-6483654-3-3

Editor: Annie Seaton
Cover Design: Charmaine Ross

Published by Fleur Blüm, Melbourne, Australia

Singular Focus

Fleur Blüm

To all the kick-ass women who have been through some stuff—we are more than the sum of our wounds.

Chapter 1

Freya hated birthdays. She woke on Thursday, the first of February, a morning that dawned bright and warm, hopeful she would make it through her twenty-eighth birthday without anyone remembering. Not because she feared growing old, or disliked presents, but because being sung to over a birthday cake filled her with dread.

She was confident no-one at work knew. Her Facebook profile was set to not remind people. Looking at the off-white paint of her bedroom ceiling, she smiled a half-smile.

She'd lived in Melbourne all her life and had her job a little over three years. The other staff were pleasant enough, her work as a financial planner was varied and challenging but not so difficult as to stress her out. Freya had pretty much got her life to a place where she was happy.

The clock showed two minutes to seven. It gave her a sense of quiet satisfaction to know her body clock was so well attuned to her routine that she woke before her alarm. She waited the two minutes until her alarm sounded before switching it off. She flung off the sheet, stood up and stretched her arms up over her head before drawing back the long red velvet curtains.

Freya had few possessions, but some things were important; like good block-out blinds; having them in deep, blood red velvet delivered a naughty thrill whenever she thought of how much she'd paid for them.

Train to work, drop handbag at desk, put lunch in fridge, make coffee; delightfully normal. She breathed a sigh of relief when there had been nothing on her desk, no card or streamers, to evidence someone had remembered her birthday.

Freya liked to arrive a little early. Not so early the company would be making money from her, she wasn't that keen on the job, but early enough if there were any delays she would still be there on time without getting stressed. She disliked high stress situations and, although she wouldn't admit it to anyone, thought of herself as nice and boring.

The morning passed quickly and without incident. She ate her salad sandwich in the lunchroom with a few other people from her floor, as always at quarter to one, and then went for a stroll around the block. Her office was on the tenth floor of a tower block in the CBD. Sometimes if Freya felt particularly energetic, she would take the stairs instead of the lift, but today was her birthday, it was not for worrying about calories and counting steps.

Sitting in her air-conditioned office Freya had forgotten how hot the Australian summer sun was. Lifting her hand to shade her eyes she blinked several times trying to adjust to the harsh light.

Singular Focus

Phone, check, wallet, check, but no sun-glasses. Stepping into the stream of pedestrian traffic she ambled down the hill toward Southern Cross train station.

'Freya!'

She turned, and people behind her frowned and muttered as she stopped. Eva, her best friend was walking towards her. Shortish, prettyish, slim, brunette; Eva was wholly unremarkable. To counterbalance this, she dressed in loud colours. Freya would never have the confidence to wear colours or patterns like Eva did. Her pants were fluorescent yellow and were teamed with an aqua and orange paisley patterned shirt, her shoes were red, pointy-toed stilettos.

'I was dropping in to surprise you!' Eva said, her swayed behind her where it was hair pulled into a severe ponytail.

'What for?'

'Your birthday, dummy.'

'Ah.' Freya had known it was coming; even after seven years of friendship, seven birthdays where she had made it very clear she didn't want to celebrate, her friend insisted on reminding her.

'I know you don't like people to make a fuss, so I came to shout you a cupcake. Out of the office, so no one would know.' Eva winked.

'Sorry, I've been on edge today. I don't want the office to sing to me.'

'I know darling, you told me. I don't understand why you hate it so much, but I guess that's why we're besties.'

'Pardon?'

'We respect our differences without really understanding them.'

Freya laughed. 'I guess that's true. This outfit is—it's very you.'

'I know. My dad bought me the shirt, and I felt I needed some extreme pants to draw focus away from it.' Eva's father was Indian, her mother, Australian, and her smooth, honey-coloured skin made every colour look vibrant.

Foot traffic had started to flow around them. 'Bakery then?' Freya said.

Eva slipped her hand into the crook of Freya's elbow. At six feet, she stood taller than most women, and a lot of men. She never wore heels; they weren't her style. Instead masculine -style tailored slacks in black or grey and a nice shirt, suited her slim figure.

Beside her Eva was chattering about something her sister had done. Eva was one of nine children, six girls. Even now Freya struggled to keep track of which sister was which.

The bakery was a single-fronted shop in a Victorian style building. It had opened six months ago and always had a queue. The owners were a French couple, both men, who overplayed their accents. Their speciality was a cronut—a croissant and doughnut hybrid.

Singular Focus

Freya looked at the neat lines of cronuts in the window and her gaze stopped on one iced in baby blue with silver sprinkles.

'Nordic Winter,' she said, reading the sign.

Eva stopped her monologue and looked at her. 'You want that one?'

'Blueberry icing with a subtle elderflower cream.'

'Elderflower? Sounds awful, but you like that sort of thing.'

'I do.'

Why they would have one called *Nordic Winter* in February was beyond Freya's comprehension. With only one left, she hoped it wouldn't be gone by the time they got to the head of the line.

Eva insisted on paying, and given this was her one birthday gesture, Freya didn't try to stop her.

'Sit with me and eat your gross cronut,' Eva said once they were outside the tiny bakery. She pointed to a large tree in the footpath surrounded by a hard green metal bench.

Freya looked at her watch, she'd been away from her desk longer than the allotted half hour break, but it was her birthday after all.

They sat side by side, there wasn't much room, but the lunch time rush had died down a little. Freya pulled her cronut out of the pink box and looked at it. From experience, the difficulty was eating them without making a spectacle of yourself. They were an inch and a half thick, made from flaky croissant pastry, covered in crystallised sugar, icing and sprinkles and filled with custard or jam.

'Cheers,' Freya said. She bumped her cronut against Eva's, a bright pink monstrosity called *Candy Crush*.

She took a bite and sweet, floral goodness hit her tongue. As she chewed, she started to feel light-headed. She took another bite; this one had a lot more custard cream in it and the elderflower flavour was overpowering. Her mouth wasn't responding properly. Time slowed down. She looked down on herself from above.

Freya's hand holding the cronut fell onto her lap excruciatingly slowly. Custard and baby blue icing smeared onto her grey slacks.

They're dry-clean only. Her mind hovered above her body. Eva turned, in slow motion, her mouth moved but she couldn't hear anything. Her body below slumped back against the tree, her eyes glazed and staring straight up.

With the silence came a sense of calm. Overhead, a raven flew, its cry tearing through the thick silence. The raven folded its wings into its body and dived towards Freya's limp form.

What are you doing?

The raven's sharp beak shone in the unforgiving midday sun, then the bird pecked out her right eye. Freya's floating self was fascinated but not concerned.

It squawked again and looked at Freya's mind-self. Everything around her faded from view and instead of the sunny street, a rolling thunderhead of clouds appeared coming towards her. Purple-black and portentous, lightning flickered in silence.

She blinked, as though waking from a dream, and she was back in her body. There was a thick warm stream running down her cheek.

'Freya.' Eva was screaming. 'Fuck, fuck, fuck. Are you okay?'

She put her hand up to her eye and realised the out of body experience had not been a dream. Her hand was covered in dark red blood.

'I don't feel well,' she said.

'Don't worry, I'm calling an ambulance.' Eva pulled out her phone and started talking urgently into it.

The sense of calm and silence lingered a little, as though Eva was very far away. The blood on her face was bad but didn't feel scared. This was supposed to happen.

Chapter 2

Freya was very groggy when she woke. Her eyes seemed to be glued shut, she struggled to open them. A warm hand landed on her forearm.

'We've bandaged your eyes. Sorry about that,' said a gravelly male voice next to her. 'It's good to see you've come around. I'm Greg, I'm a nurse.'

Freya raised her hands to her head and ran her fingers over the bandage wound around her whole head. 'What's going on?'

'You're in the Royal Melbourne Hospital.'

The rolling thunderhead flashed through her mind's eye, then she remembered the raven.

'Your friend called the ambulance. She was very worried about you, you didn't respond to her or the ambulance officers. We had to take you to surgery.' Greg hesitated. 'We weren't able to save your right eye, I'm sorry.'

'The raven was real?' Freya asked. It was eerie speaking to a man she'd never seen. She had an image of what a hospital looked like in her mind, but not being able to see it for herself made her anxious. She tried to pull up the bandage on her left eye.

A warm hand stopped her. 'Let me, I think we can probably rearrange your dressing so you can see a bit.'

Freya let her hands drop into her lap as he rearranged her bandages.

'Your eye will take a while to adjust to the light, so take it gently.'

Freya saw the light through her eyelid first and blinked her left eye open trying to take in what was around her; a thin hospital bed, a baby blue cotton blanket, grey curtains drawn around her bed. Greg was tall, thin, and bearded. He wore a dark green scrubs and a lanyard with a thousand things dangling off it around his neck. Above the curtain was dark, perhaps it was night. Even though it was not very bright, she had to close her eye almost immediately.

'Give it a couple of minutes,' Greg said.

'What time is it?'

'It's about five a.m. They had you in surgery for a while and we kept you sedated afterwards so the wound had some time to settle afterwards.'

'I don't feel so good.' Freya was suddenly aware of a dizziness and urge to vomit.

'That's the anaesthetic. It's not kind on the tummy. I have a bag here if you need it.'

She opened her eye a crack, a white plastic bag with a white plastic rim sat on the table in front of her. She closed her eye and lay back.

'Try to rest. We'll make sure you're looked after. You'll need to stay a few days for observation, to make sure the wound heals properly, and you don't develop an infection. Once it's all healed, in a couple of months, you can think about prosthetics.'

'Thank you.'

Greg pulled the curtain open and back into place, then his footsteps receded. She must be dreaming. It was very realistic though. Usually dreams had weird broken logic that give them away.

I suppose the raven thing would count. But it still didn't feel like a dream. After several minutes of pretending it was a dream Freya opened her eye again. The hospital was still there, she was lying on several crinkly pillows, she heard the steady beep of machines, footsteps down the hallway, someone snoring. The urge to vomit had passed, but she felt dizzy if she moved her head too fast.

The scene from yesterday kept playing over and over in her mind's eye, interspersed with the blackening thunderhead. Even when she had her eye open the images in her mind were there in front of her.

With her eye closed the images were so vivid she wondered if she was hallucinating. Perhaps it was the medication, but it didn't explain the out of body experience.

*

'Freya? Are you awake?' Eva said.

Freya must have fallen asleep, as the curtain had been drawn back and the room was filled with light.

'How are you feeling?'

'I don't know.' She was less dizzy than last night. 'What happened?'

'How much of it do you remember?'

'All of it, I wanted to know what you remember.'

'We were eating cronuts, I was banging on about something, can't remember what, you had one bite of yours and spaced out and then a massive black bird attacked you. It all happened so fast; I was frozen for a minute. By the time I tried to shoo it away, it was too late.'

'Too late?'

'Your eye.'

'Oh.' She didn't want to say it aloud.

'Then I was freaking out and you were still in your daze, so I called the ambulance and rode with you here and then you went into surgery.'

'Where did the bird come from?' Freya wondered aloud.

'I didn't see it before it was… on you, and then it flew away, and I didn't see where it went. It was so awful.'

Freya took her friend's hand. 'You couldn't have done anything.' As she said it, she knew it was true.

'On your birthday too.'

'At least no-one tried to sing at me,' Freya said. She smiled a little, hoping it would cheer her friend.

'Oh, babe.' Eva reached over and hugged her, the movement was sudden and her head spun and her eye socket throbbed.

'Gentle.'

'Sorry, sorry.' Eva pulled away and wiped her eyes on her sleeve. She was wearing blue jean shorts, a grey long sleeved T-shirt and no makeup. She'd never looked so frazzled.

'Did you sleep?'

'Not really.'

'You look terrible.'

'I know. I stayed in emergency till they brought you out of surgery then I went home, but I couldn't sleep.'

'I'm sorry you were worried. I'm fine, promise.'

'I called your work and let them know you wouldn't be in for a while.'

'Thanks.' Work seemed far away, so much had happened since she left the office yesterday. 'Could you go to my office and get my handbag? I didn't bring it with me.'

'Of course, babe. Anything else you need?'

'My keys are in my bag. Can you go to my place and get me some underwear and maybe some pyjamas, and undies or something?'

'Sure. Do you want your laptop or a book or anything?'

Freya looked around; a TV hung on a long metal arm in her line of sight. 'There are a couple of books on my bedside table, bring all of them.'

'Having lots of books on the go at once, don't you feel unfaithful?'

Freya laughed. 'Only you could think a book would be jealous reading another book.'

Singular Focus

It felt good to laugh. As her smile faded, Freya's vision was obscured by an image of Eva lying on her bed at home, she was on top of the covers, fully dressed, staring at the ceiling. Her eyes had lost their sparkle. Time slowed down, Freya looked down on the tableau from above. Her friend wasn't dead, but worse than dead—she was gone.

As suddenly as the vision had come, it faded again, and she was looking at her friend in the flesh.

'Are you sure you're okay?' Freya asked.

'Yes, silly. I'm not the one in hospital.'

'Of course.'

'Now I know you're okay, I'll head off. I took the day off work, but I think I might go home for a nap after I've got your things.'

'You look like you could do with the rest.' Freya squeezed her friend's hand. Her dark brown eyes were still sparkling, if a little less than usual. She hoped it was tiredness.

When Eva left, she leaned back on her pillows and tried not to cry. The vision was horrible, and the only way she could cope was to remind herself it couldn't be real. She flicked on the TV using the remote control attached to a nurse call button on her bed.

Four channels had morning shows, and one had Greek news without subtitles, even the lifestyle channels were boring. She switched to ABC and watched as a small cartoon pig went on an adventure under the sea.

Chapter 3

On her third day in the hospital, Greg came in with a doctor to visit Freya.

'Well, we're quite happy with how you're coming along,' the doctor said, smiling at her from beside her bed.

'Can I go home soon?'

'Yes, we'll release you later today. You will need to see an occupational therapist and make a few follow-up appointments with the surgical team and the O. T. We also have a few other services the O. T. might refer you on to, like counselling or social workers.'

'What do I need an occupational therapist for? Or a counsellor?' Freya was itching to leave the ward. Eva had dropped off a stack of books, some pyjamas and clean clothes. She picked at a ball of fluff on the blue cotton blanket.

'You've had a traumatic injury, Freya,' he said. She hated when people used her name, it sounded patronising.

'I'm aware.'

'You may not be aware however losing an eye will affect quite a few functions, primarily depth perception, and you may need to make adjustments in the way you do things; walking, driving, parking will be especially difficult. They can show you how to make this sort of thing easier now you have monocular vision.'

Freya sighed. 'Anything else?'

'You'll need to monitor the wound, I know you haven't seen it yet, Greg will change your dressing now and show you how to change it yourself at home.'

A ball of dread formed in the pit of Freya's stomach. Since she'd been in the hospital, she had avoided looking at herself in the mirror. She swallowed.

'It's not especially pretty right now, but not the worst I've seen. I'm confident it will heal up nicely.'

'Gee, thanks.'

The doctor nodded and left her bedside, pulling the curtain around her for privacy.

'Sorry, we don't want you to have unrealistic expectations.'

'I suppose that's fair.' Freya clenched her teeth.

'You may feel some discomfort as I take the dressing off,' Greg said.

This was an understatement. As soon as the nurse started to unwind the bandage the flesh where her right eye had been started to throb. She sucked her breath in sharply through her teeth.

'I'll try to be gentle,' her said. His gravelly voice should have been comforting but Freya couldn't stop her mind filling with images of eye injuries from movies.

The last layer of dressing was a gauze pad taped to her cheek and forehead. Greg peeled off the pad and handed her a mirror.

It was not as bloody as expected. Her eye was puffy, purple, and swollen shut. Several large cuts ran across her eyelid and upper cheek.

'We've put tape on the cuts, the socket wasn't too damaged, but you won't be able to open the lid for a while with the swelling.'

'What will be under there when I can open it?' Freya wasn't sure she wanted to know the answer.

'Nothing. You know what it looks like when you pull your eyelid down? Fleshy pink?'

'Oh.'

'It will be more recessed than the other eye, without the eyeball to give it volume. In time, we can fit you with a prosthetic. Until then you can wear a patch if it makes you feel more comfortable.'

Freya stared at herself. She raised her hand to her wound.

'Best not to touch it,' Greg said, gently pushing her hand back into her lap.

He showed her which dressings to use, and the ointment she should put onto the cuts. And then he put on fresh gauze and wound her head in a new bandage.

'The main thing is to make sure you don't develop an infection in those cuts. Don't pick at the tape or scabs, let them fall off naturally. Try not to scratch it and keep it clean and dry.'

'Whatever you say.' Freya wanted to hide. Despite her face not being as hideous as she had expected it was still frightening. She would have scars; her pale skin didn't recover well at the best of times and the face was delicate. As she stared back at herself, her one remaining brown eye looked sad.

What happens if I cry? Would her right eye still cry? Would it damage the dressing? She took a deep shaky breath and realised Greg was still talking to her.

'Did I lose you?' he asked.

'Sorry.' Her voice hitched.

'It's a lot to process. You've done very well, and in case you're wondering, crying is unlikely to have a negative effect on the healing process but try to avoid it if you can.'

Freya let out a sob and tried to cover it with a cough. He'd known exactly what she was thinking.

'These sorts of injuries can be very emotional. You're not the first to feel overwhelmed. Try not to be too hard on yourself.' He put his hand on her shoulder, it was warm and the weight of it gave her strength. She sat up a little straighter, sniffed and calmed herself.

'Thank you.'

'I'll leave you, Jacob will be by in a little while to talk about your rehab.' Greg took his hand from her shoulder and her strength went with it. The curtains remained drawn around her bed and she was alone with her thoughts.

As hard as she tried, she couldn't stop tears from coming. When she scrunched her face up the cuts stung and throbbed. She tried to cry calmly; the tears falling from her left eye onto the hospital pillow.

After a while she decided she'd had enough of this self-pity. She sat up in the bed, adjusted it so she could reach the table with her computer. She would try to get back to her old life.

She could return to work as soon as she felt up to it but had been advised to take it easy. She accessed her work emails and started to scroll through the fifty or so she'd received in the days since she'd last been in the office.

Someone was not as tight-lipped as they should have been; many of the emails were commiserations and get well soon messages. She didn't think Eva would had told anyone. It was much, much worse than having Happy Birthday sung to her.

She closed her eyes and counted to ten, getting angry wouldn't help anything in this situation. As she turned back to reading her mind's eye filled with the image of the thunderhead again, but this time the rain had broken—the grey-black clouds streaked down to the horizon.

Freya blinked and the vision disappeared. She shook her head. At least it wasn't Eva on the bed again, not dead but also not alive.

It must be the trauma.

She made her way through her emails, moving the get well soon ones into a folder without reading them. What was done was done and feeling sorry for herself wouldn't lead to anything helpful.

About an hour later, as she was reading through a financial industry newsletter, she heard the curtain slide open beside her bed. She was startled, the curtain had opened on her right side.

I'll have to get used to that. She tried to compose herself.

'Hello, didn't mean to scare you,' the man said.

'You didn't,' Freya lied. He was tall, broad shouldered and muscular. His short-cropped hair and stubble-covered chin were salt and pepper, although he wasn't much older than her. He gazed at her with hard ice-blue eyes and seemed to be taking her in.

'So,' he said finally. 'You've been in the wars.'

'Mmm,' she said.

'You probably hate that expression. It works well for children.'

Freya frowned. 'I'd like to get home, so if we could keep the chat to a minimum.'

'Of course. My name is Jacob, I'm an occupational therapist. I specialise in head injuries. I'm here to make sure you're okay to go home.'

'I'm fine.'

'Sure. Do you live alone?' he asked.

'Yes, I have a bedsit apartment. Nothing fancy, I value my solitude.'

'I hear you. Share housing can be trying.' He smiled, lifting the severity from his demeanour, and she found herself smiling back.

She looked away.

Don't flirt with the OT, even if he is dishy.

'You'll notice a few things are different. We'll have to do a driving assessment before I can sign off on letting you back behind the wheel on your own. Most other things will be fine, although you'll misjudge distances for a while.'

'Great.' *Stuck with public transport or taxis.*

'Recovery is generally about nine months. You'll be able to compensate for most things, but it will take time, try not to get frustrated with yourself.'

They talked a little more about the sort of therapy he would be doing, and they made appointments once a week for the next month.

'I'll let the nursing staff know you're right to go home now. Remember to take it easy. Deal?' He held out his hand to shake hers.

'Deal.' When their hands touched, she smiled again. Her cheeks felt hot and she let go abruptly. He pulled the curtain closed behind him and Freya was able to calm herself without his hard, blue eyes watching her.

Chapter 4

Freya took a taxi home after the nurses had finished the paperwork, late on a Monday afternoon. It was quiet in her tiny apartment after days of beeping, snoring, mumbling and squeaky nurse shoes. Her bedsit was small; one large, white-walled room with a tiny kitchenette along one wall, and a bathroom behind it. The queen-sized bed ran along the long wall next to the door, and she had a chest of drawers and an armchair. A large glass bi-fold door opened out onto a tiny balcony where she kept potted shrivelled, brittle herbs. It wasn't much, but she had called it home for four years.

Sometimes she heard the people next door pottering about, one of her upstairs neighbours wore stiletto shoes inside, so she could always tell when she was home. She pulled open the balcony door and let out the stuffy air accumulated while she'd been away.

At least nothing seems to have gone off. She sat down heavily in the armchair and closed her eyes. It was disorientating navigating her familiar apartment with one eye; the room simultaneously small and bigger than it used to be. In the hospital, when she'd walked to the bathroom or up and down the ward out of boredom, she'd had to concentrate on the unfamiliar surroundings and avoid other people, but here, where she knew the width of the apartment by feel it was much harder.

Greg had suggested she take some more time off, but Freya had refused. The longer she was away, the more she'd feel like a cripple. She'd read all the books Eva had brought and had watched more reality TV than she had in years and was both bored and exhausted.

She picked up her phone and stared at it. No notifications. A few people at work had checked in to see how she was after abruptly not returning from lunch but she hadn't told them the whole story yet. Eva had been true to her word and hadn't told a soul. Freya hadn't even told her parents what had happened yet.

Freya answered the phone to her mother's voice.

'Hello?'

'Hi, Mum.'

'I've just left work. Can I give you a ring back later?' her mother said. Freya could hear her car in the background, she must have been using the hands-free.

'Um, sure, I need to tell you something, but it's better if you're not driving.'

'Are you alright love? You sound funny.'

'Yeah. Give me a ring when you get home.'

'Alright then. Bye.' The line went dead.

Freya wasn't ready to tell anyone else the story and didn't want to sit in silence until her mother called back, so called Eva.

'Hey, babe. You home?' Eva said.

Freya had texted to say she was being discharged.
'Yep.'
'You alright?'
'Uh.'
'Of course not, silly question. What are you doing?'
'Nothing. Sitting.'
'You can't just sit. Have you got any food? Have you called your parents?'
'No and yes, but Mum was driving.'
'Right. I'm coming over now, I'll bring you dinner. I can't stay long, but it might keep your mind off things till your mum calls back.'

Freya stayed on the phone to Eva as she made her way to the apartment. Her friend brought burgers, chips and milkshakes with her from the place up the road. Not what Freya would have chosen, but it was what Eva wanted.

Freya was quiet while they ate, Eva talked about her family, her friends, work. It was hard not to think about her lying deathlike, on the bed. She shivered as she tried to push it away.

'Someone walk across your grave?' Eva asked.
'Something like that.'
'Are you sure you're alright? You look pale.'

Freya adjusted her position on the bed, Eva had taken the armchair. The remains of their meal sat in a pile on the floor, the apartment wasn't designed for company.
'I've been having, like, hallucinations. Maybe waking dreams. It's nothing really, I'm sure it's some side effect from the accident.'

'Did you tell the doctors?'

'I don't want to bother them.'

Eva frowned. 'It's not bothering them. It's their job. What if you have some weird brain trauma they didn't notice, and you drop dead in two months?'

'I won't.'

'You're not a doctor. You should tell someone.'

'Alright. I'll tell them.' When I next see them, if they haven't gone away.

'And not in three weeks when you have the surgical consult. I want to you call them tomorrow.'

Freya sighed. 'Okay.'

Despite her penchant for gossip and bright colours, Eva was often incredibly insightful. It could be irritating, but Freya knew it was out of concern.

Before Eva could press any further, Freya's phone rang. She looked at the screen it was her mother.

'I'll go. Love you, babe.' Eva picked up her handbag and kissed her friend's cheek before letting herself out of the apartment. Freya took a deep breath and answered the phone.

*

After an hour on the phone to her mother Freya was totally drained. She had been much more upset than Freya had expected. Her mother, Astrid, could be quite self-involved, and dismissive but had been uncharacteristically concerned and wanted to know details about the injury and the recovery. When her mother had finally hung up to answer another call Freya was close to weeping.

As soon as she put down the phone she lay down, fully clothed, on top of the bedclothes and fell asleep. She dreamed of the thunderhead, the mass of clouds rolling towards her. Beneath the clouds the streaking rain blotted out most of the landscape, but it looked like the ocean. Lightning lit up the clouds and zipped down to the ground; she waited for the thunder, but it never came. Her dream, like her hallucinations, was totally, oppressively silent. The dream morphed into a cityscape, standing at the top of Bourke Street, on the steps of Parliament House. She saw several people walking in a daze, one of them sat down on a bench and seemed to give up. His mouth hung open, his eyes glazed. He was gone as Eva had been.

Freya opened her eyes and was startled by the boom of rolling thunder coming in through the open balcony door. She closed the window and shivered; Melbourne's notoriously changeable weather had gone from muggy heat to chilly thunderstorm in a matter of hours. The clock showed a little after midnight.

Her dream left her shaken, she wouldn't fall asleep again easily so pulled out her laptop and trawled through her social media pages. Most of her friends were complaining about the weather and sunburn. Despite her aversion to birthdays, Freya was resentful no one had sent her a message or checked in. She felt forgotten and unimportant. Her circle of friends was small, she had always valued her time alone, but for the first time in years she felt lonely. She clicked away from Facebook and opened Netflix. She would distract herself with a children's film, something with low stakes, preferably animated. Her sleep cycle had been disrupted while she'd been in hospital; the noise and nurses checking on her had disturbed her every couple of hours. She would need to get it back on track if she was going to make it through a workday.

*

Freya took Tuesday off, and Eva texted her to ask if she'd told the doctors about her hallucinations, but she put her off by saying she'd left a message. She had no intention of telling the doctors about the hallucinations. Apart from the fact they were terrifying, they seemed to be the same set of images over and over—Eva on the bed, the oncoming storm, and people glazing over and stopping. Each time she saw them there were small details changed, different faces, but their meaning didn't become any clearer.

Against her preference, Freya took the rest of the week off. Her energy was low, and the medication made her sleepy.

She woke up the following Monday with a splitting headache. The hospital had given her two weeks supply of opioids to manage her pain and she forgotten to take any the night before. She swallowed her tablets and tried to get herself ready for work. She changed her dressing, now only a gauze pad taped to her face.

Singular Focus

When she looked at the wound under her bandage the puffiness was less but the bruises which had been purple were turning various shades of yellow and brown. The bruising had also started to migrate down her face onto her cheeks. She dabbed at it with foundation and concealer; the pain killers had kicked in by then and it was only moderately painful to the touch.

Once she had finished applying her makeup as best she could, Freya took a step back and looked herself over. She looked like death warmed-up, but she didn't want another day alone in her apartment. She needed structure, something to remind her she was still a highly competent financial planner, and not a cripple.

At least I won't be able to see all the faces people make at me on the right-hand side.

The walk to the train station looked different; she noticed small details she'd never seen before, a rosebush with its flowers brown and wilted from the heat, a little white dog barking at her from behind a white metal mesh fence, a small clump of grass growing up between the asphalt and the wooden power pole.

When she stepped into the train a smell of old sweat, floral perfume and banana washed over her. Her stomach clenched and her head throbbed as she shuffled in beside a group of high school kids. She wouldn't have been able to explain it, but the world was more intense than it had been. Harder to block it out and retreat into her mind, and not only because if she did, she was liable to be bombarded with hallucinations.

'Freya, we didn't expect you back so soon,' her boss, Talia, said.

'I got the okay from the doctor. No use sitting around feeling sorry for myself,' she replied. Technically, they had told her she shouldn't come back for another week, and if she was really needed, she could do half days. In her book that meant she was fine.

'Great. And if you need to go home early, say the word, but since you're here—' Talia listed a number of things to be done urgently. One of the things Freya liked about working for Talia was she always had a million things on the go at once. She would never run out of stuff to do but was quite highly strung and drank far too much coffee.

As Talia turned to leave, she patted Freya on the forearm. The touch sent a shiver down her spine and left her arm feeling cold. *At least it wasn't a new hallucination*. Then it hit her; faces flashing before her, all with their mouths hanging open and eyes wide and glazed.

Freya forced herself to get back to the tasks Talia had assigned and pushed the faces out of her mind.

*

Avoiding thinking about what had happened worked as she didn't allow any space for thoughts other than her job. She worked two days solidly before her first appointment with Jacob for her rehabilitation. People in her office stared openly at the gauze pad over her eye for the first couple of hours, then some attempted to hide their looks. She would catch them as they hurried to look away. Some walked past her desk slowly, but at least they weren't asking her about it.

Perhaps the office grapevine had worded them up not to bother her. Talia had not asked, except for her initial query. Freya felt strangely liberated by the fact they were all studiously ignoring her obvious injury, but another part of her felt unseen in her suffering, as though it wasn't really happening.

But it was happening. Her dreams were now filled with silent screaming faces. The thunderhead appeared in her dreams and when she closed her eyes or when she let her concentration slip.

As she walked up the long, white hospital corridor towards the rehab offices for her first rehabilitation appointment, she wondered whether she should mention the visions. It seemed like something she should keep to herself.

It's like hearing voices, there's almost no explanation where this doesn't mean I've lost my mind.

'Hi, Freya, good to see you.' Jacob was seated on a stool in the consultation room. Much like a physiotherapist's office there was a long, slim table in the centre of the room, with foot pedals to lift if up and down, anatomical diagrams on the walls; skeletal system, muscular system, one she assumed was blood vessels and one which looked like the nervous system. In the corner was a sink and an array of bottled liquids and ointments and a thin white laminate desk running along part of the wall where he was sitting.

'Have a seat,' he said, indicating the only other chair in the room. 'It's good to see you're up and about, looks like you're already adjusting well.'

'I'm fine.'

'When are you thinking of heading back to work?' he asked.

'Uhh—'

'You're already working, aren't you?'

'The doctor said it was up to me when I went back to work.'

He sighed, it was only a short, soft sound, almost as though he hadn't done it. 'I understand you're eager to get back to normal, but your normal is different to before.'

'I know.' Freya shuffled in her chair and smoothed the fabric of her grey linen slacks. She had done everything she could to prove to herself nothing had changed.

'We're going to do a few diagnostics today. I have a bunch of tasks designed to push your limits, what I want to assess is the point at which you fail. From there we can develop strategies to get you back to a place where you can function in the world as close as possible to your previous level.'

'I see.' A cold prickle of dread formed in her stomach. Failure was something she avoided at all costs. Throughout school and university, she had pushed

herself to do her best academically, even at the expense
of her social life.

'You're not a failure because you fail these tasks. We
will keep going up to the point where you struggle, to
accurately assess your strengths and weaknesses.'

'I understand.' The air conditioning in the room was
up too high, goose bumps formed on her forearms. She
swallowed and found her mouth had become dry.

'It's also fine to cry. I've been doing this a long time
and I have never thought less of someone because
they've cried. You've been through a significant trauma.
It will be hard.' He put his hand on her shoulder and she
pushed down an urge start sobbing right then. A hot,
shame-filled tear rolled down her cheek.

'Let's get on then.'

The appointment lasted a little over an hour. Jacob
tested her balance, watched her walk and run, he tested
her field of vision and her depth perception. Freya was
shocked how quickly he had found her weaknesses.

'You've done really well, Freya. It probably doesn't
feel like it, but it has been a very successful session.'

'You're right, it doesn't feel like it.'

'This is the first step on a journey towards recovery.
We must find your limits before we can push them.'

She made a non-committal noise she hoped he would
take as agreement. She glanced at her watch, she had
hoped to return to work after the appointment, but it was
four-thirty.

'I'll see you at the same time next week. Try to take it easy, I know it's unnatural for you.'

'I'll make sure I don't overdo it.' Even though it's exhaustion and work getting her through this.

'Do you have any other symptoms, anything we haven't covered?' Jacob was already standing at the door of the office, holding it open for her.

'No, nothing really.'

'Okay, let me know if anything changes and I'll see you next week.'

Did he know she was holding back?

Chapter 5

Over the next few weeks, Freya got into a new routine. She went to work, she came home, she saw Jacob on Thursday afternoons. The weather was still warm during the day, but it the days were becoming shorter

Her appointment with the surgeon was six weeks after her discharge from hospital.

'The wound has healed nicely, you can get rid of the dressings now,' the doctor said, peeling off the examination gloves, and rubbing sanitiser over his hands. His consultation room was in an office building not far from the hospital. The furniture was all beige and steel, the walls were tastefully wallpapered in a textured weave pattern in a complementary tone of beige. Freya looked at her face in the mirror, the bruising had mostly gone, and the swelling almost disappeared. Her scars were still purple and obvious, and the sight of her eyeless socket was shocking.

'I can't walk around like this,' she said.

'Medically speaking you can, but I understand you may not want to. We'll be able to give you a prosthetic down the track, but for the moment maybe a patch would be better. I'll grab one for you.'

'Thanks.' She turned back to her reflection.

This is what I look like now. She touched the lower eyelid, the scars ran across her eyebrow and eyelids, the raven had certainly done a good job of slashing her up; her scars met in the middle like a gruesome star.

The doctor came back into the room and Freya jumped back from the mirror, startled.

'The scarring will settle down and become less prominent over time. And you'll get used to the way it looks.'

'Yes, of course.' Freya turned away from the mirror. He was holding a black, satin-look eye patch in one hand.

'I found one. Let's pop it on, shall we?'

The patch was on an adjustable elasticised string which she pulled over her hair and it sat in place over the right eye socket. She looked at herself, scarring was visible around the edges of the black fabric, but overall, less conspicuous even than the gauze pad.

'If I were a man, I'm sure this would make me rugged and irresistible.' She wanted the consultation to be over. 'Can I take this with me?'

'Yes, that's yours. We will need to see you again in three months. Was there anything else?'

Like intense, repeated hallucinations? 'No, it's all as well as can be expected.'

He walked her to the reception desk before calling in the next patient, a woman whose dressing covered most of the left side of her face and who looked to be a great deal of pain.

Singular Focus

The receptionist, a young man with shaggy blond hair, looked up at her and smiled crookedly. 'Very dashing.'

'Uh, thanks.' Freya's cheeks heated. She'd spent her life trying to go unnoticed. The incident had destroyed her ability to blend anonymously into a crowd. Not that she liked crowds much these days, the hallucinations were harder to avoid when she was surrounded by people.

*

Freya's office closed for four days over Easter. This year it fell in the middle of April and it would be the first time since she came home from the hospital she'd had more than two days away from the office in a row. She had managed to fill her weekends with research, but she didn't think she could do it for an entire four-day weekend.

I need something to do at Easter, she texted to Eva. Freya hadn't seen much of her the last couple of weeks.

I'm going to Wilson's prom with Derek. I'd invite you, but it's just the two of us, she texted back. It was unlike Eva to be so quiet for weeks on end.

Have I done something to piss you off? Freya wrote back. She didn't expect an answer, but she needed to say it.

Her phone started ringing in her hand, Eva was calling. 'Hi.'

'Hi,' Eva said.

Freya waited.

'You haven't done anything. I promise.'

'What then?'

'I feel bad.'

'About what?'

'Your eye. It's my fault.'

Freya frowned. 'I don't understand.'

'It was my idea to get cronuts. If it hadn't been for me, you wouldn't have been there, and that crazy bird wouldn't have attacked you.'

'Oh.' Freya chewed on her bottom lip for a moment. 'I don't think you can take the blame for that.'

'I'm glad you think so, but it upsets me. When I look at you all I think about is that moment.'

'So, I lose my best friend as well?'

'No, I'm not gone.'

'It feels like it.' Freya closed her eyes and tried to figure out a way to demonstrate she wasn't at fault, but she came up empty. 'I need you, Eva. Work through whatever shitty guilt stuff you have and go back to being my friend. I can't lose you too.'

Eva's breath came in shallow little gasps.

'Don't cry, hun, I'm not angry. I miss you. It's lonely—people stare at me in the street. They've stopped mostly at work, but I still catch them. I need my friend.'

'I'm so sorry, hun. You know everything with you and getting caught up with Derek. I've been a bad friend. I'll make it up to you.'

'But you're still busy at Easter?'

'It's a romantic weekend. It would be super awkward. Don't your family do something?'

'Yeah, I'll sort something out. Don't worry about it.' Freya rubbed her left eyebrow; a frustration gesture she'd recently developed since she couldn't push on her eyes the way she used to.

'I gotta go, love you.' Eva hung up.

Freya wanted to cry. Her best friend was avoiding her. She understood, but it still hurt. The walls of her small apartment pressed in on her. Where she used to find comfort in solitude, she was now surrounded by reminders of how alone she was. She could call her family; they weren't so bad really. Her older brother had moved back in with their mum in Doncaster, a suburb caught in a public transport vacuum in Eastern Melbourne. If she wanted to visit either of them, she would have to drive, or spend hours on a bus. Her father had moved to Queensland with his new wife a few years ago, his third marriage, despite having never married her mother.

She had been cleared to drive, however she wasn't confident yet. It seemed absurd she be allowed to drive with one eye. *Maybe I should sell the car, I could rent out the car space to a neighbour and get a bit of extra income.* It would probably be cheaper even with taking taxis or ride shares when she needed them.

It was time to accept things would always be different. Not to mention the hallucinations hadn't abated. She'd weaned herself off the painkillers, although there had been a couple of days of crankiness and irritability, perhaps mild withdrawal. Her eye socket didn't hurt anymore, although she was more prone to headaches. Freya wore the eyepatch unless she was home, alone. The look of horror that flitted across her neighbour's face the one time she forgot to put it on to open the door was enough to remind Freya how shocking her appearance was. A prosthetic eye would be better, she could leave in when she was at home, but they were expensive, and the surgeon hadn't given her the okay to have one fitted yet.

She finished the glass of red wine and decided to turn in for the night. Her plans for Easter would have to wait till tomorrow. Since it was the next weekend, it might be too late to arrange something fun.

She brushed her teeth and climbed into bed. The winter weight doona was still in the cupboard, but nights were starting to get cold. She snuggled down and stared at the slightly paler darkness around the curtains.

This time of night, between waking and sleep, was when she was most likely to see visions. Tonight, it was the faces again, people she'd seen in the past who stopped what they were doing. They didn't change much, surely that meant something. If she knew who to ask, without them thinking she was crazy, she might be inclined to look into it.

*

The next morning, Sunday, she took herself out for brunch. She was sick of moping around at home and the place around the corner always did great pesto eggs. Her head ached and she took a couple of paracetamols, had a shower and went out. She wore skinny fit black jeans, a plain dark grey T-shirt, black cardigan and her pale grey woollen over-coat. It probably wouldn't be cold enough to wear the coat, but she never liked to be unprepared for Melbourne's changeable weather.

The sun outside was bright but did little to take the edge of the morning chill. The café was a five-minute walk away, the owners knew her, and the staff were friendly. They stopped staring at her patch quickly, and she was thankful other regular customers had too.

She sat at a table by the front window, facing out to watch the world going by as she ate her breakfast and read the paper.

'Three more hospitalised with mystery illness.' The headline caught her attention. She'd never been one to follow the news. It had always seemed quite depressing.

'Doctors are still perplexed by patients presenting with apparent total paralysis. The Royal Melbourne Hospital now has seven vegetative-state patients, and no link or cause for the condition has been found. Investigations are continuing into the phenomenon; however doctors are confident it is not contagious and hopeful the issue is isolated.'

Freya scanned the paper for more, but there was nothing. She pulled out her phone and searched online. She found several news sites with the same content and a couple of twitter conversations about the incompetence of the hospital staff.

The skin under the eyepatch prickled and itched. This seemed important, although she couldn't put her finger on why.

The waiter brought her breakfast and she folded the newspaper away.

'Freya?' a familiar male voice asked from behind her. She turned towards the speaker and saw it was the O.T., Jacob.

'Hi.'

'I didn't know you lived around here,' he said. He looked much more handsome than she remembered. It had only been a couple of weeks since she'd seen him, but the deep red turtleneck sweater he was wearing clung to his chest in a way she found very distracting.

'Yeah, this is one of my regular spots.'

He looked around; the café was packed. His eyes moved from the empty bench seat opposite her to the packed room and back.

'Would you care to sit with me? It's a busy time,' she said.

'Are you sure? I wouldn't want to impose.' He moved towards the empty seat.

'It's fine, if you don't mind me eating.'

'Of course, of course.'

He took his seat and ordered a latte and big breakfast plate from the waiter who appeared next to her shoulder.

'How's everything coming along?' he asked.

'We don't need to talk about that, you're not at work now.'

'I meant generally. But if you don't want to talk, we can read the paper.' He frowned. She'd offended him.

'I'm sorry. I don't like being treated like there's something wrong with me.'

'Understandable. I was only making conversation.'

She smiled, it felt awkward sitting with him, he was very attractive and there was no reason not to enjoy a quiet meal with a handsome man. She hadn't thought about dating since the incident but now he was here, she could do worse.

'How's work?' she asked.

'You know, same old stuff.'

Her gaze fell on the folded newspaper sitting next to Jacob on the bench seat. 'Do you know anything about those patients? The ones in a coma?'

'They're not in a coma, not properly, as far as I've heard.'

'Really?' she took a scoop of her eggs and waited for him to go on.

'They seem to be conscious, but they don't respond. Can't get them to do anything, eat, drink, talk, nothing.'

'No one has any idea what's happened to them?'

'No. Can't even figure out what's wrong. Tests all show up as normal, reflexes, brain scans, the works. It's like they don't want to respond.'

'Sounds bizarre.'

Jacob's breakfast arrived and Freya was jealous, her meal seemed small and boring in comparison. 'Yeah.

There's been a new case every day for a while and they're all the same. I hope they figure something out.'

'What will happen if they don't improve?'

'Well.' Jacob loaded his fork with tomato, egg, sausage and put it in his mouth. He chewed madly for a moment. 'They can be kept alive, glucose drips, stomach tubes and what not, but their muscles and bones will waste from disuse, if they stay immobile for an extended period of time they'll get bedsores, possibly pneumonia, they could die but they could also keep hanging on. No one's ever seen anything like it.'

Freya silently contemplated what he had told her. It sounded like a terrible thing to happen to a person, and their poor families—loved ones stuck with no explanation and no treatment.

'I've been having weird dreams,' she blurted out. She couldn't have explained why she said it except the wakeful, paralysed people reminded her of the faces she kept seeing.

'Really? Is that new for you?'

'Since the accident really. Not just weird, recurring. The same stuff over and over.' *Maybe if I tell him they're dreams it will seem less weird.*

'Trauma can do funny things to the brain. You wanna talk about it?'

'Kind of. I have dreams where people are limp and lifeless but their eyes are open. Like they're asleep but not. It sounds like that condition you were talking about.'

'Maybe you're psychic now.' He laughed.

'Maybe.' At least he didn't say I was crazy.

'Always the same dream?'

'There are a few, but the same ones over and over.'

'Same ones for a couple of months then? Do you have other dreams or only these ones?'

She thought about it for a moment. 'No, only those.' All her dreams and some of her waking moments had been taken over by these same few visions. She might have noticed before if she hadn't been so caught up in pretending it wasn't happening.

'I mean I've never heard of an injury like yours causing dreams, but the human brain is complicated. It should settle down I'm sure.'

'I hope so,' she said. She picked up the cup containing the last mouthful of her café latte and then put it back down. It was cold and she didn't want it. 'I'm getting another coffee, will you have one?'

'Sure, I'm not in any hurry.' He smiled at her and she was struck by how much his smile changed him. It was clichéd but she thought there was a light in his eyes, perhaps even a twinkle, but only when he smiled.

They chatted amiably, occasionally they lapsed into a comfortable silence and Freya watched the other patrons enjoying a quiet morning.

'This was really nice,' he said when they had finished their second coffees.

'Yes.' *Can I ask him to do it again?* 'Do you—' she started to speak as he started to say something.

'You go first,' she said.

'I was going to say; I would be glad to do this again, you know, if it's not too weird given where we met.'

'I was going to say the same. Most of my friends look at me differently since, you know.'

'A lot of people who come to see me have facial disfigurements—'

She winced at the phrase.

'Sorry. In my line of work I've become used to a wider variety of faces. Your friends might come 'round to love your face. Some will decide it's easier to feel sorry for you or stop hanging out altogether. Definitely their loss though.' He flashed a grin at her she was sure was flirtatious.

'I'd better get on,' she lied. Her cheeks felt hot and prickly and she wanted to exit the situation before she embarrassed herself further. She caught her reflection in the mirror behind the cash register and her scars stood out purple against her pink flushed skin.

There's no way he didn't notice how she blushed just now.

After they'd paid, they were both standing outside the café.

'Here's my card, it has my mobile number on it. Let me know when you want to have a coffee again,' he said.

'Thanks. I'll be in touch.'

He looked at her, he was leaning forward and had his arms hovering by his side as though he wanted to hug her.

'Would you like a hug?' he asked.

She thought about it for a moment. 'Yes, please.'

He smiled his intoxicating smile again and pulled her towards him. His large shoulders and well-muscled arms held her tight. He had put his arms around her shoulders, hers had slipped around his waist, brushing against the firm muscles of his abs and sides. Her blush returned and started to tingle its way down her chest. It had been a while since a man had been so close. Especially one with a wicked smile.

She leaned back and released her hands from his waist.

'Catch you soon, Freya,' he said, before turning to walk away down the chilly autumn street. In spite of the crisp air, Freya's ears burned, and perspiration beaded on her upper lip.

As she walked back to her apartment, she considered why she had responded like a schoolgirl. It had been a while since she'd had a boyfriend of longer than a month or two, and nearly two years since her last long-term relationship had broken down. She and Brett had been together for over a year, but there had been no talk of moving in together. He travelled for work and refused to spend more than a couple of nights a week with her. In the end she had broken it off when she realised he would never be able to give her the love she craved.

Freya always thought she would have kids, but the older she became, the less likely it seemed. Her friends were mostly in relationships, some talking about kids, one couple had their first child, a little girl, last winter.

She opened the door to her apartment, opened the balcony door, swung the armchair around to face outside and sat down. She stared into the dull grey Melbourne sky wondering if it would rain, how long she should wait to text Jacob, and if he felt the same about her.

Take it one step at a time. If it's meant to be, it will be, and if he's a friend, I need those too.

She turned his card over and over in her fingers, her mind running through scenarios where they could end up in a kiss. She shook her head and put the card away.

*

Her mother invited her around for Easter lunch on Good Friday. They weren't religious but enjoyed an excuse for a day off work. Her brother, Axel, had broken up with his long-term boyfriend a few weeks ago, and was both homeless and heartbroken. Astrid had welcomed him back with open arms. He had been dumped for a younger man; something their father had done to their mother.

The house was maze-like, three levels, and set into a sloping piece of land. Freya had been brought up in a house down the road, and when her parents had split up, her grandparents had helped her mother to buy the place. It was always too large for their three-person family, so she often had lodgers and people staying with her to help with extra income and company.

Freya suspected some of her aversion to social gathering came from how many people were in her house growing up.

Singular Focus

'You made it.' Axel stood in the front door, on the middle level, and yelled to her where she was standing in the street. He was the physical opposite of her; tall, broad shouldered and strawberry blonde. Since the breakup he had put on some weight and was looking rather more barrel-shaped than he used to.

'Yes. I managed.' Freya had taken an Uber. She walked up the external stairs to the front door and her brother hugged her rather more forcefully than necessary.

'Are you drunk?' she asked, smiling.

'Not yet. I waited for you.'

'Hullo,' a voice came from the kitchen. Their mother was more like Freya; dark-haired and slight of frame, but as tall as both her children.

'Mum's gone all out. Prepare yourself,' Axel said.

'Oh dear.'

Astrid went through phases in the kitchen. It was a hobby she picked up and dropped depending on her mood. Cooking meant comfort and having her eldest child back home had encouraged her maternal side.

'My poor darling,' her mother exclaimed when she entered the kitchen. It was the first time she had seen her daughter since the incident, since Freya had hidden it from her until she was home and then Astrid had declared herself too fragile to visit. It was upsetting to see your child come with a serious injury, but Freya was still hurt.

On the stove, all four burners had pots bubbling away on top, and the room smelled like cloves.

'What are you making?' One pot held purple cabbage, another potatoes, and the last steaming carrots and in the last pan sausages sizzled.

'A German feast! I was watching some silly detective show, you know the one with the dog. And I decided we would feast like they do in Europe.'

'Smells good.'

Axel made a face at Freya behind their mother's back and she giggled.

'It's so good to hear you laugh. I was so worried when you told me what happened. I still can't believe it. Come here.' Her mother held her face between her palms and looked deeply at her. Freya mind filled with the rolling thunderhead. The visions were set off by touch, although her brother's hug hadn't had the same effect moments earlier.

Perhaps it requires skin to skin touch.

'Come on, Mum, it's not that bad,' she said, pulling away.

Her mother sniffed theatrically and turned back to her cooking. 'We're about five minutes away from eating, make sure the table is set. George won't be joining us, he's with his own family.'

Her latest lodger was a fifty-something-year-old divorcé, George. He had adult children who weren't interested in seeing him and was on to his second ex-wife, from what Freya could remember. Astrid cooked for and mothered both men. Freya thought it was pathetic, but she was starting to understand her mother's aversion to being alone.

The meal was surprisingly delicious, and Astrid was much more interested in talking about the dramas at her workplace than asking about Freya's eye. Axel was similarly self-involved; he interrupted his mother frequently to remind her he'd already heard the story. Freya collected their plates and took them into the kitchen.

Her mother and brother continued to bicker in the other room and she sighed. With Eva away for the weekend they couldn't hang out. She pulled out her phone and scrolled through her contacts. Plenty of names; people she knew from work, from high school and university, friends of friends, but she didn't want to see any of them. They would stare at her and ask her about her eye. She wanted to complain about work or the state of politics in the US and not brace for questions about an injury she would rather not think about.

She scrolled past Jacob's name and stopped. They didn't know each other well, but he wouldn't stare at her patch. She didn't have to be defensive with him; if she admitted she was struggling she didn't think he would look at her with pity in his eyes. He knew how to help her without making her feel helpless.

Are you free tomorrow? My best friend is away and I'd be glad of some company. Perhaps we could have coffee or go to a museum? she typed. She hesitated with her finger over the send button. It sounded desperate. She deleted it and started again.

Hey. It was good to see you the other day. Are you free for a coffee tomorrow? I'd be glad of the company. It was still a little bit clingy, but much better.

'Are you putting the kettle on, Freya?' her mother called from the dining room.

'Yes, sure.' She pushed send before she could think about it again, put her phone into her pocket and filled the kettle with fresh water. She wanted to stay in the moment with her family but couldn't help wishing she was with Jacob instead. Not only handsome, but he was very easy company.

She stayed at her mother's place until dark playing the card game, five hundred.

'I hate playing with you,' Axel complained, he was only half joking. 'You always win.'

'It's not my fault you're no good,' she replied.

'Now let's not get into that again,' her mother said. She gathered up the cards and Freya knew the game had been forfeited.

'I'd better get going.'

'How are you getting home?' Axel asked.

'Same way I got here. Uber.'

He frowned. 'Will they let you drive?'

'Yeah, but I'm not sure it's a good idea. I might sell the car.'

'You'll lose a lot of independence if you don't drive, darling.' Astrid was wiping down the table.

'I don't I have much choice. My blind spot would be huge. I don't think it's worth it.'

'Whatever you think is best.'

Freya clenched her jaw; her mother's code for 'I don't agree, but I am not prepared to continue the conversation'. It was exactly the conversation she'd hoped to avoid. She rubbed her left hand across her eyebrow.

Freya took out her phone to order the Uber and her breath caught a little as she saw Jacob had replied. Ignoring it for the moment, she put in the Uber request; the driver was three minutes away according to the tiny map.

I have some family stuff to do during the day tomorrow, but I could meet you for dinner or a drink? Let me know, Jacob had sent back not long after her message.

'I'll wait outside.' Freya gathered her things, wrapped her coat and scarf around her and went to sit on the steps in front of the house. The air was damp and cool.

'Can I wait with you?' Axel asked, padding down the stairs behind her in his socks.

'Sure.'

He sat next to her. 'Mum doesn't mean to be such a pain. I think she was reminded how random life can be, you know, we could be hit by a truck at any time. She doesn't like to say how scared she was.'

Freya snorted. 'She wasn't the one who lost an eye.'

'You know how she is.'

Fleur Blüm

She harrumphed. She'd spent her childhood making excuses for her mother. Perhaps she should learn to accept Astrid would always have her foot in her mouth. 'I know.'

They sat in silence for a while, Freya checked the position of the driver on the map on her phone. He seemed to have become lost in the side streets of suburban Doncaster. She huddled into her coat, not looking forward to winter. It always seemed much colder in Melbourne than the temperature readings indicated.

'Can I buy your car?' Axel said.

'I thought you had a car.'

'I do, but yours is better.'

'Really?'

Axel leaned his body away from her, there was something he wasn't telling her. 'Yeah.'

'If I'm going to sell you my car, I need to know what happened to the last one.'

'Nothing happened to it,' he said, his voice rising in pitch. When they were kids, he would always fill silence, especially when he wanted something form her.

'I lent it to my ex and he dinged it up. I had insurance but it didn't cover other drivers, and I took his name off the policy when we split. It's not worth having it repaired and has bad memories. Plus, yours is only a couple of years old and you'll give me a good deal, right?'

'Sure.' She looked at the map, her driver should arrive any minute. 'I guess it can't hurt to give you mate's rates. I don't need the money.' Her distrust of her brother's driving ability aside, if he wanted to buy it, it would save her the effort of advertising.

'Do you miss him?' she asked.

'Of course. He's an arse-hat but I'm still hurting. I love him.'

Freya didn't understand.

'I hate him as well. I would never take him back or anything but there's a hole where he used to be.'

'You'll be okay.' She reached over and squeezed his hand. When her skin touched his she had a vision of him, standing in front of his bathroom mirror, toothbrush in hand and a vacant expression on his face, as though he'd forgotten what he was doing. She flinched her hand away.

'Sorry, cold hands,' he said. He folded his hands under his armpits. 'You be right out here? I see your ride now.'

'Yep. I'll be right. See you soon.'

'Love you,' he said, turning to walk back into the house.

'Love you too.' The cold of the autumn air was nothing compared to the chill she felt at the image of her brother being one of those slack faces. Although she'd tried not to think about it, she had been turning over the visions and the newspaper item in her mind ever since she saw it. She climbed into the back seat of the car, risked a bad rating for not being chatty and closed her eyes.

They must mean something, her dreams or visions. When she saw Jacob, she would have to take his hand and see what happened. She dreaded seeing him, slack-jawed and staring, but what if she saw something else?

She snapped her eyes open; she hadn't responded to him.

Let's have dinner, there's an Italian place nearby, Mario's, have you tried it? I've been meaning to go for a while, she typed.

She hoped it didn't sound too much like a date, but he had suggested dinner. She smiled at the idea of a date with him. They were supposed to have some follow-up appointments in six months, to make sure she was adjusting properly and fit a prosthetic eye, but she was sure another specialist she could see if they started dating. It would probably be unethical, but if she stopped being a patient it would be fine.

I've been past, but never been in. See you there at seven thirty? He replied almost immediately.

Clearly not busy then. She sent back a confirmation before she stepped out of the car. 'Thank-you,' she said to her driver as an afterthought. She gave him five stars because he hadn't tried to intrude on her quiet time, and she hoped he would be kind enough to give her the same.

Chapter 6

Freya spent all day worrying about her outfit for the evening. Despite the conundrum of the comatose people, her mind was filled only with the square jaw and disconcerting ice-blue eyes of her occupational therapist.

Ex-occupational therapist.

She searched news websites for any updates on the illness, but she found nothing new. Twitter had a few mentions, but it didn't seem to have been picked up anywhere yet. Perhaps she was the only person who was really worried.

What connected the patients? What caused them to be unresponsive but apparently awake? Why did she have visions when touched a person's skin? Were they connected?

In the end she decided to dress down for dinner; she wore slim fit black jeans, a white button-up blouse, black jacket and a grey woollen overcoat. She toyed with adding a black and white patterned silk scarf but decided it was too much.

Drizzle began to fall as she rounded the final corner before arriving at the restaurant. Jacob wasn't outside, she went in to wait for him. The interior decor was a throwback to the nineteen seventies; walls covered in pine panelling, and a low ceiling with exposed dark wood rafters and clad in woven straw mats.

The family run restaurant had been there for a long time and was clearly not suffering for the dated décor. Tables laid with red and white checked tablecloths crowded the floor, each with white taper candles stuck into wine bottles, and fake flowers. The specials boards hanging on the walls had rustic Italian fare; *osso bucco, fettucine carbonara, lasagne, tiramisu,* all the favourites.

Freya regretted wearing a white shirt and made a mental note to avoid red sauces.

'Do you have a reservation?' said a petite young woman, her dark hair was pulled back in a severe ponytail.

'Yes. Under Freya.' She couldn't see him in the crowd.

'Follow me.' They walked through the busy restaurant and the hostess pointed her to a cosy corner table. The kitchen was close by her table, and the smell of pizza and steaks wafted towards her. Her belly grumbled.

She had arrived exactly on time and waited ten minutes before she saw Jacob's head pop around the door. She raised her hand to wave him over.

'Sorry I'm late,' he said, bending to kiss her cheek before sitting opposite her. His meticulously maintained stubble was deliciously scratchy on her cheeks. She hoped they hadn't gone too red.

'I had to drop Rhonda at the airport and of course the traffic was worse than I expected. I barely had time to change my shirt and dash back out.' He was smiling sheepishly. His blue paisley shirt was open at the neck, under a deep blue jacket with blue jeans and tan lace-up shoes.

It took her a moment to take in what he'd said. 'Who's Rhonda?'

'My partner. She's flying to Darwin for a placement. She's a GP working in remote communities.'

'Ah.' Freya was dumbfounded. For all this time she'd assumed he was single. They had flirted a little when she first started to see him for her therapy and then, when they bumped into each other she was sure there was a spark of something more than platonic. But it wasn't going anywhere now she knew he wasn't available. She'd fallen for a married man before, and it had been the worst year of her life. She would not waste her time pining after someone again.

'Anyway, I'm here now. I'm starving,' he said.

'Yes, I thought the same as I watched the food parading past from the kitchen.'

They ordered, she had the carbonara special and he had a steak, although once he'd ordered the steak, she regretted not having one herself. They shared a bottle of red wine and garlic bread to keep them going until their mains arrived.

'Does your partner travel for work often?' she asked, taking a bite of the buttery, garlicy bread.

'Spends about half the year away from home. We've been together for a while now, and I should be used to it, but it's still as hard as it ever was.'

His usually sparkling eyes were downcast, and their intensity directed inwards. She put her hand on top of his and her mind's eye was filled with images of people swaying to some beat she couldn't hear, their faces enraptured. It wasn't like the other visions she'd had; they didn't feel frightened. All the other times she'd seen slack-jawed faces and glazed eyes a feeling of doom had accompanied had pervaded. This vision felt friendlier; more hopeful.

Freya pulled her hand away and the vision faded.

'What?' he asked.

'Sorry?'

'Your face—like you went somewhere else there for a minute.'

'Off with the fairies. I guess.'

He went back to telling her about Rhonda's jobs and how proud he was of her commitment to rural and remote communities. She wanted to listen, but she needed to tell someone about the visions, or she might scream.

'Can I tell you something?' she asked.

'Uh, sure.' He took her interruption in his stride.

'You have to promise you won't say I'm crazy.'

'I'm sure you're not crazy.'

'Promise?'

'I'm getting worried, but I promise I won't say you're crazy.'

She took a breath. 'I have visual hallucinations.'

The pause between her statement and his reply seemed to stretch forever. A limbo in which she thought she'd alienated the only man who made her feel comfortable.

'Okay. Is it new?'

'It started after the incident. I've never told anyone.'

He rubbed his chin, and the sound of the tiny hairs springing back as his fingers moved over them seemed loud over the background music and chatter. 'The dreams you told me about, were they actually hallucinations?'

'No, I see them in my dreams, but I see them when I'm awake too.'

He opened his mouth to respond and a waiter brought their mains. He put their plates down in front of them and the delicious smells bombarded her nostrils. Despite her hunger she wasn't able to eat yet.

'I see.' He didn't even look at his steak, juicy, seared, and accompanied with salad and chips. 'Do you get them all the time? Or only particular times?'

'I can have them any time, but lately when I touch someone. It has to be more than a brush, and skin to skin, it doesn't work through clothes.'

He nodded slowly. 'Did you get something when you touched my hand earlier?'

'Yes, that's why I looked so vague.'

'Do you have auditory hallucinations as well?'

'Voices? No, they're all totally silent. It makes it creepier to be honest.'

'I bet.' He looked down at his meal, picked up his cutlery and cut off a small portion of steak. He chewed and swallowed it carefully before speaking again. 'What was the vision?'

'A group of people, maybe fifteen, watching you, their eyes glazed, mouths slack, swaying together like there was music I couldn't hear.'

His fork stopped three-quarters of the way to his mouth. 'Where were we?'

'You were on a stage.' She hadn't realised it before. 'Playing guitar. I didn't know you could play guitar.'

'Why would you? We've never discussed it.' Jacob's face was pale, he put his fork down. 'If I tell you something, will you promise not to tell me I'm crazy?'

Freya laughed, then realised he was serious. 'I see things.'

'True.' He smiled, but it didn't reach his eyes. 'I do open mic nights; you know where people get up and do a song or two?'

'Yeah.'

'I did one on Tuesday, a place in Northcote, and the people in the bar started acting weird when I sang. I haven't been for a while. Since before I started treating you, I was in a bit of a slump, but seeing you reminded me I should get back to doing things that brought me joy. Even Rhonda seemed dazed and confused.'

'What happened?' she asked.

'I finished my three songs; everyone was so out of it they didn't even clap. The person running the night was staring off into space. It took them all a few minutes to come back down to earth. Some longer than others. I've never seen anything like it. Totally freaked me out and now you tell me you saw that in your mind? What the fuck?' Jacob was clenching his teeth, his jaw rippled with the effort.

'Why are you angry with me?'

'You're fucking with me, right? Someone told you about it and you're getting some weird kick out of scaring me.'

Freya looked at her hands where they lay in her lap. 'I wish I were. Usually my visions are awful, horrifying things. I feel panic and terror. But this time, it was like euphoria. Everyone was having a lovely time, as though they were in a trance.'

Jacob stared past her towards the front window for a long time, Freya waited. It must have been a shock to have someone inside his head. As it was a shock to her to know her visions meant something, though she'd suspected.

'I haven't been game to go back. I wasn't sure if it would happen again or if it was a fluke.'

'Did it feel like a fluke?' she asked, holding his piercing blue gaze.

'No. It felt right, even while it felt really wrong'

'I know what you mean.'

He gazed into middle distance for a while longer, and she took a sip of wine before loading a small mouthful of pasta onto her fork.

'I think you should come hear me perform,' he said finally.

'Okay.' It seemed like the only sensible way to know if her vision was true and he was putting people into a trance, was to try to replicate the effect. He nodded, as though he'd settled some inner debate, and took a bite of his steak.

*

They agreed to meet up the following Thursday at an open mic night in Brunswick, a suburb further west, full of musicians, hipsters, and migrants. Jacob had picked up Freya in his box-shaped, silver four-wheel drive.

'If I'm testing out the theory I somehow put people into a trace, which is bonkers by the way, you have to touch everyone you can.'

'Sounds creepy.' Freya didn't like the sound of having so many visions in one night.

'You can make it not creepy. Do a lingering handshake.' He turned to her as they walked up the road towards the bar. 'Or the double handshake, people do it all the time, it's unsettling but no-one will remember it tomorrow.'

'Fine.' She sighed. The only way to determine whether she got a vision from every person she had to touch a lot of people.

Singular Focus

Huddled in a bend in the road opposite a large McDonalds and a much bigger pokies pub the venue was a small bar with a tiny raised platform squashed into one corner; the main room was almost triangular. Jacob put his guitar case down near the stage and introduced Freya to the organiser.

'Mike, nice to meet you,' he said. Freya took his outstretched hand and placed her other hand over his. She held him for a long moment and braced for the vision. She was about to let go, the moment had stretched out longer than was reasonable, when it hit her. He was lying, face down on a deep green carpet, his eyes open and staring, like all the other faces. The sense of fear was not as intense with him, as though he didn't mind.

She dropped his hand and tried to smile. He hadn't felt trapped at all, he'd felt content. Jacob raised his eyebrows at her, and she shook her head, now wasn't the time.

Each person she greeted she held their hands, and each time she saw them prostrate and staring. Some were terrified, some angry, only Mike had felt relaxed. The visions sapped her energy and she sat at the bar with a bourbon and coke to take a break. She would only have one or two, she wanted to stay alert, but blunt the sensations a little.

Jacob was scheduled to perform a little over an hour after they arrived. He took out his guitar and tuned it up. She saw his hands were trembling and she smiled to him from her barstool.

Would it be worse if they are entranced? Or if they're not? Would she be affected, or did her visions somehow make her immune?

He took the stage.

'Hi, my name's Jacob, I hope you like my song.' He cleared his throat and began to play the opening of *Hotel California.* Freya smiled, she hadn't asked him what he was going to play, somehow this suited him. She looked around the room, so far, no glazed looks.

Then he started to sing, his voice gravelly and tender, a calm settled over her. By the chorus, everyone in room was swaying in time, eyes half-closed, with silly grins plastered on their faces. She was calm and happy but still alert. As Jacob finished the song he paused for applause, but no one moved. Freya clapped her hands together and the rest of the room started to clap and whoop. She frowned as they kept going, the clapping on and on.

'Thank you,' Jacob said. The crowd lowered their hands and gazed at him lovingly. His second song was *Hallelujah*, more like the Leonard Cohen version than Jeff Buckley, his raspy voice sent delicious shivers along her spine. Several thoughts flew through her mind, kissing him, making love to him. She shook her head; he had a girlfriend.

The crowd were stupefied and swaying. When he finished, she didn't clap, and they all stood there. She looked into Jacob's eyes and gave him a thumbs up. He smiled and took a deep breath.

'This is my last song. Thanks for having me.' This time when he started playing, she didn't recognise the song. The tug of the contented daze was stronger this time; his voice was a bell ringing around her head. In her mind she saw a sunlit field, with long grasses swaying in the wind. The rippling surface of the grass was hypnotising. She frowned and tried to keep her mind in the present.

He finished his song and stepped down from the stage. The people in the room stood where they were. She walked over to him.

'That was incredible,' she said.

'Worse than last time.' He seemed shaken. 'How come you're not in a daze?'

'No idea. I wanted to give in, but I kept my mind on what we were doing. What was your last song? It was really strong.'

'I wrote it for Rhonda.'

'I guess that explains it.'

He looked around the room, they were all still staring at him. 'How do we get them to stop?'

'What did you do last time?'

'I waited and they came back eventually.'

'I guess we wait.' She looked at her watch, five minutes to ten.

The people in the bar came back to themselves in increments. The first to shake off whatever it had come over them was the woman behind the bar. She looked around confused, as though she'd walked into a room and forgotten what she'd come in for. She didn't notice everyone else and vaguely wiped along the top of the bar. The fellow at the sound desk come back next, and when he realised the place was silent, he put on the backing music. When he did the rest of the room woke up, Mike stepped onto the stage.

'Everyone give Jacob a hand, well done, mate.' He hadn't noticed Jacob had packed up his guitar. 'Next up we had Pete and Shirley, if you're ready.'

Two people close to the stage unpacked their instruments. Freya grabbed the woman's hand as she was passing her, she hadn't had the chance before. The vision was instant, like being dumped by a wave in an angry ocean. She was flooded with intense emotions, and the image of Shirley standing, victorious, an almost visible aura of energy surrounded her. Freya let go and Shirley kept going up to the stage.

'That was really weird,' Freya said quietly. Jacob followed her eye line to Shirley and nodded.

'Usually I would hang around and make nice with the other performers, but we need to talk.'

'Let's go.'

Jacob said goodbye to Mike and apologised for bailing so early.

They walked back to the car in silence, Freya tried to organise her thoughts; not only was Jacob's performance effect repeatable, everyone she'd touched set off visions. Most people were variations of the same, but Shirley and Mike had been different.

Jacob slung his guitar case into the back seat and he slumped in the driver's seat, Freya waited for him to turn over the engine.

'Are you okay?'

'I'm not sure. I had expected, perhaps hoped, nothing would happen.'

She nodded. 'I hoped you were crazy. But I don't think you are.'

'I don't think so either. What happened when you touched Shirley?'

Freya shuddered. 'It wasn't like the others. It felt dirty, like she was rummaging through my emotions. Like I couldn't breathe.'

'And everyone else was the same as before?'

Freya looked out the windscreen to the slick black asphalt, it had rained while they were inside. 'It was all much the same. Blank, staring faces. I got more feelings with it this time, mainly terrified, angry, one was happy for some reason, which was weird, but nothing compared to Shirley.'

Jacob was staring at his hands as they gripped the steering wheel. 'What the fuck is happening?'

'If I knew, I would tell you. Something's changed since the whole eye thing.'

'But what does it mean? Why me?'

'I could say the same thing.'

'You had a bird peck out your eye. That's an obvious time for something weird to change in you, but nothing special happened to me...' he trailed off.

She turned to him, he was squinting, scrunching up his face. 'What?'

'Just before I met you, I had laryngitis. I couldn't speak, couldn't make any sound, I didn't have a cold; no other symptoms, I couldn't talk. And the next morning it was better.'

'My accident happened on the first of February.'

'That's the day I couldn't speak. I woke up fine, then after lunch, in the middle of a consultation and I went dry—nothing.'

'This is ridiculous. We're reading too much into coincidences. We don't know you're putting people into a trance, and I might be schizophrenic and never noticed before.'

He turned to face her; his pale blue eyes were worried. 'You don't believe that.'

'No, I don't.' She couldn't look away. She wanted so badly for everything to go back the way it had been before, but everything she did made it harder, not easier.

'We need to, umm, research or something. Maybe it's happened before?'

'Yes. Facts will make me feel better. There's plenty of stuff my understanding of science can't explain—maybe this is one more.'

Jacob nodded his head and started the car. He was quiet as he drove her home.

'See you soon,' she said as she stepped out of the car outside her block of flats.

'Yep, I'll let you know if I find anything.'

Singular Focus

Chapter 7

Freya found nothing in her research close to describing what was happening to her or Jacob. For months she spent her spare time at home following the barest threads of information down internet rabbit holes only to be disappointed when she realised they weren't what she was looking for.

She and Jacob had coffee a couple of times, but he was often busy when she proposed a catch up. He was probably avoiding her trying to deal with the idea of his hypnotic voice. He hadn't done any more open mic nights.

Her work was the same as always; giving wealthy people advice on how to become wealthier. Ever since she lost her eye, her job felt less and less important. Her waking hours were largely consumed with research materials or thinking about it and her dreams were filled only with visions. The same images over and over; the thunderhead and the slack faces.

Despite her visions being unpleasant, and filled with fear and dread, Freya would grasp people's hands long enough to get a reading from them whenever she shook hands. If she continued to have a conversation while holding them, she was met with less suspicion than if she pretended she wasn't doing it. For most people three or four seconds was enough to get the image, some were quicker and stronger, but since the open mic night, she hadn't come across anyone else who had caused a reaction like Shirley.

She watched the newspapers and news websites for anything on the new condition affecting the people of Melbourne. At first there were frequent articles about the rising number of patients in the hospitals and the doctors complete lack of understanding, but the media had become silent in the last month.

Her armchair now permanently faced the window, and craved company. Outside the grey August morning was cold, the inside of her windows had fogged up, but it was too cold to open the doors.

Freya had texted Eva the night before, she'd been trying to catch up with her for about a week now and had barely had any response. They had seemed to get past the blame Eva had been putting on herself for taking her out for cronuts, but perhaps not.

Her scars were starting to fade, dull pink now instead of angry purple, and she had had her follow-up appointment with the surgeon. Everything was going well. Without the patch, the right eye socket looked empty and strange. She wanted to try a prosthetic eye, to test whether it would make her look more normal, but she had largely stopped noticing when people in the street stared.

At lunchtime when she still hadn't heard from Eva, Freya called her at work. The phone rang and rang for a while before it went to her voicemail, Freya didn't leave a message. Sometimes Eva wouldn't answer her mobile at work, so she tried her office number; it went to voicemail too. Frustrated, Freya found the phone number for the receptionist.

'Hello, my name is Freya Gordon, could I speak with Eva in marketing?'

'Hold on one moment,' the receptionist said. There was a pause and some clacking of keys and shuffling of paper. 'Are you still there?'

'Yes.'

'It looks like Eva's not in. Do you want to leave a message?'

Freya frowned. 'No, it's okay. I've been trying to get onto her, but she hasn't been returning my calls. I'll try her another time.'

'Thank you for calling.' The receptionist hung up. Freya had a ball of worry building in her stomach. Eva hadn't said anything about taking leave, she hadn't gone away anywhere and normally complained if she were sick. It wasn't like her friend to be so uncommunicative.

Eva lived in a one-bedroom apartment in a high-rise building in the city centre. When she knocked off for the day Freya walked from her office to the apartment building and buzzed Eva's apartment. No answer. The worry in her belly grew into a roiling ball of dread. A couple who appeared to live in the building let themselves in and Freya followed them through the security door.

She rode the lift to tenth floor and knocked on Eva's apartment door. She tried a few times; no response. She knocked louder and called out to Eva. A neighbour popped her head out of the apartment opposite.

'Can I help you?' asked a slight woman in her fifties. She wore a brightly patterned parachute material tracksuit. Freya wondered if she'd been exercising; she seemed a little out of breath.

'I'm a friend of Eva's. She hasn't been answering my calls and her work said she didn't come in today. I'm sure I'm overreacting but I'm worried about her.'

The woman frowned. 'Usually we cross paths of a morning, but I haven't seen her for a while.'

'Shit.' Freya tried the door handle, not expecting it to be open. It was locked.

'I have a spare key. Do you think we ought to check on her?'

'Do you think that's going a bit far?' Freya asked.

'She lives alone, I wouldn't want her to have fallen in the shower or something.'

'She's not eighty,' she said, trying to laugh it off. 'But we could make sure she's alright.'

The neighbour bobbed her head and disappeared back into the apartment.

'I'm Freya,' she said, when the woman returned.

'Jean,' she replied. They shook hands and Freya was bombarded immediately with a powerful vision of Eva lying on her bed, the same vision she'd had in the early stages of her recovery, back in February. She shuddered and dropped Jean's hand.

'Someone walk over your grave, love?'

'Something like that.'

Jean slipped the key into the door handle and turned. 'Eva? Are you there? It's me, Jean. I'm coming in.' She stepped tentatively through the door. There was no response from inside.

'Maybe she's not here,' Freya suggested. Inside the apartment was freezing, the heating was off. Bits of clothing were strewn all over the floor, the couch, half eaten food sat on the table. There was a smell of sourness, she turned her head to see a container of milk, lid off, sitting on the bench.

Jean sniffed before moving through towards the bedroom.

'Eva? Are you here?' Freya called to the silent apartment. Jean pushed open the bedroom door and let out a squeak. Freya rushed to her side and was shocked to see Eva lying on the bed, fully clothed. She stared up at the ceiling, eyes open, not responding. A cold shiver ran through Freya.

'Eva!' She grabbed her friend's shoulder and shook her. 'Can you hear me?' No response. Now she was close to Eva's body, she smelled urine. She'd wet herself at some point. Freya put her fingers to her friend's neck, her pulse was weak and her skin cool to the touch, but she wasn't dead. Her mind was filled with Eva's bedroom ceiling, as though she were looking through her eyes. She felt no emotions at all, only a cold nothingness. It was the first time Freya had seen someone with the mysterious condition and it filled her with horror. How could Eva lie there? She pulled her hand away and turned to Jean, who stood in the doorway.

'What now?' Jean asked.

'We call an ambulance. I don't know what else to do.'

'Yes, we can't leave her like this.'

'What happened to you?' Freya said aloud, knowing her friend couldn't reply. She took out her phone to call the emergency services.

'Fire, ambulance or police?' a matter of fact man's voice answered.

'Ambulance please.' Her voice was steadier than she felt. The operator put her through to someone else.

'Tell me what's happened.' The second operator sounded like an older man, a tender fatherly type, and Freya had to fight to keep from bursting into tears.

'I don't know. She's lying here, she won't respond.'

'Eyes open?'

'Yes.'

'Is she breathing? Have you felt her pulse?'

'Yes, she's breathing steadily. Her pulse is okay, her skin feels cold.'

'Another one,' he said, his voice heavy. 'I'll put your call into the system, but you may have to wait a while. These patients are stable, and if something else urgent comes through they will take priority. I'm sorry for your loss.'

'She's not dead.' Freya was breathing heavily. *Why would he say something like that?*

'I know, but I haven't heard of a single person recovering from it yet. Hang in there and we'll send someone to pick her up. Where are you?'

Freya gave the man her details and he hung up. She held the phone in her hand and stared at it.

'What did they say? You look awful.'

'There's nothing they can do. She's gone.' Freya sat down heavily on the floor, hot tears sliding down her face.

Chapter 8

She stared at the prone body of her friend for a long time, she heard Jean trying to comfort her and feel her hand on her shoulder as though through a fog. Nothing mattered now. No one knew anything about the stupid disease, or whatever it was. The words of the triple-oh operator played over and over in her mind, 'I'm sorry for your loss.'

He knew they didn't come back. What could the paramedics do even when they got there, except put her in a hospital bed where they would keep her alive with drips and stomach tube? Freya had no idea how they did it – she hadn't seen any reports of deaths among the patients, but the media had become silent on the issue, as though the hospitals had decided to close ranks and stop talking to the press.

She shook her head and looked up at Jean. 'I'm sorry, what were you saying?'

'I asked if you were alright about ten minutes ago. You seemed like you were thinking very deeply so I waited.'

'I'm sorry, Jean.'

'It's rather a shock. I thought perhaps she'd had a fall, or food poisoning and couldn't leave the house, but this is worse.'

'Yes.' Freya sighed, and got up from her position on the floor. Her feet had gone to sleep, they felt as though they belonged to another person.

'We can't leave her like this, the ambos could take forever to get here, the guy on the phone said urgent cases would take priority.'

'So, what do we do?' Jean looked to Freya as though she had the answer. She knew no more than Jean, unless you counted her visions which were cryptic at best.

'First, we get her out of those clothes. We wash her and dress her. Strip the bed, collect the garbage, food, clothes. If they haven't come by then, we might have to take her to hospital ourselves.'

Jean looked at her hands. 'I don't think I can do that, bathe her and everything. We don't know each very well.'

'She can't do it herself.'

'What if I do the rest of the house, and you do the bathing?'

Freya nodded. She looked at Eva, although she was a slight woman, she wasn't sure they could carry her out of the building, and Freya couldn't drive even if they had a car. 'Do you have a car Jean?'

'No, I got rid of it when I moved to the city.'

'Shit.' Freya pulled off Eva's shoes and socks. The smell of stale urine wafted up as she moved her. *How long has she been like this?* She hadn't had a response since Sunday, three days ago. She pulled off Eva's clothes, her pants were stiff and hard to remove. Freya pulled the bedclothes off and placed a towel under her. She found a face cloth, and with a bowl of warm soap water washed her friend.

Eva was barely even moving to breathe. It was eerie, her body felt empty, as though the person she knew was no longer in there. When she was done, Freya redressed her in loose-fitting clothes.

'I think I've finished,' Jean said, standing at the door to the bedroom. 'She looks better.'

Freya didn't believe her but didn't say so. 'We can't move her ourselves. I don't think the ambulance is coming.'

'Do you know anyone with a car and a wheelchair?' Jean asked.

'Not really.' *Maybe Jacob would help.* They hadn't been in touch lately, Freya thought he was avoiding her. She called him, stroking a long black hair from Eva's face.

'Hello?' he said.

'Hey.'

'Uh, what's up?'

'My friend Eva…' Freya's voice cracked. She didn't want to say it.

'What's wrong?'

'We found her today. She's got—she's lying here, in one of those comas. The ambulance said there was nothing they could do.'

'Nothing?' he asked, incredulous.

'They'll come for her eventually, but I don't want to leave her here and I can't drive.'

'I'll come.'

She gave him the address; he'd be there in fifteen minutes. Her hands were trembling, and she wanted to sob; she wanted to lie down next to her friend and cry, but it wouldn't do any good. Jean was hovering.

'My friend Jacob is coming; we'll take her together.'

'Thank goodness.' Her shoulders dropped and she released her breath. 'You don't need me to stay then?'

'No, it's fine. Leave me the key.' Freya knew the older woman wanted to get away from Eva; from the smells and the morbid finality. Freya wanted to leave too, but she loved her friend, and someone needed to look after her. This creeping nothing, wasting away, whatever it was, was slowly spreading. The medics didn't know what it was, how to treat it or stop it. All they could do, it seemed, was keep them warm and alive, such as they were, until bedsores, or pneumonia or some other thing killed them. The last report she'd read said there were thirty patients in their own ward at the Royal Melbourne Hospital. That was more than a month ago, since then it had gone silent. Freya paced the length of the loungeroom trying to think but her mind wouldn't stay on any single point. The vision of the ceiling through Eva's eyes kept intruding.

Waiting for Jacob was the longest fifteen minutes Freya had ever experienced. She put the clothes Eva had been wearing into the washing machine, she would have to come back tomorrow to dry them. She didn't know where the bins were, so she sealed up the waste in the black bin liner, the apartment smelled pretty stale, despite cleaning up the urine smell was potent. The door buzzer went as she was winding open the bedroom window. Freya startled and went to let Jacob in.

'It's on the tenth floor,' she said into the speaker. The camera was busted but she wouldn't imagine anyone else coming to call on Eva on at half past nine on a Wednesday.

There was a knock at the door, and opened it to see Jacob, his blue eyes concerned under his furrowed brow.

'What happened?' he asked. She led him into the bedroom where Eva was lying on the stripped bed.

'I don't know. She wasn't responding to my texts, and she wasn't at work, so I came to check on her and we found her like this.'

'You called the ambos?'

'They said she wasn't urgent. That was hours ago.'

Jacob made a soft murmur of concern. He went to Eva's side and waved his hand in front of her face, no response, he picked up her hand and let it fall, no response, he blew gently into her eye, she closed it but when he stopped she went back to staring at the ceiling. Her breathing was shallow but constant and every so often she would blink; otherwise nothing to indicate she was alive.

'I've never seen anything like it,' he said finally. 'Did you get anything when you touched her?'

'Yeah, the view of the ceiling through her eyes. No emotion at all. It's like she's empty; her body is here but her soul, is gone.'

Jacob sniffed. 'Is that urine?'

'Yeah.'

'I guess we have to get her to the hospital.'

'She'll waste away eventually.'

'She'd dehydrate first, they'll have to put her on a drip and a catheter. I don't know much about vegetative states.' He shook his head.

'What do we do with her?' Freya had been thinking about how to move her friend since she called Jacob. If they had a wheelchair it would be easy, but unless Jacob had one handy that was out.

'If we roll her in a sheet, or doona cover, her arms and legs will be secured, then we can make a chair with our arms and take her out that way.'

'Right.' Freya went into the bathroom; the linens were stored in the top of the cupboard. She brought back a beige, teal and chocolate brown patterned doona cover. They rolled Eva onto her side and slide the fabric under her, rolled her up, not too tight, then sat her up. She was limp and loose, which was a help in some ways and a hinderance in others; unless they held her, she would fall back. After a bit of grumbling and a few false starts they managed to get her sitting on the edge of the bed looking like a human burrito. It would have been funny except for the ambulance operator's words: 'I'm sorry for your loss.'

'She's not very heavy. Might be easier if I do a fireman's lift out of here. Do you want to get a bag of stuff together for her? When she wakes up, she'll want her stuff.'

'Are you right to hold her?' Freya watched him hold her against his hip to stop her falling back onto the bed.

'I'm okay.'

She found an overnight bag and put in a few pairs of underwear, two changes of clothes, basic toiletries, and the book on the bedside table. Eva's handbag was on the floor near the couch and Freya put it in the overnight bag. It seemed woefully inadequate, but there wasn't much else she would possibly need until she woke up.

If she wakes up. 'Right, I think that's it.'

'Here are my car keys, if you can open the doors and lock up as we go, I'll take Eva.'

Freya nodded. She had Eva's keys now as well as Jean's spare. Jacob hoisted Eva onto his shoulder with ease and she held the apartment door for him, locked the deadlock and pressed the button to call the elevator. They stood silently at the numbers ticked over towards ten.

'I hope no one sees us. I'm parked out the front,' Jacob said when they exited the lift at the ground floor. Freya nodded, opened the door of the building and held it as he walked through. Outside it had started to rain, a miserable sort of drizzle which reflected the miserable mood she was in.

'Silver four-wheel drive,' Jacob said, inclining his head to the left. Freya clicked the remote locking on his

Fleur Blüm

keys and opened the back door. He loaded Eva into the
back seat and buckled her in. Freya climbed into the
passenger seat, clutching the overnight bag.

'They're all at the Royal Melbourne,' Freya said.

'Right.' Jacob's hands were gripping the steering
wheel so hard the knuckles were white.

'Relax.' Freya didn't believe it but hearing herself say
the words made her feel better. 'I guess we should tell
triple-oh we don't need them to come.'

Jacob nodded. Freya called emergency services again
to cancel the ambulance, by the time she'd hung up, they
had arrived at the Royal Melbourne Hospital Emergency
Department.

'I'll get someone to come out and get her,' she said,
jumping out of the car. She didn't like to leave Jacob
alone with Eva, but the visions were coming on strongly,
the thunderhead, the faces, the image of the back of her
own head as though through Eva's eyes all flashed
through Freya's mind on a loop.

'I need some help please,' she announced to the
youngish woman wearing scrubs.

'What's the problem?'

'I don't know what you call it, my friend is in one of
those comas.'

The woman hid it well, but there was a flicker of
unease, perhaps revulsion. She pulled a wheelchair from
a spot along the wall and pushed it in front of her
towards the car. As they walked the nurse peppered
Freya with questions; how long had she been like that,

what happened immediately preceding the coma state, was she taking any medications or drugs, Freya didn't know the answers to any of them.

'I'm sorry, I found her. I went to check on her when I didn't hear from her for a few days.' She felt like a broken record.

'I see,' the woman in scrubs said. 'You need to do the admission paperwork and then we'll get her settled.'

Jacob and the nurse manoeuvred Eva out of the car and into the wheelchair. The woman raised an eyebrow at the sheet but said nothing.

She wheeled Eva into the emergency department waiting room. 'Wait here and fill in this form.' She handed Freya a clipboard before walking purposefully away to converse with her colleagues. The flicker of concern went across their faces.

'Why do they keep making that face?' Jacob asked.

'I don't know. There's something going on with these coma cases they're not telling the public, maybe some shady government department's involvement. That face says "oh shit, another one" to me.'

Jacob looked at her. 'You're right. Maybe not about the shady government department.'

'Happy to be proven wrong.' She turned back to the form on the clipboard in front of her. They sat in the waiting room for twenty minutes before the nurse came back over to them.

'We're going to take Eva up to the ward now. If you want to follow me.' She took the handles of the wheelchair and started walking swiftly down a corridor.

The ward was on the fourth floor, six rooms and a nurse's station in the middle. Everyone in the ward was in a coma. As they walked in, Freya's mind was cluttered with images, as though every patient was screaming for her attention, she didn't need to be touching them. Much the same with Eva, she had various versions of the view of the ceiling, each of them had a feeling come with them but they were all very weak, like the volume had been turned all the way down. She shuddered, even with the low intensity of the emotions there was a lot of fear in this place.

'Is this all of them?' Freya asked.

'Everyone we can fit. Occasionally people are moved to private facilities. Some patient's families prefer them to be closer to home, or somewhere less like a hospital.'

'How long will Eva be here?' Jacob asked. He had folded his arms across his broad chest, Freya thought it looked as though he was hugging himself. The nurse with the wheelchair stopped and turned to look at both of them.

'It's not good news. Since we started being presented with patients in this condition, none of them has recovered. They show no improvement. We've tried different interventions but haven't yet isolated what caused the condition and we don't have any effective treatments. We stabilise them and search for answers.'

The words 'none of them has recovered' resounded in Freya's ears. She had known intellectually, surely the press would be going on about the miracle cure to the strange illness if they had found something, but it felt as though she'd been punched in the diaphragm; she couldn't breathe.

'Fuck,' Jacob said quietly.

'I'm sorry I don't have better news for you,' the nurse said. 'Let's get her settled in and comfortable. You can come visit whenever you like, read to her, help bathe or care for her if it makes you feel better.'

Freya followed her mechanically and watched as she and another nurse, who appeared quietly, put Eva into a narrow hospital bed. They still put up the barriers so she wouldn't fall out.

All around the ward, patients were all lying on their backs, eyes open, staring upward. She walked to the man in the bed next to her, mid-fifties, mostly bald and with a few days of growth of stubble. Silently, she took his hand and tried to feel into him. To try to use her visions to find information rather than receive images. She had no idea if it would, but she'd never tried to direct it before.

Jacob stood next to her, waiting patiently for her to finish. This man's emotions were buried deep, but she tried to search them out; anger, fear, panic. She looked for the last thing he had seen before he lost himself to whatever it was; in her mind's eye she saw a handshake with a faceless woman, felt a small jerk, as though something was tugging forwards from her spine, right behind her belly button, then images of this man coming home, dropping his things, and lying down on his bed. She couldn't find anything else, only these images over and over.

She let go of his hand and a wave of faintness came over her.

'Steady,' Jacob said, he had grabbed her around the waist to stop her falling and guided her to the seat next to Eva's bed. 'What did you see?'

'Shaking hands. He shook hands with a woman, tall, thin, dark hair, I couldn't see her face, and then he went home and went to bed.'

'I don't understand.'

'I don't either. I'll have to try the others.' She tried to stand but couldn't make her legs respond.

'Stay there. You're very pale. I'll get you some lemonade or something.'

'Okay.' Freya leaned her elbows on her knees and put her head in her hands. There was a pressure in her head like she was surrounded by noise she couldn't hear; the unspoken voices of everyone in the ward silently screaming to be let out of the prisons their bodies now were.

'Hot, sweet, milky tea. I couldn't find a vending machine.' He handed her a cup. She drank half of it in one slurp. The sugar revived her a little, but she still felt weighed down.

'We don't have to do this now. It's been a long night.'

She looked at her watch, it was nearly midnight. 'One more.'

'Alright, but I'm going to hold you this time, no fainting.'

She nodded, it felt weak having him physically hold her up, but she didn't have the strength to argue and it seemed she might need it. On the other side of Eva was a young girl, maybe fourteen, spotted with acne and greasy hair; puberty hadn't been kind to her. Freya took the girl's hand and looked into her mind. It was easier this time to find the feelings; panic and resignation, maybe she'd been here longer. In her mind's eye, Freya found the image of her lying down on her bed, she tried to play the image back to see what had happened before. It was disjointed, but she found the handshake again, this time with a man, elderly by his hands and posture, but she couldn't see his face either. She looked for more details, tried to force the girl's mind but the feeling of tugging behind her belly button was more intense the harder she looked.

'Let go,' Jacob whispered in her ear. She released the girl's hand and came back into herself. He was holding her up, his large warm body pressed against her side. 'You slumped over but you wouldn't let go.'

'I don't feel so good.'

Jacob led her over to the chair and sat her down. She was exhausted, nauseated, confused.

'It was the same. A handshake with someone whose face I couldn't see then she lay down. She's not as panicky as the other guy. When was she brought in?'

Jacob took the file from the basket at the end of the bed. 'It doesn't say, but these observations go back three months.'

'She's given up. She's trapped in there somewhere and can't find her way back.'

Jacob looked at her. 'What do you mean trapped?'

'It's like they're in there, somewhere. Weakened or paralysed. Their spirits are in there, but they are not in control of their bodies anymore.'

Jacob closed her file and put it back. He looked at the floor and sighed. 'Are you okay?'

'I don't know.'

'I think we should get out of here. I feel like I can't think straight.'

She nodded. 'I know what you mean.' She stood, her legs were a bit wobbly and she had to sit back down. Jacob took her hand a held her up as they walked out of the room back to the lift.

'Want me to take you home?'

'Let's get something to eat, I feel really wiped out.'

They stopped at an all-night kebab shop in Lygon Street. She ordered a chicken kebab and a serve of chips, Jacob ordered the lamb kebab. She lay her head down on the wood-look laminate table while they waited for their food. She felt shaky, and her mouth tasted metallic.

'You'll feel better after you've eaten. Looks like you're having an adrenalin crash.'

She took a bite from her kebab, she hadn't felt hungry, but as soon as the food hit her mouth her senses returned. She became ravenous and she ate most of the kebab and all of the chips before she started to feel full. They didn't talk, she tried to keep her mind blank, but the feelings of panic and fear she'd picked up from the patients in the hospital ward crept into her consciousness. She sat back and pushed away the remnants of food, satiated finally, and starting to feel in control again.

'I got a really bad feeling in there. I don't know if it was because they were all together, putting their fear out into the air, or whether it was something to do with the visions,' Freya said.

'I felt it too. Similar to the time I went to Auschwitz a few years back. And Port Arthur.'

'There weren't any living people in those places. The people back there are still alive.'

'Technically, but you have to admit, it's hard to hold out much hope when the first cases were in February and no one's figured out what the fuck is going on yet.'

Freya covered her face in her hands and took a breath before she answered. 'My best friend is one of those people you've given up on.'

'I—' he started. 'I'm sorry.'

'You should be sorry. You don't know any more than I do and I can't give up hope. I'm not ready to resign my friend to living death until she gets some complication and dies before she wakes up. There must be something they can do.' She looked at her hands and realised they were gripping the edge of the table so hard her fingertips were white. 'I think the visions I have, the trance thing you can do, and this condition are all linked. They all started on the same day; it can't be a coincidence.'

Jacob chewed for a moment. 'It's very unlikely for all three things to have happened at the same time. But other than timing, we have nothing to link them.'

'Give me your hands.' Freya held her hands out, palms upward on the table. Jacob frowned a little but put his hands over hers. She concentrated on trying to find the moment he lost his voice in his mind.

If I believe I can control it, then I can control it. Images flashed in her mind, a child on a beach running after a cricket ball as it rolled into the surf, a teen crying over an older woman in a coffin, and then she found it. Jacob was sitting in his office, watching an older woman do proprioception exercises; she had her left eye bandaged up, as well as her left arm which ended at the elbow. Freya could see his mouth moving, although as with all the other visions this was soundless. He put out his hand to hold hers to steady her, then he made a face, confusion followed by more mouth moving, then he put his hand to his throat and coughed.

'Did you lose your voice the moment you touched that lady's elbow?' Freya asked.

'I felt you looking through my memories. It was weird, like watching a movie.' Jacob had pulled his hands away.

'But was that the moment? The moment you touched her elbow?'

'I guess so.'

'Had you touched her skin before?'

'Yeah, I'd seen her a couple of times before then. And I'm pretty sure we shook hands when she came in.'

Freya thought for a moment. 'It must not have been the skin to skin contact then. What time was it?'

'I dunno, after lunch.'

'Can you be any more specific?'

'My first appointment after lunch is quarter past one, but I think she was a bit late. So maybe twenty past?'

'I lost my eye at twenty-four minutes past one on the first of February. I think that's the time everything changed. Something happened at exactly then.'

'You sound crazy.'

'I know. But you can put people into a trance, and I can see into people's minds, so...'

'Yeah.' Jacob was quiet. He looked past her shoulder out and of the kebab shop window. She turned to follow his line of sight but couldn't see anything. She turned back to Jacob and waited for him to finish thinking. She was exhausted and her best friend was as good as dead. She couldn't mourn her, it would be morbid, and she didn't want to give up hope, but the medical staff had nothing to offer.

'Let's say you're right,' Jacob said. He was still staring behind her. 'Something happened on February first and it changed the world as we know it. You got visions, I got the magic voice, and people started falling into comas.'

'Right. Should we give it a name? No one's given it a name.'

'The Emptiness?'

'Sounds too passive. And they're not empty they're stuck somehow.'

'The Shrivelling?'

'No, that's not right either.'

'What about The Withering?' Jacob suggested.

'The Withering. I dunno, it's not quite right but it will do for the moment... the Withered?'

'So, the Withered, the magic voice and the visions all started on the same day.'

'Yes.'

'Is there something special about that day?'

'Nothing, other than it being my birthday,' Freya said.

Jacob looked at her for the first time since they'd started talking again. 'You lost your eye on your birthday?'

'Yep.' She twitched her mouth up on one side in an attempt to smile.

'Fuck. You didn't tell me that.'

'I was busy dealing with my lack of an eyeball at the time. Plus, my date of birth is in the file.'

'True. I only take notice of age, I don't usually look at the date of birth, doesn't mean much to me.'

'Clearly.' Freya smiled, hoping he would see she was trying to lighten the mood. He took no notice.

'It's all so crazy.'

'You said that already.'

Jacob looked at her and half laughed. 'It's been a long night.'

'You can say that again.'

'It's been a long night.'

Chapter 9

It was nearly two in the morning when they arrived at Freya's place. She didn't invite Jacob in, although the desire to be wrapped in his strong, warm arms all night was almost enough to make her weep. He had a partner and she would not be that person. He was a good friend; he'd been there for her when she needed him.

She showered and washed her short-cropped hair. She went to bed with it still damp even though on a cold night in August it was the sort of thing her grandmother would have told her not to do. Despite her exhaustion, she lay awake thinking. She tried to name the feeling in the hospital ward and the closest she could come was impending doom. A sense something was about to go horribly wrong and she needed to do something but didn't know what it was.

Jacob was taking it harder than she was. It wasn't fair, he hadn't lost his best friend or been forced to feel everything they were feeling and more every time he touched someone. She needed more information, someone to explain what was happening to; a conveniently placed wise woman or sage to explain the plot to her, but this wasn't a novel or a game of dungeons and dragons, this was real life.

*

Freya had vivid dreams and slept fitfully. She lay in bed pretending to sleep for a long time before getting up. Then texted her boss to say she couldn't come in.

Freya was restless and agitated, despite her poor sleep. Her head was pounding, so she took a couple of paracetamol. Had something happened the day she lost her eye, something newsworthy, to explain why everything pointed back to that day? If she could figure out what had started it, maybe she would be able to work out what was going on. Freya refused to give up on Eva, or the others and decided to do everything she could to bring them back.

The State Library in the city held back issues of all the major Australian newspapers and access to newspapers from around the world. A grand sandstone building built in the mid-nineteenth century, the library was a monument to the era. She had used their microfiche facility once before, while at university. In the eight or nine years since then, they might have moved it all online, she hoped they would have the information she wanted.

The tram ride into the city was quiet, but she still caught a few stares from curious children and impolite adults at her eye patch.

I'm going to look at newspapers from Feb first. Fingers crossed I find something interesting, she texted Jacob.

Inside the library she passed under the great, white-domed room to the newspaper section in the back near

Russel Street. Large tables and comfortable looking chairs were placed around the airy and spacious room. Tall shelves were interspersed between the tables. These days libraries were exchanging book stacks for access to the web, but she doubted paper books would ever be obsolete.

The Australian newspapers for February second were quite easy to find, and as she flipped through the pages there was the same old nonsense: politicians ignoring climate change, commentary on the pre-season of Australian Rules Football, the women's football still took up a much smaller space, some cricket, and tennis, and local interest stories. She skimmed over the conservative pundits spouting racist rubbish. Nothing in the Australian papers to indicate something catastrophic had happened at twenty-four minutes past one the day before.

Newspapers from around the world didn't have anything either. She read over the ones she could find in the United States and Britain. Her belly rumbled and she rubbed her hand over her face. She hadn't done this much intense reading since she'd lost her eye and the left one had started to throb. It was almost three in the afternoon and despite spending hours researching she was no closer to solving the mystery.

Jacob had replied to her message. **Good luck. Anything yet?**

With a loud sigh, the disillusionment came out; too hungry to keep going and too dejected to reply to Jacob. Leaving the library Freya crossed Swanston Street into

Melbourne Central shopping centre. Inside a huge light-filled atrium stood a brick tower; back in the 1890s the tower was used to form molten lead into perfectly round pellets for shotguns. They dropped the lead down the inside of the tower into a pool of water. By the time the drop had travelled all the way down it would have solidified into a sphere of solid metal. The weak winter sun shone down as she looked up at the brick tower and the glass cone above it.

No one here seems troubled by the fact something really weird is happening. She took two sets of escalators up to the food court. Food courts were never a first choice, and this one held even less appeal than others. Her belly growled as she walked past rowdy groups of young people, students from the nearby RMIT University, and the University of Melbourne. Some students were younger, wearing school uniforms. Considering the pizza and pasta, she then walked past a sandwich shop but the line was too long. In the end she settled on an Asian place selling food from *bain-maries*. The sauces were lumpy, and the vegetables seemed on the verge of collapse, but the service was fast and the cost inexpensive.

'Sweet and sour pork, and noodles please,' she said. The young woman behind the counter nodded and started piling food into the transparent plastic container. Freya took the container, her flimsy plastic fork and a couple of napkins and looked for a place to sit. The tables and chairs were mostly occupied, the only spot was on a high table with an uncomfortable looking wire chair.

She consumed most of the meal without thinking or tasting anything before looking at Jacob's text message again.

Nothing obvious in the newspapers from Feb second. At least not in English. Could try some of the other languages, she wrote back.

Freya looked at the remains of her late lunch and couldn't bear to finish, pushed it away and closed her eye. She steadied her breathing and tuned into the emotions of the people around her. Since learning she could control her ability a little last night, she had been wondering what else she could tune into.

For a while there was only the sound of her own breathing and the hum of conversation around her. No visions came. She was about to give up when image of the oncoming storm filled her mind again. Letting the image wash over her, she imagined herself diving through the storm as though to get through a wave, and then another image filled her mind: three figures standing on a beach.

It wasn't much, but it felt important. Freya opened her eye, took out her phone and called Jacob.

'I had a new vision,' she said when he answered.

'Freya? I can't hear you, what did you say?'

'Sorry, I'm in a food court.' She looked around for a less noisy place where she might have better phone reception. 'Hang on.' She walked back towards the shot tower and found an unoccupied section of the rail looking down on the open atrium.

'Is that better?'

'Yeah. What did you say?'

'I had a new vision.'

'Okay.' Jacob sounded strange.

'Three figures standing on a beach. I think the storm is at a beach.'

'That's great,' he said quietly.

'Are you alright?'

'I can't talk now.'

'I'll come around later. When is good?'

'Uh…'

'Seriously, are you feeling okay?'

'I'm not sure I can do this.' Jacob said, his voice barely more than a whisper.

'What do you mean?'

'After I saw Eva, I dunno. I don't want to end up like her.'

'That's why we have to keep going. We don't know what's causing it and if we give up, we're as likely to end up in the ward as she is.'

'I can't go back in there.'

'I know it was super creepy. I considered going in to touch some more people, but I think I might leave it for a while. I think I can control the visions, at least I'm trying to.'

Jacob was silent, apart from shallow panicky breaths coming down the line.

'It's okay. I can't do this without you, you keep me sane. It's intense, I agree. We don't have to go back to the ward. If we do nothing Eva may as well be dead, and I'm not ready to let her go.'

He sighed. 'Thanks.'

'What for?'

'For talking me down. I thought you would be really angry.'

'Why would I be angry? It was awful.'

'I'll be home about six, come over and I'll make us something to eat. You wanna bring some wine?'

'Sure, red?'

'Yep. See you soon,' Jacob said. Despite her poor sleep and her dead ends in the library Freya felt hopeful. She and Jacob were a team, and as long as she kept her libido in check and didn't make things awkward it would be okay.

She briefly considered going to see Eva but decided against it. The feeling in the ward, the desperation and silent panic were more than she could handle, especially alone. Eva's condition wouldn't change, Freya would go when she'd had time to catch up on her sleep.

*

Jacob's place was an apartment in a small block of flats five minutes' walk from Freya's place. Yellow brick with a walkway along the front and a white metal latticework in front of the apartments on the upper floor. A long, thin pot with mint and other herbs sat on the sill of the front window.

She knocked and looked haggard when he opened the door, but he smiled when their eyes met.

'Thanks for inviting me over. I got a Shiraz, I hope that's okay.' She held out the bottle. 'The fellow in the bottle shop said he liked this one, I'm not much of a wine drinker.'

'Great.' He showed her into the apartment. It was neat, fastidiously so, the furniture had a mass-market Scandinavian feel to it, as though she'd walked into a display at Ikea. The front door opened onto the loungeroom, with the kitchen to the right, two bedrooms and a bathroom.

'I like your place,' she said.

'Rhonda did the decorating. I had a few pieces when we got together but we've mainly replaced them so it's all of a matching mood.' He put air quotes around the word mood.

'You don't think it looks nice?'

'I didn't say that.'

'But you don't really like it?'

'Feels a bit sterile. And if anything is out of place it feels messy. Rhonda's a neat freak.'

He keeps it tidy even when she's away. He hadn't made the space his own and felt out of place in it, so he kept it clean as though he were a guest in his own house. The kitchen had a two-person dining table.

'Come have a seat,' he said.

'I'm sorry I'm not much good company today. I went to work even though I barely had any sleep. I feel like a zombie.'

'I know what you mean. I called in sick.'

'Wise.' He sat opposite her, resting his head in his hands and his elbows on the table. 'So, you had a new vision?'

'I don't know what to make of it.' She described the vision she'd had earlier. 'I can control the visions, or at least, give them some direction, which is interesting.'

'And you couldn't make out the faces of the people on the beach?'

'No, I was sort of above them. They were standing in a circle. I couldn't see faces.'

'Mmm, interesting.' He stood, grabbed two wine glasses down from the cupboard above the stove and poured them each a glass.

'What are we eating?' she asked. She never liked to drink too much on an empty stomach.

'I was going to order pizza. I'm too tired to cook.'

'Good idea.' They ordered a pizza each, so they would have leftovers for lunch tomorrow, and Freya's mind returned to what the cover-up could be about. 'Were you able to find any mention of the Withered patients in the newspapers today? I didn't look in today's issues.'

'I scanned them quickly at lunchtime, but I haven't seen anything about it for a few weeks.'

'Maybe they've put an embargo on it, or they don't want to let on how many people are up there in the ward.'

'And that's not counting the ones whose families have moved them out.'

Freya took a sip of her wine. 'There were six rooms, each had eight beds, so forty-eight if they're all full. Let's suppose ten have been moved, which is nearly sixty people with a condition no one is talking about, which has no treatment, no cure, no recovery, and no one knows what causes it.'

'Fuck,' Jacob said.

'We really need to do something.'

'Like what? I'm not a doctor. I don't even know how I'm involved—'

'You can put people into a trance with your voice. I have visions. It's connected somehow. The Withering didn't start until the day we changed. It can't be a coincidence.'

'Then what is it?'

She shrugged. This was the place she had got to and didn't know how to go forward. 'Do you believe in the supernatural?'

'I don't know. Why?'

'Bear with me. What if there is something going on outside of what modern science can explain.'

'Like what?'

'These people are having their life force drained somehow.'

He raised an eyebrow and took a sip of his wine.

'That's what it felt like. As though the volume was turned down, they were still in there, but far away, stuck inside themselves. Did you ever see the movie "*Get Out*?"'

'Where the mother hypnotises black people so they were trapped inside their own minds and white people could take over their bodies?'

'Yes.'

'And you think that's what's happening? Except instead of being possessed, they're empty.'

'Not exactly empty but, yeah.'

'Why would someone do that? In the movie they get a new body, what's the pay off in your scenario?'

'I don't know. They must get something out of it. Maybe it's not just a one-time drain, they're feeding off the life force somehow.'

'Psychic vampires?' He shook his head.

'I know what it sounds like, but we're both way past what we used to think was sane.'

Jacob scrubbed his face with his hands and stood up. He pulled out two placemats, plates, knives, forks, and serviettes and laid them on the table. 'Let's assume you're right, and there are psychic vampires running around Melbourne, who were made—activated? Anyway, who started doing their thing on your birthday. Why only sixty people in six months?

'I don't know.'

'How do they feed? How many are there?'

'I don't know.'

'If we're going with a crazy theory, we need a lot more information.'

Freya clenched her fists in her lap. 'Do you have any other ideas?'

He looked away. 'No.'

They sat in silence for a long time. Freya took long slow breaths. She'd drunk half her glass of wine and told herself she wouldn't have any more until the food arrived. She picked at her fingernails nervously, the pulled a piece of fluff off her black woollen skirt.

'How would we get proof your psychic vampire theory was true?' Jacob asked.

'I'm not sure. I probably have to go back and touch some more patients. The two I touched last night had both shaken hands with someone. I don't think I would have been shown if it wasn't important.'

'We're making some pretty intense jumps in logic.'

'I know.'

Jacob exhaled, but said nothing.

'Maybe it's happened before. Looking in the newspapers for something on February second was a good start, but we have to go back further. If this sort of thing is really happening, maybe there's evidence in the past.'

'Where would we start?'

'Psychic vampires? They're mostly made up, but maybe something out there is true.'

'Mmm.'

There was a knock at Jacob's door, he went to open it and returned with their two pizzas. 'They threw in a garlic bread for free.' He smiled.

'How about we stop talking about the Withering for now, sleep on it, and we can start doing some research tomorrow?'

'Deal.' Jacob picked up his wine glass. 'Cheers.' They clinked their glasses together and Freya had a vision of them doing the same thing, but at a different time; Jacob's hair was longer, and his face seemed older. She shook her head; wishful thinking.

'Do you rent here?'

'No, I own it. Rhonda pays the mortgage with me, but she's essentially renting from me.'

'Cool.' Sounds like it could get messy when they break up.

She tried to keep the conversation on light topics, and away from anything which mentioned Eva, her eye, her visions, the Withering, but it was hard. The conversation was stilted, and she couldn't think of anything to say to fill the long silences.

'It's hard here on my own,' Jacob said after a particularly long pause.

'How long is Rhonda away?'

'Depends, this time it's been three months, but she hasn't even been home for a visit.'

'Do you talk on the phone a lot?'

'Yeah, we talk pretty often…'. He seemed to be holding back. 'I shouldn't complain.'

'It's okay. I haven't had a boyfriend for a while. And since, y'know, the eye, I haven't been looking. Who'd want to date someone with one eye?'

'Don't be so hard on yourself. You're a hot, vivacious, charming woman. Any man would be lucky to have you.' Jacob put his hand over hers. She knew she should pull away; she had told herself she wouldn't encourage anything romantic between them.

'I'll get back on the dating horse when I get the glass eye and don't look like a dodgy pirate.'

'You don't look like a pirate. But I wouldn't want to come across you in an alley, or on a ship.'

'Arrgh,' she said, making her hand into a hook shape and waving it at him. 'Sorry, the wine's gone to my head.' She looked at her watch, it was almost nine-thirty. 'Maybe it's the sleep deprivation catching up on me.'

'I'd better have an early night. One more day of work, then the weekend. I'll have a think about where to start with research into psychic vampires if you like,' Jacob said. He drained the remains of his wine and started to clear away the plates.

'There's an occult book shop in the city, I could go tomorrow. They might have some ideas.'

'It's going to be hard to work out what's real and what's nonsense.'

'We'll know real when we see it. Anything that starts to describe similar symptoms to the Withering and we'll know we're onto something.'

Jacob leaned against the kitchen sink. 'You're a good friend.'

'Sorry?'

'Doing all this to help Eva.'

'That's not the only reason.'

'Well, she's lucky to have you as a friend. Some people would want to get on with their lives. It shows strength of character.'

'Thanks, but there was never any other option.'

Jacob closed his eyes for a long moment and Freya knew she needed to leave. 'I'll head off. Thanks again for hanging out with me. It's really hard not being able to talk to anyone about the stuff going on.'

'I know what you mean.'

They both stood, and he walked her to the door. 'I'll let you know how I go tomorrow,' she said. They hugged goodbye and Freya caught a whiff of shampoo from his hair.

As she walked home the scolded herself for not being able to control her physical attraction to him. He smelled of musk and wood, he was calm under pressure and had taken all the stuff they had discovered in his stride, but he was committed to someone else and no matter what her feelings were, they could not be reciprocated. Becoming romantically attached would only lead to pain and disappointment later, she needed to get over this schoolgirl crush.

*

Singular Focus

The occult bookstore was in Little Bourke Street between a camping supplies store and a skateboard shop a couple of minutes' walk from her office. She scoffed a sandwich from a convenience store as she walked over. The front door was painted deep maroon, the name of the fellow who ran it printed above the door in peeling gold letters: Mr Theodore Halloway, Esq.

Freya had looked it up after giving up on a productive morning. The bookshop had been there over twenty years, they led ghost tours around Melbourne and the building had a reputation for being haunted. She'd Googled Halloway too, he seemed theatrical, all the photos she could find were of a thin-faced man wearing black Victoriana outfit, a top hat and long hair dyed black. She hoped the performance didn't indicate he was more show than substance.

She pushed open the door and walked up a narrow wooden staircase to the bookshop on the first floor. It was brighter than she had expected, the usual array of New Age magic shop paraphernalia, crystals and candles set up along a front counter down the left side of the room. A female mannequin dressed in Victoriana held a ceramic skull with a lit candle inside. The whole room smelled overwhelmingly of patchouli and nag champa incense; she almost choked as she walked into the hazy room.

'With you in a moment,' a voice called from behind a deep red crushed velvet curtain.

'Thanks.' Freya ventured further into the shop; the section nearest to the door catered to tourists and was full of witchy gift wares, then shelves of books and tarot cards, all of which looked very new. She pulled out a book on reading angel cards and, as she had suspected, it was overpriced.

'Are you looking for something in particular?'

Freya turned back to face the man who had spoken. He looked exactly like his picture but about ten years older. He'd let his hair go grey and the outfit looked a little worse for wear, but his green eyes were keen behind his small round glasses.

He stepped back and assessed her. 'It's you.'

'Have we met?' she asked.

'No. I've been expecting someone. Ever since I heard about the first person in that living death coma. I didn't know what you'd look like, but I knew I'd know you when you came into my shop.'

Freya shivered, either this man was great at cold readings or he had some psychic ability himself.

'I'm sorry, I'm sure that's very off-putting for you. I'm Theodore. It's a pleasure to meet you.' He held out his thin hand to shake hers, his fingernails were long and painted black.

'Freya.' As soon as she took his hand, she was overwhelmed with a vision stronger than any she'd had before. As though his entire life was flashing before her inner eye; a small thin boy playing with dolls, a teen ostracised at school, his first book on magic, and the feeling he'd found his place in life. She snatched her hand away.

'Interesting,' he said.

She stood reeling for a moment. Her heartbeat slowed as the flood of images in her mind faded and Freya found her way back to herself.

'I didn't realise you would be so strong,' he said.

'I didn't mean to, I'm sorry.'

'No control yet.' He was looking into her eye intensely. 'Can you take off the patch?'

She put her hand over the patch. 'It's not very pretty.'

'Naturally. I know what happened to it, that much I had knowledge of in advance.' He raised his hands toward her. 'May I?'

She dropped her hands and nodded. His long slim fingers were delicate as he peeled the black satin eye patch away from her right eye socket.

'It all started when you lost the eye,' he stated.

'Yes. How do you know all of this? How do you know me?'

'All in good time. I think I'll close the shop. We need to have a chat.' He pushed the eyepatch into her hand and trotted down the stairs. He snibbed the door and he came back up the stairs with a lightness she wouldn't have expected of someone in his late sixties.

'Come through here, I have a little spot to sit. Can I offer you tea?'

'Uh, okay.'

He pottered around the little kitchenette, flicked the kettle on to boil and pulled out two mugs. The space was cramped but didn't have the witchy aesthetics of the bookshop beyond. 'It's mainly for show you see,' he said. 'I've had a moderate psychic ability since I was a child. Knew things I shouldn't have known, was able to guess the outcomes of things and sometimes items of news would be what I'd dreamed about. Sugar? Milk?'

'Milk, no sugar,' she said.

'When I was a teenager, well, you saw, I found magic. I realised it was real, at least some of it. The more I found out the more I knew I'd found my calling. Of course, a lot of the stuff I sell isn't worth the paper it's written on. There is a big market for nonsense to make people feel better about their pedestrian lives. I digress.' He sat down on the folding chair opposite her, placing her tea in front of her. Freya didn't know what to say, so sat in silence.

'I knew someone would come. Since the first day of February my ability has been ten times what it was. I've been able to see things further into the future, I don't have to touch people to get a reading from them; I used to need physical contact but now I don't even have to be in the same room for people I know well. New people I still have to touch the first time. I felt you.'

'You felt me?'

'Yes, I knew there was someone with a new and intense ability. I knew it would have something to do with these, what do you call them… the Withered?'

'How did you know that?'

'I have some small talent for clairvoyance, remember—it's an apt name. And there is another yes? A man?'

She nodded.

'What have you come to ask me?'

'I have a theory. About how these people become as they are, Withered. But I don't know what I'm doing. You can control the visions?'

'Yes, but that's for another time. You have a theory.' He took a sip of tea. His intense green eyes didn't move from her face.

'They're being drained. I touched two of them and saw them shaking hands with someone. I know they're still in there. I think we can rescue them, but I know nothing about psychic vampires.'

'Mmm.'

'And what happened on my birthday?'

'I didn't see that coming,' he said. 'I suppose it makes sense it was an important day for you, why you were chosen.'

'Chosen for what?'

'One thing at a time. I believe someone did something, think of it as though they flipped a switch and turned on a bunch of latent magical abilities. People like me who already had some ability have had an increase. I believe someone, or a group, has done this purposefully, for reasons not yet clear.'

'They wanted to turn these abilities on. Why?'

'Same reason anyone does anything; power, revenge, money, status. Human beings are dreadfully predictable.' His shoulders sagged, as though he were tired.

Freya sipped her tea; it was strong and floral. 'What has flipping the switch got to do with the Withering?'

'Along with your visions, and your friend's abilities, there are people, or entities, who are now draining others, as you suggest. This is what is causing the Withering. Whether it was intended by the person who flipped the switch is not clear to me.'

'I see.' Freya thought for a moment. 'Do you have visions then?'

'Sometimes. Mostly I just know things. It's not as clear-cut as having an image in my mind as I believe you do.'

'It's as clear as if I saw it with my eyes. My eye.' She corrected herself.

'Anything else?'

'I get feelings. When I touched the patients, I felt their emotions.'

'Any other senses?'

'No. The visions are always silent, sometimes I see things clearly, like when I touched you earlier, it was so clear, but mostly the details are sort of vague, like things are a bit out of focus.'

'Mmm.' Halloway nodded.

'Can you tell me what they mean?'

'I may be able to help, but the visions are likely to be unique to you. They will mean something more to you than I will know. Wherever your information comes from, it's coming to you specifically.'

'Right. You can't tell me about the thunderhead then?'

'I haven't seen anything like it. Other than the obvious metaphor a storm is coming, I can't tell you.'

Freya sat quietly for a moment. She was grateful to Halloway for his insight, but she was suspicious that he knew so much about her and the situation but nothing helpful. She would need to keep her wits about her to ensure she was not sucked in by his kind demeanour.

'Do you have any ideas how someone might go about, uh, flipping the switch.'

He narrowed his eyes and regarded her over his mug. 'Of course, you don't trust me yet. Why would you? You don't know me from a bar of soap. I've been in this game a lot longer than you have. I know the sort of thing that would need to be done, the books one would need. Only one teacher in Melbourne crazy enough to take on a student who wanted to do it.'

'You can't do it yourself?' she asked.

'Can't and won't are very different. In this case these are powerful magicks and they require a lot from the practitioner. It's hard to understand from your perspective, you had your ability thrust upon you, I've had mine since birth and I'm sure we've both, at some point, wished we didn't.'

Freya nodded. Only last night she'd been thinking it would be better for everyone concerned if she didn't have the visions, but then she wouldn't know about Eva; she wouldn't be able to save her.

'There are people in this world, in the occult community, who have always been jealous of the power of others. Small people, low status for one reason or other, who believe the world owes them something. I'm sure you've come across their type. These people are dangerous because they will stop at nothing to get what they want. They feel justified to do almost anything.'

She thought back to the boss she had a couple of years ago who would take credit for work she'd done and pass on all the blame if anything had gone wrong. She had always known he would put himself first in everything. If he had believed in magic, she was sure he would have both coveted it and no natural ability.

'I don't keep those sorts of books myself, of course. I have a few which provide some background you might find useful. Even if I had the desire to do something like that ritual, I wouldn't know exactly how it was done.'

She looked at her watch. She'd been in the little shop for at least half an hour.

'You'll need to go soon. I have some books for you to take home. Your path will not be easy, I'll help you where I can, but I can't do the work for you. This is your task. You must find the people to help you.'

'Great.'

Sounds like the sort of cryptic nonsense I expected from an occult bookshop owner.

Theodore stood, his thin crow-like hands dangling from his wrists as he walked back into the shop. He went to one of the shelves in the back of the store and pulled out three old, tattered-looking leather-bound books.

'These are the only real books in here, I've been keeping them for you,' he said. 'Very few people are genuinely talented, although there are more now, more's the pity.'

She nodded. The number of people lying in the hospital ward would continue to grow until someone stopped it.

Until *she* stopped it. Freya took the volumes; they were heavy and a little dusty, it made them seem more authentic. She thanked Mr Halloway and he followed her down the narrow stairs to reopen the shop.

'Come back to see me whenever you need to. I will do everything I can to help.'

'Thank you,' she said.

'Except actually doing the work.' He laughed. 'Even if I hadn't foreseen it otherwise, I couldn't do it myself. Too scared. Bye now.' He waved to her and turned back up the stairs.

Chapter 10

When she got back to her desk Freya put the heavy books into her desk drawer and determined she would have a productive afternoon. With everything going on she didn't want to put her job in jeopardy too.

Met with the occult book shop owner. Bit of a weirdo, mostly helpful. Talk later, she texted Jacob. Placing her phone in the drawer with the books she went back to work.

There were a couple of simple tasks to get through before the end of the day. Given it was Friday she would make up the extra time spent with Theo next week instead of staying back late.

She held the books against her chest standing on the busy train home. Once inside her apartment, she made a cup of green tea and sat with them in the armchair. Three books, two thick dark brown ones and one thinner red one. All from the same collection; their worn leather covers were the same style, and the faded gold lettering was the same typeface. The first volume, the thinnest, was called *The Elder Edda.* Inside were embellished and illustrated verse poems. She flipped through the pages and read a few familiar names: Thor, Odin, Loki, as well as a number she didn't; Baldr, Heimdallr, Vali. Even a version of her own name, Freyja. It was a book of creation myths of the Norse people. She had known some of the stories from her childhood, her mother's family were from Norway, but had never paid much attention. They were all pretty insane, like the time Loki turned himself into a female horse and got pregnant.

The second book, titled *Seidhr*, was a book of magic, specifically woman-centred seeing magic. Holding the book in her hands sent a tingle through the scar tissue around her right eye socket.

This one seems promising. She put it aside to check the third book. This last book was the most used of the three, delicate and worn. She opened it and a small piece of paper fell from between the pages.

Cher

I hope this gives you what you need. The journey to righting this wrong is dangerous. Do not tread it yourself. This is feminine magic; you must find the woman who will set it right.

Hettie.

The hand-written note dated from May of this year. Theodore had been telling the truth about knowing she was coming. He'd got hold of actual books of magic from this Hettie, a woman in the occult scene, Freya assumed. She flipped through the pages; mostly handwritten in the same wobbly block letters as the note. *It must be Hettie's spell book, why didn't he point me to Hettie herself?*

Each page was dated, the first was 1978, more than forty years ago. She took notes of the rituals she undertook, the purpose, who was there, what was done and the outcomes. Perhaps the *Seidhr* had the instructions and these were her experiments. Freya flipped to the end of the book and found the last entry. It was the same date as the note to Theo. She turned back to the first of February.

Today I did no work. There was an enormous disturbance in the flows and I'm afraid of what it could mean. I've seen the coming storm; and this is the first clap of thunder. The Woman and The Girl are called to action by the events of this day. My own power has strengthened but I feel it will be the end of me. It burns too brightly.

Freya looked up out the window to the dark spidery branches of the tree outside. If Theodore had read this journal, he would know exactly who she was without needing to have a gift himself. She had assumed Cher was a term of endearment for him, but it could be someone else. *What if he had taken the book by force? What if he'd started this all, done the ritual and was trying to set it straight after things went too far.* But she hadn't had any of those feelings from him when she shook his hand. Something so big would have come through. Even the Withered, with the tiny amount they were able to send to her, conveyed their fear. If he had been trying to right his own mistake, she was sure she would have known.

Singular Focus

The outline of a large, black bird soaring appeared against the evening sky. It circled around and landed heavily on one of the bare branches. The raven stared at her; she felt a shiver of recognition. That was the bird who had taken her eye. She stood up and pulled the curtains closed, hiding the black raven from sight.

From inside her handbag she heard her phone ringing.

'Hello?' she said.

'I got your message.'

'Hi Jacob.'

'Sorry, yes, hi. What happened with the bookshop owner?'

She sighed and thought for a moment. 'It might be better if you come look at the books he's given me. Come to my place.'

'Text me your address and I'll be over in five.' He hung up before she could say anything in response. She had enough time to change into comfortable clothes and put the kettle one. She hadn't eaten but wasn't hungry; her mind was too busy trying to make sense of the spell book. She wanted to read the entries leading up to the end of the journal but waited for Jacob.

She jumped at the sound of knocking on her apartment door. 'How did you get in?'

'Snuck in behind a neighbour.'

'Mmm. You got here quick,' she said.

'I ran,' Jacob said. His cheeks were flushed from the cold evening air, but he was only a little out of breath.

'You didn't need to. Tea?'

'Water would be good.'

She poured him a glass of water from the jug she kept in the fridge. Jacob drained half of his in one gulp, then reaching over to top him off before turning to the kettle to make herself a green tea.

'Have a seat on the armchair. I only have one chair, apart from the bed.'

He nodded and sat down. 'Tell me about this bookshop.'

She took her tea to the bed and settled herself leaning against the wall. She told him the story of what had happened that day and about the books Theodore had given her.

'Did you get any vibes off the books?'

'I only get visions from people.'

'Right. Are these the books?' He looked at the pile next to the armchair where she had dropped them after seeing the raven.

'I've looked through them a little.'

He picked up the spell book and started to look through it.

'That one's a spell book cum journal, by a woman called Hettie. I haven't figured out how she and Theodore know each other. The vibes I got from him were honest but at the same time, I don't trust that he knew who I was, and what I was looking for. It seemed a bit convenient.'

'Sounds like it saved you a bunch of time looking through irrelevant stuff.'

She took a sip of her tea. 'I'm not ready to take his word for it he's on our side yet. The only people I really trust are you and me.'

'Pretty cynical.'

'It might be, but there is something going on, putting people in hospital, no one will talk about it and no one seems to know anything.'

'A year ago, I would have laughed at the idea of a magical disease and a conspiracy of silence, but I've seen the ward. And I haven't been able to get any information out of anyone. What's in the other books?' he asked, not taking his eyes of the spell book.

'One is Norse mythology. The other is Norse Magic. It seems Hettie was using the magic, *Seidhr* it's called, and using the spell book to record her rituals and experiments. I only got to read a couple of her entries before you rang.'

'Anything good?'

'I looked at February first. She felt something; thought it was going to bring her undone.'

'Interesting.' Jacob flipped to the last page in the spell book. 'Listen to this: I have been losing my wits and my will over the last few weeks. I have done what I can to find the culprit, for I know it is something powerful and unnatural that drains me, but I have nothing. My powers are failing me, and I know soon I will succumb.'

'What were you up to, Hettie?' Freya wondered aloud

Jacob flicked back a couple of pages. 'I called the circles together again tonight, we are down to four now, having been picked off by this other power. We have tried to pinpoint the source, the practitioner who invoked the Awakening and started us all on this cursed pathway—'

'A bit dramatic, isn't she,' Freya interrupted.

'We have found traces of the ritual in the sands. A great scorched place in the scrub. It looks to have been a lightning strike of some sort, but the scent of magic was on it. The marks on the earth radiated outwards in nine strands; scratched and burned into the ground like a scar.' Jacob stopped reading and looked up at her. 'Take off your eye patch for a second.'

'You're the second person today to ask me to do that.'

'Do you mind? I want to check something.'

She sighed and pulled off the eye patch.

'Shit,' he said.

'What?' She held her teacup between her knees as she wrestled the patch back in place.

'There's a drawing. Of the lightning strike.' He turned the book around to show her. 'It looks like your scar.'

Freya looked and the drawing in Hettie's wobbly, spidery hand and shiver ran down her spine. He was right, the sketch looked like her eye. There was even an almond-shaped hollow in the middle, filled in with black, could have been an eye. 'I don't like it,' she said.

'This got way creepy.'

'Is there anything about a raven or a crow?'

He scanned the pages in front of him and flicked backwards through the book. 'I don't see anything. Why?'

'I saw one on the tree outside. It's not unusual except I felt like it was looking at me.'

'Are you afraid of birds or something?'

'I never used to be, more indifferent, but a raven did this.' She pointed to the place where her right eye used to be. 'I guess I have an aversion to black birds now.'

Jacob shuddered. He'd never done that before, in all the therapy sessions even when her injury was new and much gorier. 'I'd forgotten.'

'I wish I could.' The experience replayed in her mind; floating above herself, watching the raven pluck out her eye, her mouth open in a scream she couldn't hear. 'I bet he's still sitting out there, waiting for me to look around the curtain.'

'I'm sure your imagination is getting the better of you.' He laughed.

'I dare you to look,' she said.

He put the spell book down on the floor, stood and turned to the balcony window. He pulled the curtain aside a little and was silent for a long time.

'It's still there.' He sat down heavily. 'It just stared at me. I tried to tell it to get lost with my mind, but it didn't work.'

'I think you have to be singing for it to work.'

They were quiet for a while. Freya considered opening the *Seidhr* but she was very tired and wanted to cry. She didn't know what any of it meant, the visions, the Withering, Jacob, the raven, Hettie and Theodore. The more she learned the less she could control.

'Halloway said he couldn't help me. *Wouldn't* help me,' she corrected herself.

'Why not?'

'He said it was not his path. What if we put the books in a box somewhere and let things sort themself out?'

He levelled his gaze at her, the intensity of his eyes made her shiver. 'Do you really want give up on Eva?'

'I don't want to do dangerous stuff. I'm not brave, or good at conflict. I've always been the fun, agreeable one. Since this happened,' she pointed to her eye. 'I've become a different person and I don't like it. I used to be a people person and now I look forward to sitting alone in my apartment.'

'You're scared.'

'Of course I'm scared. I have no idea what we're coming up against; it's all spooky nonsense.'

'Having visions and singing people into a trance are spooky, but we've established both are normal now.' He softened and smiled at her. 'It's all new, and I felt like you do yesterday. But I realised my whole life has been leading up to this; I became an occupational therapist to help people, to recover from traumatic experiences. Why would I turn my back now when there are people in the ward who need our help? No one else is doing anything. Maybe no one else can.'

'Why did it have to be me?' Her words came out as a whine.

'You have a strength in you. You came to me and you were determined to be normal, to do the work and make sure your recovery was good. I think you're better suited than you give yourself credit for. If someone did flip some switch to unleash latent powers, you had it in you from the beginning.'

Freya made a harrumphing sound. How dare he make sensible arguments when she wanted to hide under the blankets and never come out.

'I know you don't want this to be happening, believe me I wouldn't have chosen this either…'

'What?'

'Nothing.'

'Doesn't seem like nothing to me.' Freya put her hand on his shoulder. His brows were drawn together.

'Rhonda and I have been fighting.'

'What about?'

'She's jealous.'

'She has nothing to be jealous of,' she said, trying to keep an appropriately serious look on her face. Trouble in his relationship meant he was unhappy, and she was unhappy on his behalf, but underneath she was also a little hopeful she was one step closer to having him for herself. 'It's hard to understand why we're so close if you don't understand the "we have to save the world" bit of it.' She smiled.

'I've told her about your visions. And my singing. She thinks you're crazy and I'm no better for letting you convince me I was part of the secret project to rescue all these coma patients.'

Freya squeezed his shoulder, she didn't get a vision from him as she usually needed skin on skin contact, but she got his feelings in waves; confusion, anger, exhaustion. 'It's not the first time she's done something like this, is it?'

Jacob flinched away from her. 'That's not fair to get visions without telling me.'

'I didn't. I'm guessing. Based on what you've told me and the fact you're more dejected than I would expect if it was the first time.'

He laughed bitterly. 'I should have known you'd be perceptive even without the visions. She's never supported stuff I want to do. When we got together, she told me I should have become a proper doctor.'

Freya scoffed. 'Like her?'

'Yeah. And then when she got this job doing remote work, she said I should come with her, she'd find me a job, and if she didn't her salary was enough for both of us anyway.'

'Doesn't put much stock in your life.'

'She doesn't think it's important. Doesn't like my friends and won't come to stuff even when she's in Melbourne. I feel alone, more than when she's away.'

'Do you love her?'

'I thought so.' Jacob looked down. 'Wow, I don't know why I'm telling you this, it's not important in the scheme of things.'

'It's important to you, so it's important to me.'

He hung his head running his fingers over his forehead and into his hair. Before he looked up again, he wiped his eyes and sniffed loudly. She walked over to the kitchenette, busying herself with straightening the things on the counter to give him time to compose himself.

'I can't remember the last time Rhonda said that to me.'

'I'm sorry. Sounds very isolating.'

One side of his mouth pulled up in a goofy crooked grin. 'I'm sure Rhonda wouldn't agree.'

'What are we going to do now?' she asked. She was conscious she'd been making the decisions possibly treating Jacob exactly the way Rhonda did.

'I'm still not clear why it was done,' he said.

'They wanted to unleash latent magic, but why? Why now? Why here?'

'I think we take some time to study the texts. We have to assume this stuff is literally true,' he pointed to the spell book where it lay on the pale wood floor next to the armchair. 'Maybe we'll find something to help you control the visions and explain what's happening with me.'

'Sounds like a good plan.'

'Tomorrow is Saturday. Maybe we spend the day reading through the spell book and this other one—'

'The *Seidhr*,' she said.

'Yeah. Might give us a better idea of what's going on, and then we can try to figure out how to stop it.'

'There's one thing.'

'What?' he asked.

'The note in the front of the *Seidhr* talks about the women who will fix things. There's someone else we're supposed to find.'

'That might be a question for later when we know more about what we're dealing with.'

Freya nodded. Her belly rumbled loudly, and she remembered she hadn't had anything to eat since the sandwich she scoffed at lunchtime.

'You wanna order something and get started now?' he said.

Having said it all out loud for Jacob she knew she wasn't crazy, which was a relief. She needed some time to think about the spell book, Hettie, Theodore, the *Elder Edda* and the *Seidhr*. Maybe look into some forums and see whether anyone else was talking about the same things.

She wanted time to go over the note a couple more times. She could do it with Jacob in the house but now she knew Rhonda was not happy about it. Sitting on her bed trying not to think of how good his skin smelled when she had her hand on his shoulder. 'Let's get started fresh tomorrow. I'll meet you at yours. And I'll bring coffee.'

'Done.'

It pained her to see him so sad.

He stood and went to the door. 'Thanks for saying that before, about being important. See you tomorrow.'

Jacob was out the door before she could say anything else. He obviously needed space to think as much as she did. She pulled a lasagne from the freezer and put it into the microwave. If she'd been chosen for a reason, some underlying ability, then he had been too. It had to be done in his own time, but the relationship with Rhonda was ending. She seemed to treat him as an accessory rather than a partner. Whether or not Freya was able to give him what he needed, he deserved more.

She snuck a peek behind the curtains; the raven was still sitting there. It looked straight at her and her mind was filled with the image of the rolling thunderhead. She was standing on a beach, she felt the sand between her toes and the wind whipping past her skin, making her robes flap wildly around her legs. She looked down it was not her own thin, female frame, but a robust, male body wearing a black kaftan. There were two others, both with their hands outstretched, forming a circle

The vision faded and she was back to staring at the bird. It bobbed its head and took off. The raven had given her the vision, she was inside it this time, rather than above it. The microwave pinged. She decided to write the experience and pulled out an old journal she

Fleur Blüm

used to keep after her last relationship broke down. She turned to a new page and started writing.

When she'd finished four pages in hasty, sloping handwriting, her stomach growled again, and she remembered the lasagne. It was lukewarm, but she ate it all the same.

Chapter 11

The next day Freya woke early, the grey skies outside didn't bode well for good weather but would be ideal for a day spent inside researching ancient magic.

She pulled open the blood red curtains and was relieved to find the raven wasn't there. Silly to think it would be back so soon. The warm water of the shower roused her and kept the chill morning air from creeping into her. The comfort of her favourite black jeans and a dark grey knitted jumper with her woollen overcoat gave her courage for the day ahead. Texting Jacob she was on her way. Freya headed to the café to pick up a couple of proper coffees and something to nibble, although whether she would be able to eat for the bubbling nerves, half fear, half excitement, in her belly was unclear.

Twenty minutes later she stood at Jacob's door with two lattes and two blueberry and white chocolate muffins. She wouldn't usually eat something so sweet for breakfast, but today sensible eating seemed less important.

Jacob's shirt was crinkled and only one half was tucked in, and the stylish stubble on his chin seemed longer and scruffier than usual when he opened the door.

'Sleep well?' she said, walking inside and dropping her cargo on the little kitchen table.

'I had nightmares. I'm also not great before I've had coffee.' He reached for the cup and took a long swig.

'Good thing I come prepared. What were the nightmares?'

'I dreamed I was standing on a beach, looking at a storm. It was vivid, and really windy—what?' he asked.

'I had a vision of the same thing, after you left. I wanted to see if the raven was still there and I could have sworn it sent me that vision. It was the same as the vision I had before, but I was inside it.'

'I don't usually dream, but this seemed really ominous. I woke up a couple of times through the night but each time I fell asleep again it was the same thing over and over.'

'We should keep records of weird stuff that's been happening. Like Hettie.'

'I guess it couldn't hurt.'

'You've never had a dream like that before? I've been dreaming of the thunderstorm for months now.'

'No, never.' Jacob ran his hand over his chin, the stubble made a soothing scratching sound. They sat in silence for a moment; he sipped his coffee but didn't touch his muffin, Freya's belly had settled enough that she was hungry. She pulled the top from her muffin and bit off a small piece.

'I guess we start reading?' she said after the pause had gone on long enough for her muffin to be mostly gone.

'Yep.' He looked up at her. 'Sorry I'm not hungry, the muffin looks delicious.'

'If you're not hungry later I might have to eat yours too.' She smiled. He didn't return it. He looked tired and anxious; his brows were drawn together, shoulders hunched. 'Are you alright?'

'I had another fight with Rhonda.'

'Really?' Between last night and now? No wonder he looks tired.

'I told her we were spending the day together, texted her, and then she called me at midnight to yell at me.'

'I'm sorry.'

'Not your fault.' He sniffed and rubbed his hands across his eyes. 'She's got this pathological need to control what I do. I have to check in with her constantly and let's not even talk about what happens if I don't return her texts or calls for more than an hour. I'm sick of it, but…'

Freya waited. 'But?'

'It's my place but the furniture is all hers now. I'd have to start again.'

'Ah.'

'Yeah.' He stared at the takeaway coffee cup and poked it with his right forefinger.

'Not much of a reason to let her stay. She'll find somewhere to live, and you might be happier.'

'Probably.'

Freya finished her coffee and muffin and stood up. She put the cup and wrapper in the bin and pulled out the three old books. Jacob continued to stare straight ahead; Freya left him be for a while.

She took the books to the loungeroom, kicked off her shoes, and curled her legs under her on the couch. She always felt better curled into a ball, there was something soothing about it. If she'd had a blanket it would have been even better. She started with the journal; Hettie's wobbly writing stared back at her. She went to the entry for her birthday.

The Woman and the Girl.

Was she the girl and Hettie the woman? Or was she the woman and someone else was the girl? Hettie already had power, so hadn't included herself in the two.

Perhaps it would be more useful to find out more about the power, this *Seidhr*, where the magic came from. Freya opened the second larger book and started to read.

She lost track of time but looked up when Jacob scraped his chair back against the kitchen tiles.

'You alright?' she called.

'Yes. Sorry. I'm back with you now.' He put the kettle on to boil and brought his muffin into the lounge. He sat at the other end of the couch and Freya's feet were almost under his firm bottom.

'I've been reading about *Seidhr*.'

He nodded.

'It's a predominantly female kind of magic. There were male practitioners, but they were in the minority and less powerful than women.'

'Interesting.'

142

'It only works as a communal thing; a single practitioner is pretty useless; the more people you add the more power you can wield. Exponential growth it sounds like, in olde worlde language.'

'I guess it explains the three figures on the beach.'

'In your dream?'

'I was one of them; standing in a circle with two others.'

Freya shivered. 'That's creepy.'

'It didn't feel creepy at the time, it felt amazing, the best I've ever felt. If that's what magic is, I know why they're chasing it.'

'Yeah.' The vision she'd had, standing on the beach watching the oncoming storm had not been filled with glee or euphoria. She had felt paralysed, powerless and frightened. 'Maybe it works differently for you. I didn't get that feeling.'

'Maybe.'

She went back to the book. 'The ultimate number here seems to be nine; the best for doing rituals. Three circles of three; each with the girl, the woman and the crone.'

'I've heard of those three before.'

'It's pretty standard in magic lore, I'm not surprised this version of magic has some similar stuff.'

'What am I?' he asked.

'I don't know. I haven't got to anything involving men in ritual. So far it discourages them from getting involved.'

He laughed an empty humourless laugh. 'Course it does.'

'I'm telling you what is says. I don't know any more than you.'

'Sorry. I'm bitter about Rhonda.' He paused. 'I'm going to have to end it. I don't want to be my own, but I can't go on like this. She's supposed to be back in mid-November.'

'That's a fair while away.'

'I don't think I want to wait that long. She'll have to find somewhere else to go and I should give her some warning. I can't lie if I know it's over.'

'What will she do?'

'She's said before if she can't have me, she wants nothing to do with me. I've threatened to end it before, I thought it might make her treat me with more respect, but she wasn't interested in compromise.'

She reached out to put her hand on his shoulder, he was shaking, she saw the pain and confusion in his face. He seemed to be struggling to make a decision, as though he knew he needed to end it but didn't want it to be over at the same time.

'If you want to be alone, I can come back.'

'Don't go,' he said. 'Would it be okay if I sit here quietly? I'm not up to saving the world today, but while you're here I feel helpful.'

'Of course.'

'Cup of tea?' he asked.

'Always.'

He patted her foot and padded back into the kitchen. He moved slowly as though physically weighed down. He put on some music, quiet and classical, and sat with her, hands wrapped around his cup of tea, staring into space. She felt his eyes on her a few times, but when she looked up, he looked away.

Freya went back to the journal and flicked to the last few entries. The sketch of the beach was confronting; it was the same pattern as the scars on her eye with a black hole in the centre. She traced her fingers over the pattern and felt a tingle in the scar tissues. The shape was tied to the *Seidhr*.

Hettie had taken a couple of friends with her; Sylvie and Ingrid.

We encountered a young man who gave me the willies as we were walking away from the beach. His presence felt wrong. He introduced himself as Craig, an insufferably common name, but when I shook his hand, I knew he was feeding. When he let me go, I was too weak to do anything but watch him walk away. Sylvie and Ingrid shook his hand too and were dazed and weak. We made it home, I drove on autopilot. He knows me now and I must make my preparations. This will be the end of me.

Freya turned the page; it was the second last entry. Despite her tendency for the melodramatic, Hettie stopped writing only two days later.

Sylvie and Ingrid succumbed today; they have joined the others in the hospital in the city. My own strength is leaving me, I will follow shortly. Theo is the only one who can find the Woman and the Girl now. Perhaps he will be less susceptible as he is a man. The feminine power has been defiled and balance must be restored else we are all doomed.

That answers one question at least, Theodore was the intended recipient of the books.

'Something interesting?' Jacob asked. He looked much brighter after having sat in comfortable silence for some time.

'You look better.'

'I feel a bit braver, but still not looking forward to it.'

'Hettie seems to think there's a girl.'

'Not you?'

'I think I'm 'The Woman'' she said, putting air quotes around the words. 'I think the girl is likely to be pubescent or younger. There's a fair amount about the onset of menarche.'

'What?'

'Getting a period,' she explained.

'Oh.'

'I got mine at twelve, so we might be looking for quite a young girl.'

'Jesus. That's a lot of responsibility for a kid.'

'I guess that's what we're here for.'

Jacob made a sound which could have been agreement. He didn't seem himself at all. Freya excused herself to use the bathroom and have a look around.

Rhonda had put her stamp on everything. The products in the shower were matching; shampoo, conditioner, body wash, body milk, which Freya assumed was fancy moisturiser, all looked expensive. In the cabinet behind the mirror were makeup and other items. Shoved at the bottom of the cupboard under the sink were a beard trimmer and a few masculine looking items. One toothbrush sat on the edge of the sink. It felt as though Jacob didn't live here, even though Rhonda was only there part of the year. A nugget of sadness settled in her gut.

She sighed, Jacob needed to sort it out for himself, she only hoped he would get over the initial shock quickly so he could help her on what was turning out to be more like an epic quest than simply getting her friend back.

When she returned to the lounge room Jacob was flipping through the *Seidhr*.

'I have an idea where to look for the girl.'

'Oh?'

'Yeah. If you're the women, and Hettie is the crone, we only need the girl, right?'

'Right, although it sounded like we needed nine to make it work properly.'

'Maybe. Listen to this: The youngest, the girl, of the circle must be related by blood to at least one, and preferably both the other two. Linkage by bloodline allows power to flow through the circle with less resistance, finding its resonance more easily among related practitioners.'

Freya sat on the couch. She was surprised Jacob had managed to shake off his funk so quickly, but perhaps he was good at compartmentalisation. 'My older brother has a child, but she's only five.'

'I think more like twelve or thirteen. The onset of menarche, as you said, seems to be a good time.'

'How did you find in the time I was in the bathroom?' she asked.

'It's on the second page after where you were. I was skimming, but the heading was '*On casting powerful circles*', so I read that bit.'

She smiled, it would be his luck to find exactly the right section of the book, one which incidentally had no chapters and no index, after five minutes when she'd spend hours and only scratched the surface.

'Any early teen girls related to you?'

'I have a cousin who'd fifteen, but she lives in New Zealand,' she said.

'Hmm.' The energy which had been animating Jacob's frame, buoying him dissipated as she watched. He slumped back into the couch.

'What about someone related to Hettie?'

'She's not part of the circle, if she's Withered,' he said.

'Plus, we don't know where she is or how to find her. Maybe we need a different third for the circle.'

'Know any crones you're related to who would do magic with you?'

'Apart from my mother?' She chuckled. 'Even if the end of the world depended on it, my mother would never agree to it.'

They sat in silence for a moment. Freya fought her own disappointment; they had barely begun. The book said it was a feminine power, but there was nothing in it to say the circle had to be made up of women. The girl was required, the onset of puberty in boys was not easily marked, but surely, they could replace the crone.

'What about you?' she asked.

'What about me?'

'Do you know any teen girls?'

He thought for a moment, his hand absently rubbing the seam along the arm of the black leather couch. 'My sister's thirteen, half-sister. Dad remarried. But that doesn't help us, she has to be related to someone in the circle.'

'You could take Hettie's place. Nothing says you can't.'

'Uh uh,' he said. He rifled through the pages of the book he'd read. 'It all talks about the circle being women.'

'But does it say specifically the circle can't have men?'

'No, but didn't you say?'

'I said it was usually women, it was unmasculine. That's not the same as always women. Plus, if you're secure in your manliness, you'll be fine.'

He spluttered and made a sound almost like a laugh. 'You're serious?'

'I think it would work.'

'Fuck.'

'And half-sister is a pretty good match. I dunno if it's stronger than niece, maybe about the same. I get confused by lineage stuff.'

'It's not a skill I've had to use often.'

Freya sat forward on her seat. 'Can we visit her? Your sister. I'm sure if I laid hands on her I'd know whether she was right for the job. And we'd know you're supposed to be in the circle. It can't be coincidence your songs can put people under a spell, you have a sister of the right age, and we met a couple of days after this all started. It's fate.' She jumped up from the couch and started to pace up and down in front of the coffee table. She felt an energy tingling in her fingers, and groin; a fizzing as though she would create a spark if she touched anything. It was unlike any other feeling she'd had; she was giddy with it.

'Earth to Freya?' Jacob said.

'What?'

'I've been trying to tell you my sister won't work. She's deaf.'

'I'm half blind and I seem to be at the centre of this whole stupid thing. Plus, as long as we can communicate to her how much we need her it will be fine. I have to meet her, it's the only way we'll know.'

Jacob look at his hands and sighed. 'Alright. I'll text her. We can probably go around today.' He looked at his watch. 'I don't think she has any activities on a Saturday afternoon, she plays soccer in the morning.'

Freya clasped her hands together in front of her in an effort not to pounce on him; as though moving in slow motion, he reached for his mobile and typed out the message. She turned to look out the front window of his apartment. She moved the lace curtain aside to see better.

I wouldn't have thought Rhonda would allow such an ugly curtain in her house, but I guess she values privacy over aesthetics.

Outside the late winter afternoon cast a pall of dull light over the open, concrete carpark and the road beyond. The world was waiting for something important to happen. She looked along the balcony rail and was startled to see a raven alight on it. It hopped sideways along the railing until it was directly in front of her. It let out a short mournful caw and looked at her.

The sense of urgency drained from her; she was suspended in time. She had felt something similar the day she'd lost her eye. As she tried to turn back to Jacob the world faded and she was thrust into an immersive vision.

She sat at a large green leather covered writing desk. In front of her was Hettie's journal, and what felt like her own hand was writing in those spidery, boxy letters, quickly across the page.

It was hard to write; it was one of the last days Hettie was able to function. The document was a letter, but not to Theodore.

I don't know what is in store for me, or anyone else. I want you to know I have always loved you. Even when you did not love me, all those times you tried to have me committed. You were not touched by the magic running in our family. Even with the events of the last few months, nothing has awakened in you.

If I am not here, or something happens to me, know only I have always loved you. I am proud of you, and I forgive you, my only son.

She shuddered as the vision left her. Her legs felt shaky she wanted to sit down. The raven cried out again, bobbing its head before taking flight.

'Hettie had a son,' she said.

'How do you know?' Jacob asked. 'I texted my sister, she's usually pretty quick to get back to me.'

'There was a raven outside. I had a vision of Hettie writing to her son. She knew she was on the way out, putting her affairs in order. We have to fix this.'

'We will. It'll be alright.' Jacob stood and came over to her. He gently steered her back to the austere black leather couch in the middle of the minimalist living room. He sat and when Freya laid her head in his lap, he stroked her short hair. She should stop him; but being touched, the soothing feeling of his fingers in her hair, the fact she wasn't being bombarded with his feelings or incomprehensible images even though his skin touched hers was a luxury she couldn't give up.

His phone buzzed on the table. She sat up and he reached for it.

'She says she's free. I guess we go see her and figure out if we have a circle.'

Freya nodded. It was one thing to find the members of the circle, but what they were supposed to do afterwards remained a mystery.

Chapter 12

Freya and Jacob drove over to visit his sister, Dinah, who lived with her parents in St Kilda.

'I don't get on much with my dad, but I try to keep in touch with Dinah. She's kind of an only child even though there are three of us older siblings,' Jacob explained.

'Are they older or younger than you?'

'I'm the youngest of Dad's first lot. He left my mum when I was fifteen and moved in with his secretary, what a cliché right? She was sick of his shit after three years and he ended up with Josie after that. She was a bit younger and wanted to have kids, but Dad didn't so they compromised by having one.'

'I see.'

'That's Dad's story. We suspect Josie got pregnant accidentally on purpose and Dad was stuck with it. At least they're still together. Occasionally I worry he'll leave them like he left us, but so far they're going strong.'

The house was a single-front terrace house in a quiet suburban street. The front garden was barren, and the tiled veranda had two white wicker chairs which looked a bit worse for wear.

'Dad's got a brown thumb, and Josie has no interest in the garden,' Jacob said. Sometimes she wondered if he'd picked up more than his singing abilities when he said things like that.

'Dinah has a cochlear implant, she can hear you, but she finds it easier if you face her when speaking to her.'

Jacob knocked on the red front door and then rang the bell, it seemed rude to use both, but it was his family. She heard footsteps thumping down the hallway, either a very large person or someone wearing noisy shoes.

The front door opened to reveal a young girl, not tall, she would have reached Freya's shoulder, with long straight brown hair, parted in the middle and hanging loose around her face. She had the same intense ice-blue eyes as Jacob's and wore black track suit pants, slung low around her hips, a skin-tight T-shirt with what Freya assumed was a band logo on it, and a silver sequinned bomber jacket. The laces on her huge army boots were undone, explaining some of the noise coming to the door.

'Hi,' she said, it was moderately more eloquent than a grunt.

'Hi Dinah, this is Freya. I told you I was bringing her over to talk to you about something.'

'Mmm.' Dinah turned and stomped back down the long hallway toward the lounge room.

'After you,' Jacob said, holding his arm out to indicate she should follow Dinah.

The hallway ran the length of the house; the sort of place which always put Freya in mind of a train carriage,

155

two bedrooms at the front of the house, one was very neat and probably belonged to her parents, the second was a smaller and looked as though clothing store had exploded in it. The loungeroom was mostly neat, apart from the empty packet of chips on the coffee table, a plate with the remains of a sandwich and several glasses with varying levels of liquid in them.

Dinah sat in an enormous armchair which looked like it was trying to swallow her and was already back playing something on her tablet device.

'Can I offer you a tea or something, Freya?' Jacob said.

'Sure, that'd be nice.'

Jacob waved at his sister. 'You want anything?'

'Nup.'

He disappeared into the kitchen beyond the lounge. Freya felt awkward standing and took a seat on the vast sofa near Dinah. She wanted to reach out and touch her, to see if she got a vision and try to figure out if Dinah the right person but needed to wait for the right moment. She was engrossed and Freya was uncharacteristically nervous to interrupt her.

Jacob pottered around in the kitchen, opening cupboards and clinking cups and spoons. Freya sat back, took a few deep breaths, and tried to calm herself.

'What'd you do to your eye?' Dinah asked. Her voice was slightly muddy.

Freya jumped; she hadn't realised the girl had stopped playing her game. 'I lost it.'

'Cool. Is it gory?'

'Not anymore.'

'Can I see?' Dinah had become much more animated now she was focused on the potential goriness of Freya's eye.

'It's a bit gross. I don't think your brother would approve.'

'Never mind him,' she said quietly. 'I wanna see.'

'You have to promise not to be traumatised.'

'I won't be. I've seen heaps of gross stuff.' Dinah sat forward on her chair and leaned towards her to get a better look. Freya hesitated a moment, then lifted her eye patch away to show the girl the scars and the empty pink socket where her right eye used to be.

'Eeewwwww' she said, smiling. 'That's so gross.'

Freya let the patch flip down again. 'I told you.'

'What happened?' she asked again, and Jacob came in with two cups of tea.

'Freya doesn't need to be grilled the moment you meet her. Morbid.' Jacob stuck out his tongue at his sister, and she returned the gesture.

'Why are you here? You haven't been for ages and you never bring people.'

'Let me answer this one,' Freya said. 'I want to ask for your help with something. But before I get too far into it, I wanted to ask if you've noticed anything different about yourself in the last, say, six months?'

'Is this a puberty talk? I've heard this one.'

'I wasn't thinking of puberty, but has something else been happening, with your body maybe?'

'I don't really want to talk about it with him here.' She jutted her chin in Jacob's direction.

'I'll make myself scarce,' he said, and walked down the hallway and out onto the front veranda. Once he was out of earshot Dinah dropped her voice and went on.

'I started my period about six months ago.'

'Okay. Anything else? Maybe something you weren't expecting?' Freya didn't want to put ideas in the girl's head, but she was sure there was more to it.

'You'll think I'm crazy.'

'I promise I won't.'

Dinah stared at her hands and picked at her fingernails for a moment. 'I can tell what people are thinking sometimes.'

'Really? Can you tell when I'm thinking now?' Freya brought the image of the rolling thunderhead into her mind and concentrated on it.

'A big storm?'

'Anything else?' Freya probed.

'Big black clouds, rain and sometimes lightning. Maybe a beach, I'm not really sure though.'

'Okay, what about now?' Freya thought of the vision of Hettie's handwriting out her last letters; the wrinkled skin on her hand, the boxy, spidery writing.

'An old lady writing a letter.' Dinah frowned. 'How come you're the old lady?'

Freya was convinced. 'Before I tell you the rest of the story, I need to hold your hand. I have a gift too, but I need to touch you. Is that okay?'

She shrugged. 'Yeah alright.'

Freya took both of Dinah's hands between hers and concentrated. She cleared her mind and tried to be open to whatever the universe wanted to show her. The skin on her hands prickled, like static electricity, and she had a feeling in the back of her nose as though she needed to sneeze, but instead of the sneeze she had a powerful vision. She, Dinah, and Jacob were standing on a beach, it was night. She could feel her mouth moving, as though chanting, but as with her other visions, it was silent. The wind whipped rain in her face, and she felt a ball of panic rising from her belly.

She dropped Dinah's hands and the vision subsided.

'What the hell was that?' Dinah asked.

'What do you mean?'

'I can tell what you're thinking, remember? Especially when you're thinking so loudly. Why were we at the beach?'

'It's a long story; I think we should get Jacob back here. He needs to know about your new talent.'

'He won't like that I already got a couple of things from him.' She giggled.

'Don't tell me. Can you turn it on and off?'

'Sort of. Sometimes I get things even when I'm not trying, like before with you, but mostly I have to think about it.'

'Jacob,' she shouted. 'You can come back in.'

She heard him close the front door and clump down the hallway.

Perhaps everyone sounds like an elephant in this house.

'Finished with the secret women's business?' he said.

'Yes, mostly. Sit.' Freya patted the overly squishy cushion next to her. 'Dinah can read minds.'

'Ah, shit.'

'I didn't get anything juicy. Anyway, I wouldn't tell her if I did.' Dinah said. Jacob's cheeks flushed bright red and he looked away.

'I took her hand and got a vision of the three of us, on the beach. I think we were doing the counter ritual.'

'What makes you say that?' Jacob said.

'What's a counter ritual?' Dinah asked at the same time.

'I'll tell you everything in a minute, Dinah,' she said, then turned back to Jacob. 'We were chanting on the same beach as I saw in the vision last night. The one the raven sent me.'

'There's a raven?' Dinah interrupted. Freya waved her hand to shush her.

'You really think she's the girl we want?' Jacob said, as much to himself as anyone else. 'I guess that means I'm the third in the circle. Fuck.'

'Don't swear,' Dinah said. Jacob shook his head.

'She's the right age, she's demonstrating remarkable abilities, she's related to you and you have your own abilities.'

'What can he do?' Dinah asked.

'Your brother can put people into a trance state.'

'Cool,' Dinah said.

'We haven't worked out the full extent of anyone's abilities: yours, mine, Jacob's. We'd need to do some experiments. But more importantly, have you heard about the people in the hospitals who are in a sort of coma?'

Dinah's face fell. 'Yeah.'

Freya put her hand up to Jacob, gesturing to him to wait a moment. She thought Dinah had more to say.

'A girl in my class, she got it.' She looked askance at Freya.

'We're calling it the Withering. It seems to be connected to the abilities. Go on.'

'Not much more to say, one day she was at school, next day she didn't come in, then a week later we get called into assembly and told she's won't be back any time soon. She's in hospital. We all had to promise not to annoy her family. It's so unfair, no one tells us anything.'

'We don't think anyone knows much. Even the people at the hospitals are stumped,' Jacob said.

'What makes you think I want anything to do with it? It sounded pretty scary and full on. I don't wanna be a hero.'

'Here's the thing, kiddo,' Jacob began. 'I don't wanna be a hero either. I was quite happy being Joe Bloggs, but when I went into the ward with all the Withered patients, it was like—you remember the time we went to the RSPCA to adopt a kitten? Dad was keen but your mum wasn't. Remember the feeling you said you felt in there? All those dogs and cats waiting for someone to take them home and love them? You said it felt like they knew they were waiting to die. It felt like that, but ten times worse.'

Dinah shivered and put her hand over her mouth. 'They were so sad. I wanted to take them all home, and them Mum said we couldn't even have one kitty. I was so mad at her.'

'You felt powerless right?' Freya said.

'Yeah.'

'That's how I feel now. But I've been given these visions, been chosen for some reason, to help set these people free. To help right whatever was done to them, and to put things back to the way they were.'

Dinah folded her arms.

'If you could have taken all the kitties home, would you have?'

'Of course.'

'So now you know you have the power to help the Withered, will you?'

Dinah blew out her breath loudly and unfolded her arms. 'It sounds hard.'

'I know Deens,' Jacob said, getting up from his position on the couch and perching on the armchair next to his sister. 'It will be hard. But Freya and me will be with you. We're a team.' He hugged her to his side, and she allowed him. She couldn't appear to need reassurance, but Freya was sure it helped.

'What now?' he asked.

'We fill Dinah in on what we know and figure out a plan.' Freya pulled the three books from her backpack and laid them on the coffee table. Jacob had to move two glasses to make room. They showed Dinah what they'd learned and explained the importance of creating a circle.

'The image of the three of us, in the rain, on the beach, I think that's the future. We have to figure out what the hell we're doing there and find the right beach,' Freya said.

'Jeez, should be easy,' Dinah said.

'What did we say about it being easy?' Jacob said.

'Don't be too hard on her. She's just found out she has to save the world. I'd be a bit snarky too.'

Dinah smirked at her older brother; pleased Freya had sided with her. There was a sound of keys in the front door.

'We should probably put the books away,' Jacob said.

Freya quickly gathered them into her backpack. 'Why?'

'Dad's very against anything he calls "woo".'

'What's woo?' Freya asked. Before Jacob could answer, his father walked into the room. The resemblance between the three of them was clear; he was tall, broad shouldered and heavyset. His salt and pepper hair was thick, relatively short, and he had the piercing blue eyes shared by his children. He wore a charcoal pinstriped three-piece suit and a blue tie and matching pocket square. If Freya had met him at a work function, she would have assumed he was in charge.

'Dinah, have you been sitting on your arse all day?' he said when he came out of the hallway. 'Hello Jacob. You've brought a friend.' He arched one eyebrow in disapproval.

'This is Freya, she's—'

'We're working on a research project together for the hospital. Jacob thought it would be good for Dinah to get experience on a project like this. What with her aspirations.'

'Yeah, I was thinking about interning, or whatever,' Dinah said. Freya smiled at her thankful she had picked up on the deception so seamlessly.

'You're going to be an occupational therapist too, now are you?' their father said.

'I haven't decided. I might do medicine, or law, like you, but, like, it sounded fun.'

'Fun?' he repeated.

'Y'know, not fun, but like, a good idea?' Dinah was floundering. She was clearly not used to standing up to her father, and Freya couldn't blame her, he was an imposing man.

'If you don't think it's good for her, obviously we'll be able to find another student to take the role, but a girl with Dinah's background would be a good fit.' Freya injected as much authority into her voice as she could muster, sitting bolt upright in the alarmingly soft couch.

'You'll be there to keep an eye on her at all times, I assume.' He addressed his question to Jacob.

'Course, Dad. She'll be doing literature reviews and paperwork.'

'Mmm,' he said. 'If you say so.'

If anything goes wrong, he'll blame Jacob. She focused on keeping her expression neutral.

'Are you staying for dinner?' he asked, abruptly changing the subject and signalling the conversation was closed. Jacob looked at his sister briefly.

'No, we'll be off. I can send her the stuff she needs via email and we'll be back next weekend to start work.'

'Good to see you then. Freya.' He nodded and went through to the kitchen. She looked from the one to the other sibling, some unspoken communication was going on she didn't understand.

'We'd better head off,' Jacob said in a low voice.

'Did we do something to upset your dad?'

'He thinks I'm a bad influence. Better to get out of his hair before he has a reason to stop Dinah from getting involved in the research project we've made up.'

'I was thinking on the fly. Sorry I didn't come up with a better cover story,' she whispered.

'We'll talk soon,' he said to Dinah. Jacob stood up and started toward the door.

'Bye,' Dinah replied.

'Do we need to say bye to your dad?' Freya asked.

'He's already dismissed us.'

Freya was silent as they walked out the front of the house and got into the car, mulling over the family dynamics. She should leave it alone, but she couldn't resist.

'I wonder what I'd get from him.'

'I wouldn't recommend it. He's a cold fish, is my father.' Jacob pulled out and gunned the engine.

'I gathered. Who wears a suit on Saturday?'

'Doesn't believe in casual wear or time off. You could say he was a workaholic, but it's the only thing he's any good at.'

'What does he do?'

'Barrister. He would have been briefing a client or something today. That's an "important client" suit.' Jacob's fingers were gripping the steering wheel much tighter than necessary.

'Relax. We've found the girl.'

'It could have been any girl,' he said without looking at her. 'Why did it have to be her? Why did it have to be me?'

Freya reached over to put her hand over his. 'I'm sorry this is so hard for you. It must be weird to have all this stuff thrust on you. Especially now your little sister is involved. And lying to your dad must have been hard.'

'I've lied to him for years. He knows I lie, and he prefers it to having a real conversation.'

Freya waited. 'But?'

'But she's thirteen. I don't want her to end up trapped in her own body, or worse. We don't know anything, and I don't like it.'

'It'll be alright,' Freya lied. She knew in her bones they had to do something. No one else would.

Chapter 13

Over the next week, Freya read the leather-bound books in every spare moment. The *Elder Edda* was almost impenetrable; filled with confusing poetry and allusions to various gods and goddesses of the Norse mythology. She became so confused she went to the internet to find a family tree of Norse deities to help her keep track of the more important characters. Even so, the relationships were often blurred and depended on which source you believed.

The *Seidhr* was much easier going, perhaps a modern translation. Together they revealed a rich and vibrant world of magic and myth, which someone had believed strongly enough to invoke powers which brought the Withering into her life.

Several passages mentioned most people's potential in *Seidhr* magic was not realised but needed to be unlocked or released in order to do great works. This unlocking was vague and required sacrifice. Freya was unsure if it meant blood sacrifice, metaphorical sacrifice, or something completely different.

Jacob checked in once a day, he had been looking for additional material online, now they had a better idea of what to search for. He and Dinah had created a group message on their mobile phones where they argued about recent activity on one obscure online forum or other. Freya mostly took a back seat to these conversations, occasionally adding a titbit of information to direct them.

The *Seidhr* was a magic of seeing into others' minds, into the past or future. From this 'seeing' the practitioner derived their power or influence. If you could predict the outcome of a fight or horse race, you could be rich, and if you were rich you were powerful.

What she didn't find was any reference to devouring people's energy and making them into husks.

Perhaps this is the sacrifice. Not an offering at the time of the ritual but constant feeding to maintain the new level of power.

Any luck with finding out what's causing the Withering? she texted Dinah and Jacob on Thursday night.

Nah. People on the forums are talking about it, but they're as confused as we are, Jacob wrote back.

Check this out, Dinah replied. She had found a website where someone calling themselves VisionMage was claiming responsibility for the increased magical activity in Melbourne. It was from May, and since the original post, VisionMage had gone silent.

I did it. I brought on the storm and released the potential of all you puny try-hard 'practitioners' out there. You should be thanking me and giving yourselves up to my hunger. These people in the hospitals? They're the ones I sacrificed so we could

169

**keep the party going. If I stop the feeding, this all
stops. All hail VisionMage.**

**Wow. Try to find out what you can about the
original poster, and we'll meet up on Saturday,** Freya
wrote back. The comments below the original post were
both enlightening and full of hatred and trolls; others
claiming they were responsible, or VisionMage was an
imposter. But one person said she was there.

Freya searched for her other activity online and found
she was active in a few clairvoyant circles and much less
boastful than VisionMage. Freya created an account and
contacted WitchPrincess34.

**Hey, I wondered if you could help me. I have been
getting visions since February, I think it's something to
do with what VisionMage was talking about. Do you
know him? I'd like to ask him some stuff about what
I've been going through. Thanks.**

She could only hope WitchPrincess34 would be
willing to talk, if not about VisionMage then about how
she was involved.

*

Saturday morning came around WitchPrincess34
hadn't replied. Freya was to join Jacob and Dinah at his
place to go over what they'd learned and come up with a
plan. It was the end of August and the pressure of time
was bearing down on her. Despite feeling they knew very

little she felt something was building to a point after which the Withered couldn't be saved.

She'd woken from disturbing dreams most nights, images of people trying to claw at her as she passed, ghostly images of the Withered reaching for her. The worst was Eva, her mouth wide in a soundless scream and pleading with her eyes for Freya to rescue her. Despite the chill weather, she woke covered in sweat.

When she left her apartment, the raven was hopping from foot to foot on the roof of a nearby car. She turned away; if it wanted to tell her something, it would, and if it was an ordinary bird, she didn't need to pay it any attention. She shivered every time she saw a raven now, not only had one taken her eye, but also often filled her with overwhelming and indecipherable visions. Part of her blamed the raven, though she knew the three figures on the beach had brought it on.

She stopped off at the café on the way and picked up two lattes and a hot chocolate for Dinah. The raven was waiting outside the café when she left, and then as she approached Jacob's apartment building, the bird alighted on the balcony.

'Alright, I see you,' she said aloud. She climbed the stairs and knocked on Jacob's apartment door.

'Hey,' Dinah answered.

'You see the bird, right?' Freya asked.

She narrowed her eyes. 'You think he's following you?'

'How did—yes. I think it's the same raven as… sometimes I get visions from it. Nothing so far today, maybe it's keeping an eye on me, like a creep.'

'I dunno, he looks friendly.' Dinah stepped around her and approached the bird. Freya flinched as he hopped closer to Dinah's outstretched hand. 'Hey there. Who's a pretty boy?' The raven stood up proudly and edged closer. Dinah moved her hand steadily towards him, and when he didn't fly off, she gently stroked her finger down his breast.

'Are you someone's pet? Is that why you like people so much?' she cooed.

'I think he's involved.'

'Or he's your familiar.' She turned and flashed a cheeky smile at Freya.

'We'll see. Come back inside. I don't like you touching it.'

Dinah shrugged and headed back into the apartment. 'Bye, Mr Raven,' she said.

'Who's Mr Raven?' Jacob asked, taking a coffee from the cardboard tray in Freya's hand.

'He's following Freya around. I think he's cute, but she's scared of him.'

'You would be too if a bird had pecked out your eye.' Jacob said.

'I guess.' Dinah looked at her feet. Freya couldn't blame her for being excited and curious, but she did wish the girl would be a bit more thoughtful.

'I got you a hot chocolate, Dinah,' Freya said, holding the tray towards her.

'Awesome.' Dinah smiled and took the cup. They sat in Jacob's loungeroom, sipping quietly.

'I haven't heard back from the woman on the forum. I'm starting to wonder if she's ever going to reply,' Freya said.

'She might not. It's not the end of the world. I did some more digging and found some stuff about damage to a beach down in Rye. The Bureau of Meteorology put it down to a lightning strike apparently. I couldn't get any photos, but there was a tiny article in the local paper. We'll have to go down there to check it out.'

'I wonder why they chose there,' Freya thought aloud.

'I suspect they wanted access to the ocean; it's on the Bass Strait side. Maybe an elemental thing; earth, air, water, fire. If I was going to find a powerful link to air and water, it would be a beach.'

'The visions are all windy.' A tightness grabbed Freya's chest as though she couldn't breathe deeply.

'Are you alright?' Dinah asked. 'You've gone all pale.'

Freya snapped her attention back to the room and took a deep inhale. 'I felt really strange.'

'Felt like you were panicking,' Dinah said.

'Maybe I was a little bit. This whole thing scares the shit out of me.'

'Me too. I have no idea who we're dealing with or what their powers are, but you said we can't sit around and wait for more people to become Withered.'

Freya nodded.

'We've found our circle, we're on the right track,' Dinah added.

'I wish we knew what we were supposed to do.' Freya sipped the last of her latte and tried to bring her thoughts back into line. She felt morose and defeated.

'We have to work with what we're given. No one else is going to do it,' Jacob said.

'I hope we're enough.'

'Come on, misery guts. We get to play with magic!' Dinah said. Freya couldn't work out why she was so enthusiastic; perhaps the frisson of lying to her father, or merely the illicit nature of doing magic, something a lot of teenaged girls dabbled in.

'What else did you find?'

'The same local paper did a story on a spate of recent robberies. Not much of value was taken; things of significance, a wedding album, a vase filled with human cremains, a baby blanket, weird stuff.'

'We still haven't figured out what is meant by sacrifice. It's possible they needed things of value to perform the ritual, but maybe not of monetary value, instead emotional value,' Freya said.

'What if this wasn't the first time they'd tried it?' Dinah asked. 'What's the last thing you did perfectly the first time?'

'She's got a point,' Freya said.

Jacob opened his laptop on the coffee table and put it on his lap. 'What should I look for? I can't search police records or anything, and I wouldn't have thought the lightning would work until the ritual was really going well.'

'Try the forums,' Freya said. 'Maybe look for conversations about sacrifices. VisionMage can't have popped up out of nowhere a few months ago, if he'd been active before it might have been using a different name.'

Jacob typed a few things into the search function, his brows drawn together in concentration. Freya caught herself thinking about how lovely his mouth looked, his top teeth digging into the fleshy lower lip.

Stop sexualising him! He's with someone else. The quiet in the loungeroom drew out and Freya became restless. She walked to the front window and moved aside the net curtain; the raven was still on the railing, silent and watchful. She wished it would deliver whatever message it had and go. Dinah had started flipping through the *Elder Edda*, and seemed to be making good progress, which left Freya with the spell book and the *Seidhr*. She'd spent so much time with them already she didn't know what more she could possibly find.

She closed her eyes and held her hands over the spell book, palms down.

Tell me what I need to know.

Freya stroked her fingers along the fore-edge, letting the pages flutter through her fingers. After a moment they stilled, she opened her eyes and pulled the book open to the page where her fingers had stopped.

Spring Equinox. A time of life, balance of light and dark, the coming of warmth, the power of the Woman coming into maturity. It's not as harsh here as in other parts of the world it's true, but the hope and promise of summer are always well received. I felt something today, I'm not entirely sure what, a ripple in the flow of power. It bodes ill. The flow should not ripple—whoever it is runs the risk of tearing apart the universe trying to do whatever it is they're doing.

Hettie's entry for the day filled Freya's belly with tension. Nearly five months before they succeeded on her birthday, who knows what mistakes they'd made along the way or what the consequences might be. Maybe the Withering was not an effect of the successful ritual at all but had come from one of their earlier experiments. Freya shook her head. The Withered were feeding whatever power they'd unleashed; an ongoing sacrifice to keep magic where it was not supposed to be.

She'd read in the *Elder Edda* of the various afterlives of the Norse pantheon. The mortal realm wasn't meant to have as much magic as it did right now; it was outside the natural order and would possibly need more and more souls to feed on to keep it going.

'I found something in September last year. A ritual calling for nine people; Celebration of the Moon.'

'What does it say?'

Seeking practitioners for Moon worship ritual. We'll be working on a beach at midnight. You need to be committed to the ritual no matter what happens. We've never done something this powerful before, hold onto your hats. Genuine Seidhr practitioners only. This is real.

'Sounds like VisionMage. "This is real".' Freya laughed.

'Only fakes ever put "this is real" on stuff. People do it at school all the time.' Dinah said. 'This says Odin did *Seidhr*, even though it was considered feminine. I guess that means it's okay for you to get involved bro.'

Dinah held the *Edda* in her hands. 'Odin gave up his eye to drink from the well Mimir to gain cosmic knowledge. And he had two ravens, Huginn and Muninn who were his spies. Maybe that's why those birds follow you around.'

'Don't be ridiculous,' Freya said. As though Odin, and his spies were real entities.

'Being able to see the future is fine. And I can read people's minds, but that's totally normal.'

'Enough, Dinah,' Jacob said. A ball of emotion rose in Freya's throat. She was struggling to hold herself together without Dinah making fun of her. Her breath was ragged and shallow.

Without another word, Freya opened Jacob's front door and raced down the stairs onto the footpath. She didn't turn, even when she heard him calling her name.

She wanted to cry but didn't want him or Dinah to see her tears. It was hard enough to reconcile having involved a child in this quest, with unknown dangers and no plan, and now Odin?

She kept walking, not paying attention where she was going. She stopped at a small, narrow park running between the houses on either side. A playground in the middle with a couple of hardy children climbing on the chilly metal equipment while their mothers huddled with coffees nearby. A little way further into the park was a bench under a drooping oak tree.

Freya sat on the bench, elbows on knees and head in her hands. She tried to slow her breathing, to allay the encroaching panic.

Deep inhale through the nose, blow out through the mouth.

As her breath calmed she started to cry; not the ugly sniffling cry she had been worried about, but a despairing release of tension. She didn't know what she was doing, she didn't want to put anyone in danger but the more she found out, the surer she was they would never be the same. But they had to. Hettie and Eva had already fallen prey to this idiot and his quest for power.

She'd run off without her coat and was shivering when she heard her name called.

'Freya!' Jacob and Dinah were coming down the path towards her.

'Are you okay?' Dinah asked. Jacob held out her trusty grey woollen overcoat and she gratefully wrapped it around herself.

'We didn't know where you'd gone. Dinah could feel you were close but wasn't very good at directions.'

'It was like playing hotter and colder, you know?' Dinah said. She was smiling as though she was pleased with herself.

'Thank you for coming,' Freya said. She brushed her fingers across her face, sweeping the tears away from underneath the slightly soggy eyepatch. She probably looked like she'd had a breakdown, and perhaps it was true.

'It's a lot to take in,' Jacob said. He sat next to her on the bench, Dinah sat on her other side. The girl snuggled up to her.

'It's too cold to stay out here. Come back to Jacob's.'

Freya sighed heavily and pulled the lapels of her coat up around her throat. Jacob stood, putting his hand on her shoulder.

'Come on, you're the chosen one. We can't do this without you,' he said. Freya nodded and allowed him to pull her up from the bench. Dinah slipped her arm into Freya's and walked alongside her back to Jacob's place. They walked a little behind Jacob and Freya's eyeline kept being drawn to his muscular bottom. Each time she flicked her eyes away quickly.

'I've never liked Rhonda,' Dinah whispered.

'I don't know what you're talking about,' Freya whispered back.

'I can see what you're thinking about. You should go for it.'

'I don't think that's very fair.'

'If you're going to be all moral about it. He likes you too, you know.'

'Ssh!' Freya squeaked.

'You've gone bright red.' Dinah giggled and squeezed Freya's arm. 'When this is all over, he'll know Rhonda's a controlling bitch and he should go out with you. You'll have to be patient if you insist on waiting till she's out of the picture.'

'Keep your voice down.'

'He's thinking about the beach, he's not listening to us.'

'You're getting very comfortable with this new talent of yours.' Freya looked down at the younger girl, her bright blue eyes twinkling in the chill air.

'Since last week I've been working on it. Now I know I'm not going mad it's a lot easier to play with, y'know?'

'I guess so.' Freya hadn't spent much time trying to hone her skill. She was quite frightened of the results. She had no way of knowing if the emotional fallout was more than she could handle.

'I don't think you need contact,' Dinah said. 'I've been doing experiments, and it's easier to read someone when I'm touching them, or they're close to me, but I've tried my grandparents in Mildura, and I think I got them.

Nanna was thinking about scones in a very concerning way.' She giggled. 'Plus, you said you get them in your dreams and from the ravens.'

Freya thought about it. She had been averse to using her powers since the hospital. The draining of her energy, the shakiness, and the panic were overwhelming. She had also avoided touching people most of the time in case she was exposed to something she didn't want to see. She didn't understand the rules and became quite anxious even thinking about it.

'Alright. When we get back you and I will do an experiment.' Freya told herself as much as Dinah.

The raven was sitting on the railing and bobbed its head in greeting when she arrived. She approached it her hand held out as she might to a dog she didn't know.

'I don't know if you're Huginn or Muninn or some random bird. But I'm sorry I've been rude to you,' she said.

The bird squawked and adjusted its wings. She continued to approach it steadily, calmly. If it was just a bird, it was very tame, but could still take a good nip out of her fingers if it wanted to. She stroked the glossy black feathers on the bird's breast and braced herself for a vision, but none came. Instead a feeling of calm and welcoming flowed through her, as though her veins were filled with warm honey. She closed her eyes, intoxicated.

The sun broke through the clouds over the beach, two birds flying in a circle, high in the air, then they swooped and called; they were celebrating, playing. Freya opened her eyes and dropped her hand. The bird bobbed its head again and flew off.

'Bye, bird.'

Inside the apartment was warm and comforting. 'That one is Huginn, he's 'thought', the other one, Muninn, is 'memory'. Did you get the gooey feeling?' Dinah asked.

'Yes, it was weird. I wonder if it happens every time. I don't remember it from the eye incident. That was an out of body thing, but I was strangely calm, so maybe I did in a way.' She grinned as though drunk.

'I think it means we're doing the right thing. If they are Odin's birds, they would know if we're on the right track.'

'What are you on about?' Jacob asked from the couch.

'The ravens. Haven't you read any of this stuff?' Dinah asked.

He shrugged. 'So, the beach is here,' he pointed to the screen where the little red pointer showed up near the ocean in Rye. 'It's an hour and a half drive. If we left now, we wouldn't have much time before dark.'

Freya looked at the time, after two o'clock, she didn't know how the day had slipped away. 'If we don't go today, when would we go? We need all three of us. I want to join hands around the mark, when we find it, and see what I get.'

Dinah beamed at her. 'Let's go now. Dad won't let me hang out with you tomorrow, he's suspicious so we have to try not to push his buttons too much. If we're back late, I'll tell him we went to a movie after.'

'That's settled then.'

'Can we get Maccas on the way?'

'No, but we can get something to eat,' Jacob said. 'Maccas is nutritionally void and an evil corporation.'

Dinah sighed. Freya put the books into her bag and collected her coat. Dinah insisted on being in the front seat and having control of the music, Freya agreed, as she would have time to sit with the books and see if she could get anything from them using her gift.

Jacob had narrowed down the band of beach where the mark should be, to a couple of hundred metres based on the scant information in the local paper. The road to Rye was freeway for the first hour or so, and Freya stared out the window, her mind churning over what she knew and the visions. She'd never had one from the books, nor from any other inanimate object.

She held the spell book in both hands, closed her eyes and thought of opening herself like a flower to the universe, or Odin, or wherever the visions came from. For a while she felt nothing, she tried to tap into the warm honey feeling she'd had with the raven.

The music faded away and her mind filled with silence, the gentle motion of the car on the road was like she was floating. She saw the beach from above, the black stain scorched into the foreshore, deep black cuts through the scrubby grasses and the abyss in the centre. The hole pulsed with energy that felt wrong. The gooey feeling protected her a little from the wave of fear she felt looking into the hole, as though she was looking into another place.

'Dinah,' Freya called. She turned down the music and looked back towards her.

'Yes?'

'Is there something in the *Edda* about boundaries between worlds?'

'Hmm. There are the nine realms, and Yggdrasil, the tree of the world, connects them. There are a few worlds which might be interesting, like Vanaheim, where the old gods come from. They're at war with the Aesir, who are the new gods, like Odin. The *Edda* doesn't say where Vanaheim is. It's a bit vague to be honest.'

'Give me your hand for a minute,' Freya said. She took Dinah's hand in both of hers and concentrated. She brought the image of the pulsing black hole to mind and focused on it. She focused on the fear and darkness in the hole, she tried to go deeper into it, to fly her hovering self through the hole, but it didn't seem to work.

'You're the raven. Or you're in the raven. You can't go in the hole because the raven can't go in the hole.'

Freya opened her eyes. 'You saw all that?'

'Perks of my thing.' She winked.

'What are you two doing?' Jacob asked, not taking his eyes off the road.

'Mind melding with Freya, so we both see the vision. It's cool.'

'You think I'm the raven? Is that where the visions come from?' Freya asked.

'I have no idea, but you were flying. Those other visions were inside yourself or inside the guy who started the whole thing.'

'I can't just see the future; I have to see it through someone who's there.'

'Makes sense, well as much as any of the rest of it.' Jacob laughed. They stopped at a service station with a café attached. It was mid-afternoon but none of them had had lunch.

'Have a go at getting a vision off these people,' Dinah said as they sat down to eat.

'I don't know if I should on an empty stomach,' Freya replied.

'Excuses,' Dinah said. Jacob raised his eyebrows.

Freya put down her cheese and salad sandwich and tried to calm her mind. She did her slow breathing, let her eye go out of focus, and imagined putting tendrils out into the world. For a while nothing happened, the sounds of conversation and coffee machines droned on in the background.

As she sat there, almost in meditation, Freya noticed the sounds of the room around her fading. She started to see images in her mind which were not her own. The cash register where they bought their lunch, the slim hands of the woman behind the counter busily tapping away. She was bored and dissatisfied but smiled for the customers. Freya tried to feel back into the woman's past, not knowing if she could.

Fleur Blüm

A skinny young man lying next to her, she felt flushed and happy as though they had just made love. Another image in a classroom surrounded by scraggly teens, they looked about fourteen, all rowdy and jostling. She felt sadness and anxiety. The woman was afraid of something, her eyes kept darting to one of the boys in the group. He had been giving her a hard time.

Freya exhaled heavily and reached further back into this woman's past; a small child, blonde and chubby and wailing. There was a broken glass vase lying on the floor in front of the little girl and Freya saw her own hands, smaller and childlike, trying to clean up the broken glass. A sharp intense pain as the glass slashed her hand and blood poured out.

Freya shook her head and dragged herself back to the present. She felt slightly shaky but immensely proud of the control she'd shown.

'What happened?' Jacob asked.

'She went into the mind of the girl at the cash register. Felt like you went digging through her brain. It was so cool.' Dinah said.

'I think they were memories from her past, but I didn't choose her. She was, I don't know, the easiest person to go into.' Freya sighed.

'That was a really brilliant first try. And it proves you don't have to have physical contact. What did I tell you?' Dinah beamed at her. Freya couldn't help but feel proud of her effort.

'I did okay, didn't I?'

'Better than okay.' Jacob had finished his sandwich and tapped his fingers on the top of the table. 'We should push on.'

Freya and Dinah stood up, and with a weary acceptance, followed him out to the car. In the back seat a wave of fatigue come over her. She rested her head back against the seat and closed her eyes.

She slept fitfully for the rest if the journey, waking when Jacob turned off the engine.

'This is as close as I could get. I thought maybe you could, feel the rest of the way?'

Freya nodded. She felt drained but this was their best chance. The spring equinox was only a couple of weeks away and they needed to find the place of the original ritual to reverse it. This was an important step. Her gut said today was the day.

The beach was miserable, the late afternoon sun barely made it through the clouds. The whole area was bathed in a sort of dull silver light. It felt surreal, almost dreamlike.

They parked in a lot behind some scrubby grey green bushes. A lone picnic table sat with rubbish stuffed into the gaps between the palings. A sandy path lead from the foreshore to the beach. Freya hesitated, if this was the right place, she would probably have an intense vision. She turned back to the others.

'If I faint or have a seizure or something, make sure I don't injure myself. I don't know what's going to happen. If anything,' she said.

Jacob took her hand; his fingers were warm against the biting cold wind. 'We'll look after you.'

Freya nodded. She headed down the path towards the dark grey water. The sea was choppy and turbulent. As she approached, a tingle began in her fingertips and across the skin on her face. The closer she got to the water the more intense it became. Looking left and right along the sand she was drawn left. There was nothing obvious that way except more beach, a few clumps of seaweed, one seagull puffed up against the cold and a log, washed smooth by the water.

The salty sea spray fizzed in her mouth as she breathed it in. The tingling feeling in her skin intensified as she walked. Still nothing to see, but she knew it was the right direction. Jacob and Dinah followed her silently.

Freya continued along the hard-packed sand about two hundred metres, then stopped. The tingling had gone, and she looked around. To her right the rough grey sea extended to the horizon without interruption, to her left was a hill covered in scrawny looking grass. She walked up the hillock.

Behind the grassy dune was a hollow of about ten metres in diameter, at the centre of which was a large black hole. The sort of black you might expect from a fire pit, but it had no coal or ash in it, only smooth, liquid blackness, and radiating lines exactly the shape of the scars on Freya's eye.

As she passed her eyes over the scene, Freya became nauseated. She bent down, placing her hands on her knees and tried to breathe. The world spun, everything slid in and out of focus.

'Sit down,' Jacob said, his voice calm and deep. She felt him put his large warm hand on her back. Her knees crumpled and she fell heavily on her left side. Her mind didn't seem to work, half-formed images and thoughts swirled around her.

Jacob positioned himself behind her, his hands resting on her shoulder. He whispered soothing words she couldn't quite make out. Dinah sat next to her head and took her hand. A jolt of electricity fizzed through her as they touched.

'Mhymhm,' she mumbled. She took a breath and tried again. 'We need to form a circle.' She forced herself into a cross-legged seated position, with Dinah sitting on her left and Jacob on her right.

The three of them joined hands and suddenly everything around the faded from view. It was a bright day, the breeze was cool, but the sun burned down on them. Freya looked around, they were still three but no longer Dinah and Jacob. She saw their faces clearly but did not recognise them. A stocky blonde woman, in her late fifties, and an equally stocky girl, in her late teens. The ground was unblemished.

Freya felt invincible; the power she channelled through the hands which were not hers was intoxicating. The two women were mouthing something, chanting, but as always, the vision was silent. The wind picked up and started to whip sand into their legs; she felt the sting. The thunderhead gathered over the ocean; the air was thick with electricity. Then there was a blinding flash and a boom she felt vibrate through her chest.

She struggled to open her eyes; a long, crooked streak burned into her retinas. She had fallen when the lightning struck, as had her two companions. The circle was broken, the earth was scarred, and the ritual was done. The power ran through her, she could feel people's thoughts inside her head as though they were whispering secrets in her ears.

The vision faded. The ritual had been done on this spot. Two women and one man had made a circle in the middle of the day and brought the storm. It must have been the time the raven came down and took her eye. Perhaps the only way she could gain access to her power was through sacrifice.

'Did you see that?' Jacob asked.

'What did you see?' Freya let go of his hand and wrapped her arms around herself. She felt a cold which had nothing to do with the dismal weather.

'Three of us on the beach, but it wasn't you two; one was an old blonde woman, and the other an angry black-haired man.'

'I saw the same, but I was the man.'

'I must have been the blonde then; I saw the man and a blonde girl; older than me but not a lot.'

Freya swallowed, she strained to keep her thoughts focused, she was exhausted. 'That was the moment they did the ritual. It was more complete than any vision I've had before; less like a movie in my mind and more like I had become the other person.'

'I've never felt anything like it. No wonder you were anxious to experiment, Freya, they really knock you around,' Dinah said.

She nodded. The hole called to her. She needed to touch it, perhaps she would be able to figure out where the power came from and why it needed so much feeding. She shivered at the thought of putting her hand on the opening, but it had to be done. The skies were darkening, night would come on fast and she didn't want to be here in the dark.

She stood up, stumbled a little before righting herself. Above her two ravens circled, knowing they were there made her braver.

'Let's look in the hole and get out of here,' Freya said. Jacob and Dinah followed her to the centre.

Inside the hole looked like black glass. Freya bent to touch it and found it was sticky, black gloop. She tried to punch her hand through, but it felt as though she'd punched something solid. Next, she tried sliding her hand into the gloop slowly and, like a non-Newtonian fluid, it let her in. She saw a star-filled sky, and a cold purple planet below her. She was not welcome in this world, but a part of her was called towards it, like she belonged.

She withdrew her hand and was surprised to discover it was clean. 'You try,' she said, her voice husky and weak with fatigue.

Dinah put her hand into the puddle, and her face went blank, as though she was no longer in her body. She remained motionless for a long time.

'Did I do that?' she asked.

'About three minutes. It was weird.' Jacob stuck his hands under his arms, perhaps to stop from trying to pull his sister's hand out of the puddle.

After what felt like an age, Dinah pulled her hand out and blinked life back into her eyes. 'Did you see the planet?' she asked.

'Yes. What else did you see?'

'Sort of floated around. It felt good, but I knew I had to go eventually. A part of me didn't want to stay, and a part wanted to be there forever.'

Freya nodded, mulling the words over in her mind.

'Do I have to do it?' Jacob asked.

'It's not unpleasant. Or not entirely unpleasant,' Freya replied.

'It's weird but fine. Do it and we can compare notes after.'

Jacob sighed and slid his fingers into the gloop. His face went blank and Freya turned to watch the darkening sea. Several minutes passed in silence.

'Wow. What is that place?' Jacob said.

Freya turned back to he and Dinah. 'I think we should get off the beach, I could do with a nice hot cup of tea and then we can talk.'

'Good idea,' Dinah said. She took Jacob's hand and walked off, back towards the car. Freya took one last look at the bottom of the hole. She couldn't close it up yet, but she felt very uneasy leaving it there.

Chapter 14

They piled back into the car and took off back towards the nearest set of shops. The sky darkened, long streaks of purple cut across by deep blue where the clouds hung heavy.

As they drove by Freya saw many places were closed. Perhaps there would be a restaurant or pub where they could stop and debrief. She looked at Jacob, he seemed okay, but she worried about his energy. He'd had his first vision, two if you counted the scene inside the hole. She had not seen the face of the leader; it if had been the other way around and Dinah had been this VisionMage, the one leading the ritual, she could have shared the image of his face. It was all so frustrating.

'What about there?' Dinah said, pointing to a small bar. A large mural of a woman looking through binoculars ran along one side and a few smokers sat at the outdoor tables.

Inside, the ceiling was exposed beams and boards, the floor of polished concrete, and the décor a mishmash of mid-century and seventies styles. Attempting to affect a retro chic which set it apart from the standard takeaway places close by.

Small tables with an array of chairs were mostly full of diners, the music kept low and the customers quiet gave the room an eerie feeling. As the three of them walked in, the locals turned to them briefly before going back to their drinks and meals. The smell of hot chips and tomato-based pasta sauce filled Freya's nostrils and her mouth watered despite their late lunch.

'Let's get food,' Dinah said to Freya, leaning in conspiratorially.

Freya nodded. No staff appeared to seat them, so Freya chose a table at the back, near the kitchen. They were a little way from the other customers, a good spot to have a private conversation.

A waiter arrived with menus, slightly sticky laminated black sheets. Burgers were the specialty and they each ordered one. Dinah also ordered onion rings, pushing her luck to see whether Jacob would allow it, but he was distracted, as though he were more interested in his thoughts than his surroundings.

'You saw the purple planet and the stars and stuff, in the gloop?' Freya asked.

'Yeah I saw what you saw.' Dinah answered, 'and Jacob seems to have seen the same.'

Freya frowned for a moment. 'Is he alright?'

'He's coming to terms with this whole thing being real. You know, it's been real for us for a while, it hasn't been for him. Not the same. He knew in his head, and now he knows in his heart.'

'Mmm,' Freya said. It seemed indulgent for him to be struggling with the idea so much. He'd put people into trances, he'd seen the hospital ward, and had apparently gotten over it, but the vision had set him off again.

'I think the gloop is a portal,' Dinah said.

'To where?'

'Vanaheim.'

'What makes you say that?'

'Feels like old magic. Something that shouldn't be on Earth. Something the new gods don't want us to have or keep.'

Perhaps that's why it requires so much to keep the power here; it's unnatural.

Their meals arrived, and Jacob was still in his own head. He ate, but Freya would have been surprised if he tasted any of what he'd eaten. When they were done, Freya looked at Dinah. Neither of them could drive home, but Jacob was still far inside himself.

'Jacob?' Freya asked.

'Sorry. Miles away,' he said. Some of the light came back into his blue eyes.

'Are you alright?'

'I think so.' He sighed. 'What was that?'

'We think it's a portal to another world. The magic is coming from there. That's why it felt like home,' Dinah explained.

'Right.' He sat still in his seat.

'Are you okay to drive home?' Freya asked.

'Yep. A bit tired.'

'Okay, because I can drive but my blind spot makes me really nervous.'

'I know, it's fine. I promise.' Jacob smiled, but it did not reach his eyes. Freya told herself she would watch as he was driving to make sure he stayed focused and present.

'Shotgun,' she called. Dinah looked annoyed for a moment, and then glanced at Jacob and nodded.

*

They arrived at Jacob's place after eleven and Freya was falling asleep in the front seat. Dinah had been dropped home on the way. Jacob turned off the car and turned to her.

'I'm sorry about before.'

'What do you mean?' she asked.

'I freaked out. After I saw what was in the hole, everything was too much, like we might actually get hurt. Before it seemed like...not a game, but I didn't think I could wind up dead, or withered. Not really.'

'And now you do?'

He nodded.

'Do you want to stop?'

'Now I know who started it, that it will never stop, and I'm one of the few people who can fix things? I can't walk away.'

Freya sighed. 'I'm so glad you said that.' She closed her eyes for a long moment, then pulled the door handle open. 'We both need to rest. Difficult times lie ahead. It's better knowing we're in it together.' She squeezed his hand and slid out of the car. The air was cold and still, her nose tingled a little in the chill. Jacob sat still in the car, perhaps deep in thought again. She turned and walked the few minutes back to her place.

Her hands were shoved deep into her pockets and her head bent down under the hood of her coat. Despite having a lot more information, Freya felt further away from a solution. It seemed too hard; even with the other two helping her, she would never defeat this man and his cronies.

Then she remembered Eva, alone, trapped inside her own mind in the hospital. She could help her. If she gave up now Eva would be stuck forever, or until her body gave up. Freya tried to channel her emotions into something useful. Theodore, the bookshop owner, would have better knowledge of how to best tackle the counter ritual to close the portal and stop the unnatural flow of magic into this world.

When she arrived at her apartment building a raven was sitting in the bare branches of the plane tree. She inclined her head towards it in greeting; the black bird bobbed its head, squawked and flew off.

Knowing they were Odin's emissaries helping her alleviated some of her fear of large black birds. Maybe she'd watched too many Stephen King movies.

*

Despite a weariness seeping into her bones, Freya woke the next day as the sky was lightening. She opened the curtains to look out at the world, then crawled back into bed. Her dreams were of the purple planet. She felt it calling to her, as though putting her hand into the portal had marked her to Vanaheim.

The last thing I need is more people coming after me. VisionMage didn't know who she was yet, but her investigations wouldn't remain secret for long. If she could work out a way to get the image of his face into her mind, or out of Jacob and Dinah's, she might be able to ask Theodore. Perhaps if WitchPrincess34 replied they might have another lead.

It was seven in the morning, the other two were unlikely to be up, but she sent them a group text anyway.

We need to get a sketch or picture of the leader of the group. I couldn't see him, because I was inside him, but you two did. Either of you any good at drawing?

She made herself a cup of tea and opened her laptop, she had a private message from WitchPrincess34 through the web forum.

I don't know who you are, or why you're looking for VisionMage. If you want to join him, don't bother, he's a phony and a dick to boot.

Freya bounced with glee, nearly spilling her hot tea over the keyboard and the bed. She put the tea down and started to compose a reply. It took her several attempts to get it right.

I wasn't interested in joining him. I'd heard a few things about him that made him sound fake and I wanted to meet someone who knew him in real life. I'd love to meet you – you seem to really know about all

this stuff. I'm new and don't know who to trust. Hope to hear from you, Freya.

She wasn't likely to reply straight away, but Freya refreshed the browser several times over the next half hour anyway.

The occult bookshop didn't open on Sundays and Freya would usually have had brunch with Eva. She sighed and got up, showered, dressed and headed to the hospital. The least she could do was visit her friend, even if she didn't know whether Eva would know she was there.

*

The ward was fuller than last time. The couple of patients she'd seen when she was there were still lying near Eva. She tried to close her mind to their suffering; she would go mad if she was bombarded by all their emotions and cries for help.

Eva looked pale, lying on her back, eyes open, staring at the ceiling.

'Will she hear me if I talk to her?' Freya asked the nurse administering medication to the old man in the next bed along.

'We can't be sure but assume she can. If she hears you, great, and if not, there's not harm in it.' She smiled, her eyes weary. Freya wondered how she could stand to be in this ward all day, the desolation of the rooms full of comatose patients no one knew how to treat, must be depressing.

Singular Focus

Freya turned Eva's head to look in her direction, perhaps she could see out of those staring eyes, and she took Eva's hand. She sat in silence for a while, trying to instil a sense of calm in her friend.

We're going to fix this. We're going to find the people who put you here and make them pay. I promise.

Eva blinked, a single tear rolled down her cheek, Freya wiped it away. 'It will be okay I know you're stuck in there. You probably can't hear me, but I will make it all right. If it's the last thing I do, I will make this right.'

She opened her mind and reached out to Eva, she tried to become her, although she had never done it deliberately before. At first nothing happened, then she felt something akin to a balloon between herself and Eva; she imagined herself slipping her hand through slowly, as she did with the portal, and she felt a jolt. She was looking back at herself, through Eva's eyes.

I did it! she thought to herself, and as soon as she did, she lost the connection and was back in her own body. Freya took a slow breath and tried again; she felt the balloon and pushed gently through it.

She was inside Eva's mind. A feeling of panic started to rise in Eva, and Freya thought of the gooey blissful feeling she'd felt when she stroked the raven. She gave this feeling to Eva, and her friend calmed.

Freya cleared her mind and focused on receiving information. Now she had the connection Eva would be able to show her whatever she needed to, perhaps it would be useful in their mission, perhaps not.

A long leather couch appeared in her mind, floating in deep blue pricked with white dots. This was space, or some sort of representation of it. She approached the couch and sat. Eva appeared next to her; she looked thin and haggard, much more so than her physical body did.

Can you hear me? Freya asked with her mind.

Eva nodded in response.

Perhaps you can't speak back, I don't know where we are, but I'm coming for you. I'll find a way to bring you back from here, to the real world, to your body. I love you and I won't leave you like this. She put out her hand and tried to squeeze Eva's but their hands passed through each other. Wherever they were, Freya was not really there.

Somewhere on the periphery of her senses Freya felt a vibration; a slow throb like a giant's footstep. She couldn't have explained why but she had to leave. She relaxed her mind and drifted away from Eva. There was one last flash of her own face from Eva's perspective and then she was back in her own body.

'That's new,' she said aloud. She looked around, none of the other patients had moved, the nurse had left the room, she was on her own. Letting go of Eva's hand, she wiped her face, and was only half surprised to find her cheeks wet with tears. It had been so lonely, and Eva had seemed so unwell.

Her energy is still flowing out of her, Freya thought. Maybe the initial feeding is done by a person here in this world, but these Withered people are tethered to the Vanaheim, their souls in exchange for the magic here.

Her hands were shaky, and she felt very weak. It was time to go before she ended up tethered to the Vanaheim herself.

Freya left the hospital and walked down Elizabeth Street back towards the train station. The chill air helped focus her mind. Her hands were in the pockets of her grey overcoat, and she had wound her black cashmere scarf up around her chin.

The sky overhead was grey with featureless, low hanging clouds. She heard the caw of a raven and turned to see she wasn't alone on her walk. Huginn bobbed his head and skipped sideways along the branch where he sat.

'Are you here to tell me something? Or keeping an eye on me? Hmm?' she asked aloud.

The bird squawked again and puffed himself up.

'Keeping me company then.'

If he had something to tell her it would present itself. She was sure one or both the ravens were near her most of the time now. She wondered if they would be of any use during the reversing ritual.

Will I have any power after it's been done? Once the gateway was closed and the switch turned back off perhaps her power would be gone. She had hated her visions for a long time, but now she was used to them it would be like losing her eye all over again.

Without the power would she have any reason to remain friends with Jacob? They had become close despite her inappropriate desire, she would be sad to lose his friendship. If the ritual worked would he still be interested in her? What if the ritual didn't work, or worse one of them was Withered of killed in the attempt? He'd never want to see her again.

A light drizzle began to fall, and Freya took shelter under the awning of a nearby café. It was surprisingly empty for a Sunday afternoon, and she decided to go in for a takeaway hot chocolate to restore some of the energy she'd lost in the hospital.

The café seemed to have been styled on a French aesthetic; green and beige patterned wicker chairs and red and white checked tablecloths set for two filled the tiny space. A barista stood behind a high black painted counter and seemed not to notice Freya's entrance.

Despite the cosy elements Freya's skin prickled as she approached.

'Yes?' he asked, his nose held high in the air in disdain. He was thin, tall, with thinning black hair and a pencil moustache.

'I'll have a hot chocolate please.'

'Hmm.'

Freya moved a couple of steps away and pulled out her phone and scrolled through the notifications. WitchPrincess34 had replied:

I'll talk to you as long as it doesn't get back to him. And you promise you're not going to try any of his crazy bullshit. I'm not into that.

Freya was so excited she almost dropped the phone. As she took a breath to compose herself, she was covered in a tingling sensation as though the room had suddenly become cold and dark. She looked up at the barista and felt as though he was pulsing, dully, the same throb she had felt with Eva. Freya shivered and as soon as it had started the vision, if that's what it was, had cleared.

'Hello? Your hot chocolate is ready. Five fifty please.' The thin man was standing on the balls of his feet and bouncing in agitation.

'Sorry, away with the fairies.' She pulled out her purse and handed him some cash.

'Clearly,' he muttered.

Freya cupped the hot chocolate in both hands and took a sip. It was scalding hot and she burned the tip of her tongue on it. She coughed a couple of times trying to cover the shudder of pain from the thin man, despite his demeanour she didn't want to offend him.

Outside Huginn waited for her, he bobbed his head and the warm sense of ease flowed through her.

Something important just happened. I need to talk to Jacob and figure out what the pulsing is. But before that she needed to send something to WitchPricess34 to convince her to meet.

As she walked the short distance to Melbourne Central to the train station below the shopping centre

Freya felt the slow rhythmic pulse in everything; her body vibrated with the frequency as though all the world was permeated with whatever energy it was.

It must be the magic flowing from Vanaheim. Strange I hadn't felt it before, does it mean it's getting stronger?

She stepped onto the escalators down to the train platforms, her hot chocolate had cooled down enough she was able to drink it, and the caffeine and sugar hit did a great deal to restore her energy and brain power.

She replied to WitchPrincess34 from the platform:

I don't want to get into what he's into. I'm scared, and I'd really like to talk to someone who knows what's going on. Would you meet me sometime? I work in the city we could have lunch or something, here's my phone number, give me a ring.

It was a bold move laying it all out so openly, but something told her it was the best way.

*

There was no reply for several days. Freya was sure she'd blown her one chance and WitchPrincess34 had been scared away. Then, as she was packing up to leave work on Thursday night, Freya's phone buzzed. She didn't recognise the number, but she knew in her gut who it was.

'Hello?' Freya said in a soft voice.

'Uh, hi. Freya?'

'Yes. Who's this?'

'My name is Pam, but you would know me as WitchPrincess34.'

Freya's breath caught in her throat. 'I was hoping you would call.'

'I nearly deleted your message.'

'I'm glad you didn't.' Freya didn't want to say anything in case Pam got spooked.

'I...we should probably meet up.'

'Yes, sounds great.'

'I'm at Flinders Street station. I thought I'd see if you were around.'

'Now?' Freya's mind started turning over everything she wanted to ask Pam, she thought she would have more time to plan, more time to research specific stuff, but it seemed Pam had psyched herself up to talk to her and it might be her only chance. 'Okay, I can be there in ten minutes.'

'Cool.'

'I'll meet you under the clocks near Swanston Street, I'll be wearing a big grey overcoat, we can go find a quiet spot to chat.'

'I'm wearing all black and my hair is blonde.'

Before Freya could say anything else the call dropped out. She hoped Pam hadn't decided not to wait. She was supposed to be at work for another half hour, but Freya closed her laptop, shoved everything into her enormous handbag, and dashed out of the office without a word to anyone.

Late afternoon in August was often dim, windy, and frigid, and today was no different. Freya wrapped her black cashmere scarf around her neck and head to keep her ears warm, and shoved her hands under her armpits, she had left her gloves at home.

The streets were busy with people leaving their office jobs and her walk up Collins Street towards Flinders Street station involved navigating around slow walking groups. As she approached the front of the station, the grand yellow stone façade, red accents, with its green bronze dome were pulsing with the same heartbeat of energy.

Spotting Pam proved to be easier than she had feared; the only woman standing still in the streams of people flowing in and out of the station. Pam looked nervous, and was older than Freya thought she would be, at least mid-forties, plump and short, matronly in a way. She had obviously been a Goth in her youth and had never let it go; her blonde hair was teased into a spindly bird's nest on top of her head, her eye-makeup was heavy and black, she wore black eight-up Dr Marten boots, black fishnet stockings under a long, multilayered black velvet dress. Her black wool overcoat was so long it almost touched the ground around her. She looked cold, but had not buttoned her jacket, Freya suspected it was so people could see her outfit.

'Pam?' Freya said, approaching the woman who seemed oddly familiar.

'Yes, Freya?' She looked up to greet Freya's and a flicker of fear rippled across her face.

Freya put out her hand to shake Pam's, neither of the women were wearing gloves and she hoped to get a good reading from her before the other woman realised what she was doing. Pam took her hand.

Immediately, Freya's mind was filled with a jumble of images and emotions; mainly guilt, fear and shame. Flashes of people's faces ran through Freya's mind so quickly she couldn't get a good fix on whether any of them were VisionMage.

Pam pulled her hand away. 'Hey!'

'Sorry, I can't control it,' Freya lied. Pam dropped her shoulders and exhaled.

'I didn't expect you to be so strong. I was expecting a normal practitioner, but—' Pam looked thoughtful.

'Let's go somewhere quiet,' Freya said, putting her hand on Pam's elbow to steer her towards the street and into a quiet café.

They went to the old-fashioned pub across the road, where the post-work crowd were not yet in full swing. They sat in the fancy tearoom at the front and ordered hot drinks. Pam looked around her as though expecting to be caught at any moment.

'No one knows you're here. It's okay,' Freya said.

'I'm not—' Pam broke off. 'I don't want him to find out I'm talking to you.'

'I certainly won't tell him.'

'No, I don't suppose you will.' She reached up and adjusted her hair. 'You know the touch thing works both ways, I suppose?'

Freya was taken aback, of course she had been read by Theo, but she hadn't thought to protect herself from Pam's intrusion. 'I thought it might.'

'I see now you're the one who's supposed to set this whole,' she waved her hand in front of her, 'situation right. I saw things in you I've never seen before. You have a connection to something big, and if you can't fix it, we're all in trouble.'

'Yes.' Freya wasn't reassured to hear she was "the chosen one". It was clear she had to fix things, but knowing it and having another stranger, tell her it was all up to her threatened to crush her with the pressure of it.

'The man you're looking for is called Victor. He's a hack, well, used to be a hack.' She paused while the waitress put their coffees on the table between them. 'Only had enough power to light a candle, real basic stuff, but he always wanted more. He was jealous of anyone with even a hint of real power, thought he deserved it, Lord knows why.'

'How did you meet him?' Freya reached into her bag for her notepad and a pen. She wanted to let Pam talk but couldn't contain her questions.

'He came to me, about five years ago wanting to learn. I thought I was ready to take on an apprentice, how wrong I was.' She shook her head and took a sip of coffee.

'Victor was only twenty, a baby really, but with ambition burning inside him. He'd come from a poor family, had to fight for everything, he saw magic as his way to a better life. His maternal grandmother was a powerful practitioner and he thought he should be too, although his mother hadn't inherited the gift and he had even less.'

'Where did he find you?'

'The forums where you found me. He approached me, said he wanted to learn everything he could about magic, specifically *Seidhr*, and would I teach him. Of course, I thought a lot of myself at the time, I'd been practicing for twenty-odd years and thought I could show him the path.' She shook her head. 'I should have paid extra attention, when a man wants to learn *Seidhr* one needs to be very careful. The power can be corrupting to masculine practitioners.'

'Corrupting?'

'It's a feminine energy, and for a man to practice it he has to give something up, the practitioner is a conduit, you can encourage the power to do what you want but if it doesn't want to it changes you to force it.' Pam's eyes roved around the room. 'I'm not explaining this very well. What I mean is a part of you is destroyed every time you try to force the power, it's much more common in men than women but anyone can be seduced by the idea of absolute power. Eventually it will eat you up, of course Victor had to find a way to change all of that.'

Eat you up—the words clanged around inside Freya's mind. Had Victor opened a portal to Vanaheim, created these zombies, all so he could force the *Seidhr* to bend to his will?

'Now, when I realised he wanted to take power from another world, and force it here, I hoped the ritual would kill him, more fool him for trying to bend the universe to his will, but of course it didn't.'

'No.' Freya sipped her coffee. Pam knew a lot about what had happened for someone who claimed not to have been a part of it. The cogs of Freya's brain seemed to be turning incredibly slowly. 'She's your sister.'

Pam stuttered. 'She used to be in my circle. Ten years younger than me, not as powerful but much more easily swayed by smooth talking, attractive young men. It was going to be the three of us doing the ritual, I thought it wouldn't work and it didn't matter if I didn't stop him, but all at once I knew it would work and I had to get out of there. I haven't spoken to Barb since then.'

'She used her daughter instead.' Freya said, remembering the young woman in the circle on the beach.

Pam hung her head and didn't speak for a long time. 'Poor Mia. I should have stopped him.'

'There was nothing you could have done,' Freya said. She didn't believe the words, but she wanted Pam to stay and tell her more about Victor. 'Do you have notes or spell books or anything I can use to reverse what he's done?'

Pam shook her head without looking up. 'He took them all. I thought he would kill me. He's not right in the head, you see. Greed and spite had made him irrational.'

Freya waited in case Pam would say any more, but she seemed lost in her thoughts. Perhaps ashamed of what she'd done. 'Do you know what he wants? Now he has the power, what is he using it for?'

'*Seidhr* is primarily for seeing and shaping the future. He wants to be rich, powerful, respected but most of all feared. Everything he wasn't as a child.'

Freya had to use all her willpower not to roll her eyes. Victor was a spoiled brat, grasping for things he hadn't earned and didn't deserve because he'd convinced himself he was entitled. Freya had never understood why someone would seek power over others, it had always seemed as much a burden as a boon to her.

Perhaps she was imagining things, but Pam seemed nostalgic talking about Victor, the son she never had or maybe she thought she could bring him around, but the boy Pam cared for was no longer in there.

'So how do I stop him?'

Pam laughed. 'I have no idea. I nearly didn't come because I don't think it can be done.'

'That's what you thought about opening the portal too.' Freya spoke before she was able to check herself. She knew it was a mistake before she'd even finished the sentence.

'I didn't come here to be judged. I've given you everything I can. The rest is up to you.' Pam picked up her tiny black satin handbag and stood up.

'Don't go. I'm sorry.'

'No, I can't risk him seeing me here with you any longer.'

Freya stood and took Pam's hand. 'What's his last name? How do I find him?'

'It's Mikkelsen. He still hangs around the forums, using a different name, but he likes to watch us all scrambling to work out what's happening with all these zombie people.' Pam pulled her hand out of Freya's grasp and walked out.

For a moment, Freya's mind swam with everything she'd been told. Pam walked past the plate glass window and she decided to follow on a whim. She left a twenty dollar note on the table for the coffees, more than they had cost but she couldn't wait for change.

Pam walked slowly, her short legs and small strides were no match to Freya's long powerful walk. She had almost caught up by the time Pam was halfway up the short flight of stairs into Flinders Street Station. It occurred to Freya she needed to stay out of Pam's sight if she was going to follow her.

At least she seems too busy hurrying to notice me.

Pam went to Platform 2 and waited for a train bound for Blackburn. Freya wasn't familiar with the eastern suburbs.

She got into the train in same carriage as Pam, it was crowded, and she had the advantage of height over most of the passengers. Freya stood, her back to Pam, and watched her in the windows. Pam stayed on until the last stop, Blackburn, about thirty-five minutes away, each stop Freya waited for her to get up and disembark, by the end of the trip the train was nearly empty, and Freya was sure she would spot her.

Luck was on her side, or perhaps something else. As she followed Pam around the station and down a large suburban road Freya saw her raven companion. He bobbed his head in greeting but had no visions to share with her. She nodded her head back and let a little more distance fall between her and Pam. Now there were fewer people she was afraid her footfalls could cause Pam to turn around.

After a few minutes Pam turned into the driveway of a low-rise Californian bungalow. It was almost entirely grey; the weatherboards lifeless, their paint flaking and peeling, the window and door trims were a darker grey, the roof tiles were charcoal, the darkest grey of them all. Freya put her head down and continued at a steady pace past the front of the house. She walked a couple of houses up before she turned around, crossed the road, and made her way back down the other side.

From where she stood in the dusk of a late winter evening, Freya was confident she wouldn't be seen, even if Pam looked out. There was no-one else home. Lights came on and went off through the house, eventually the front of the house was lit only with the warm yellow glow of lights on in the back of the house. The blinds half-way down the front windows looked like half-closed eyes.

A raven called from a tree nearby. 'Hello Huginn,' Freya said. Despite her fear of the birds initially, she was becoming used to their constant presence. Perhaps she got some of the warm honey feeling whenever they were around, or as a sign she was on the right track.

The bird flapped its long black wings and swooped over to Pam's front fence. In one swift movement he flipped open the lid of the letterbox, removed a letter and was on his way back to her before the lid could fall closed.

He landed at her feet and hopped over before dropping a letter. Freya picked it up, Pam Flanders.

Now I can find her sister. The feeling of warmth spread through her from her fingers up her arm. Huginn bobbed his head as though to say she was on the right track.

'Thank you, my friend. I'd better get on before she looks out the window and spots me.'

The raven cawed in response and flew off into the darkening sky.

Chapter 15

On the journey back home, there were only two other people in the carriage with Freya. It took her over an hour to get back to her little apartment, she looked out the window at the bare silhouettes of the trees where Huginn watched her.

She needed to eat and process what Pam had told her. Victor wanted to make himself important, rich, perhaps famous by manipulating the future. She'd been thinking about how she would do it, if she had the power. She could buy stocks in whatever company was about to make it big, she could bet it all on horse racing and make sure she always won, or she could go to the casino and keep winning until the owners threw her out. It all seemed so empty.

Up to a point, money made life easier, a nice house, a nice car, maybe a nice holiday house with a pool and a fireplace, but after that having more money didn't make much difference. She wanted someone to spend her money with, or on.

Her mind drifted back to Jacob, to his perfect jaw line and the stubble he always had. She longed to run her hands over his cheeks, to feel the tiny bristles against her fingertips. She told herself to stop, he was not an object to fantasise over and indulging herself would only make their friendship awkward, but the heat in her groin remained.

Leftover lasagne would have to do for dinner, she had no energy left to go out or to cook something. She wanted to tell Jacob what she'd learned but was she coming up with reasons to visit him? They were having brunch on Saturday to talk about what to do next, she could wait until then. Perhaps she could find Victor or Pam's sister, Barb, by then.

*

Friday went by without Freya noticing it, she went to work and back again in a daze. She had texted Jacob first thing in the morning to tell him she'd had a breakthrough, but she decided to wait till they met for breakfast on Saturday to tell him exactly what it was. Dinah was coming around after her hockey game.

Despite her pleading, her father refused to let her skip anything to work with them. The scam of it being an internship was wearing thin, and Freya and Jacob were wary of pushing it too far.

She put on her grey overcoat over a long, black woollen skirt and grey cable-knit jumper, her pale grey scarf wound around her throat and up over her ears. As she approached Jacob's apartment, she could see two figures inside. Apprehension scratched at her belly, then she spotted the raven sitting on the railing in front of the net-covered windows.

He bobbed his head and launched from the rail flapping down to where she stood.

'Is something going on?' she asked the raven. The vision slammed into her as soon as the words left her lips. Without trying she was inside Jacob, watching a short, slim woman wave her arms emphatically.

Rhonda, of course, back from her trip. Freya hadn't expected her for some time, perhaps something had happened, and she'd rushed home. Her visions had no sound, but she understood what was going on. Jacob was filled with quiet anger, waiting for her to finish yelling so he could tell her he hadn't changed his mind, he was leaving her.

Freya felt she was intruding on a private moment but couldn't work out how to get out of Jacob's head. She pushed the images away, as she had with the faces in the crowd, and as before nothing happened.

She grounded herself, felt her cold fingers, the wind on her cheeks, hunger tugging at her belly for breakfast and she was back in her own body. The raven bobbed his head again and started to skip across the ground in the direction of the café around the corner.

'I guess I'll meet him there, will I?' she said. Huginn didn't respond but kept hopping along. Freya texted Jacob:

You look busy. I'll meet you at the café, you can tell me about it if you want.

She wouldn't lie to him, to pretend she didn't know what he'd done or how she knew it. She hoped he would understand she hadn't meant to do it. She shivered; he might be angry at her too.

The café was busy and the only place she could find to sit was out the back in the courtyard. A tall gas-fired stood heater nearby, which made her upper back and head uncomfortably warm but didn't touch the coldness in her feet and legs.

She ordered a latte to sip until Jacob arrived. All the materials were either at her apartment or at Jacob's. Usually they ate at his place to discuss their plans before Dinah arrived. He was a fantastic cook though apparently Rhonda never liked his food.

For the thousandth time she wished she could text Eva. It had been months and she still forgot sometimes. Freya closed her eyes and though of Eva; her skin, her long black hair, the loud, aggressively patterned clothes Freya could only wish she was brave enough to wear, her straight talking and generous heart.

She held the image of her best friend in her mind, focussing her energy on the idea of her. Once the image was so solid, she could almost touch it, Freya reached out in her mind towards the Eva. There was no way it would work, but without something to occupy her it seemed as good a task as any to fill in the time.

Eva hung suspended in a sea of black, but then the image started to pulse, the deep heartbeat of the universe, and suddenly she was inside Eva's head. She was so surprised she immediately blinked open her eyes and the connection was broken.

'Latte?' the waiter said, placing her coffee down on the table.

Freya shivered and wrapped her hands around the warm glass in front of her.

That shouldn't have worked, she thought, but it did. On the branch of a nearby tree the raven was bobbing up and down in a pleased sort of way. It gave a caw and flew off into the grey wintery sky.

She looked back towards the café and saw Jacob approaching. He looked pale and sweaty with two red spots of colour on his cheeks. Perhaps he had jogged over in the frigid morning air. Freya raised her hand to wave him over.

Jacob slumped into the chair opposite and for a moment she thought he might slide right off the chair and onto the floor.

'Hi,' she said. He didn't respond. She took a sip of coffee, now lukewarm.

'Did you hear?' he asked.

'No, I—' she hesitated, there was no use trying to hide it. 'The bird showed me.'

'Oh.' He shifted in his chair to sit ramrod straight. 'I would prefer you didn't use your power to spy on me, Freya.'

She had expected this, but it still hurt. 'You know as well as I do I'm not entirely in control. Not to mention, I don't know what was said, all I got before pulling myself out of your head, was you'd made your mind up about something and Rhonda was not happy. I assume you told her you wanted to end it?'

'I hadn't meant to.' Jacob looked up and waved over the waiter. He ordered a big breakfast and a coffee. Freya took the opportunity to order a cheese and ham croissant and a second cup–hers was barely worth drinking now.

'She came home early,' he went on. 'I thought she'd be gone at least another three weeks, but some conference came up here she had to speak at the last minute. Only gave me twenty-four hours' notice.'

Freya nodded and said nothing.

'She arrived late last night, crawled into the bed, her skin cold from outside, and I freaked out a little.'

'What do you mean freaked out?'

'Well, I was half-asleep and, in my mind, alone then there was a cold body in my bed. I thought she might have been something to do with Victor or a murderer or God knows what. Anyway, I scrambled out of bed shouting and managed to punch her in the face before she could get the light on and have my senses come back to me.'

'Ah.' I wouldn't have been impressed either.

'She was livid, going on about why wasn't I waiting up to see her, why hadn't I offered to come get her from the airport, blah blah blah, y'know and I kind of blurted it out.'

'What?'

'I don't love you anymore.'

'Ah,' she said again.

They were silent for a time, around them other café patrons continued their low buzz of conversation, the clinking of cutlery against plates, unobtrusive music being piped into the courtyard from speakers hidden behind pot plants.

'Once I'd said it, I couldn't un-say it. And I knew it was true. I don't love her, I haven't for a while. So, I asked her to move out.'

'All that was last night?'

'Yeah. I slept on the couch.'

The waiter came back to their table with their breakfasts. Freya waited until he had turned back to the kitchen before looking into Jacob's ice-blue eyes. She saw they were blood-shot and red-rimmed. He clearly hadn't slept much on the couch.

'And this morning?' she prompted.

Jacob took a large sip from his coffee. 'She came out this morning and acted like nothing had happened. Made me coffee and wanted to snuggle. I told her we needed to talk, to work out logistics. I suggested she stay in a hotel or and Air BnB, I'd pay, till she goes back to the outback in a week.'

'She didn't take it well, I guess.'

'No. Started yelling about not being given a right of reply, and not having any warning and whatever. I wasn't listening. I've had enough of doing what she wants. She's hardly home but she replaced all my stuff with her stuff. It's my house but it doesn't feel like my house.' Jacob put his knife and fork down neatly on the plate, his hands were shaking.

'It will be okay.' Freya put her hand on his and gave it a squeeze. She wanted to wrap him in the warm honey feeling she'd had from the raven, she concentrated on sending out rather than letting anything in. After a few long moments she took her hand away.

'Thanks. It felt…nice.'

'I tried not to read you, I think it worked, I didn't get anything, usually I would with skin contact for that long.'

He smiled for the first time and Freya felt some of her apprehension lift. 'Maybe you're getting better at controlling it.'

She ate some of her croissant, glad he seemed to be feeling better.

'What's your news? What were you coming to tell me?'

Freya finished her mouthful before telling Jacob about meeting Pam, following her home and what she'd found out about Victor. Jacob listened quietly.

'What do we do now?'

'I don't know. Try to find Barb, but I have no idea how. We can use Barb to lead us to Victor. Although I don't know whether we want to go straight at them. What would we do if we find them?'

'Finding Barb and Victor is important, but we need to know more about what we're up against. And how we're supposed to reverse the spell.'

'We've got a couple of weeks before the equinox. The power should be at a peak then, it's a special day according to Hettie and the *Seidhr*.'

'It might be time to get Theo to tell us what he knows, although I don't trust him.'

'You've never even met him, have you?' she said, almost to herself.

'No. Maybe we should rectify that.'

'We could take Dinah and he would have the whole circle there—'

'Is that safe?' Jacob interrupted. 'Having us all there?'

'I'm pretty sure Theo is on his own side.'

'Pretty sure… I don't like it.' Jacob's phone rang on the table. 'Hello?' he answered it, and mouthed Dinah at Freya. 'Yep, we're at the coffee shop. Wow, I didn't realise it was so late. You know where it is? Yep, see you in a second.' He hung up and looked back at Freya. 'She's at my place.'

'Time is moving strangely today,' Freya said.

'You can say that again.'

They had talked a lot, but she felt no further forward in their quest. 'I suggest we all go to Theo. When Dinah arrives, we'll do a vote.'

'Okay.' Jacob drained the last of his coffee and put the cup down on the saucer with a little too much force. Freya's brows drew together, he was so angry, but after the morning he'd had perhaps it was understandable.

Dinah bounded over moments later wearing a navy-blue tracksuit. She had a bright pink puffy jacket on the top that looked much too big for her. Her cheeks were flushed, she must have run from Jacob's to get there so quickly.

'Hiya!' she said, beaming.

'You're perky,' Jacob said, like it was an accusation.

'Aw, haven't you had enough coffee yet, bro?' She ruffled his hair and the grimace that swept across his face made Freya laugh aloud.

'Better give him a break, hun, he's had a rough morning,' Freya said.

'I know about Rhonda. He's basically broadcasting it. But your news is harder to get.'

Freya held out her hand, palm up, for Dinah to take. It was much easier than telling her everything to share her mind. At first the idea had seemed frightening, like something they shouldn't be doing, Jacob hadn't taken to it, but the bond between the women was strong and their gifts more compatible.

Dinah's energy shifted immediately when she took Freya's hand. She had to concentrate to make the link work well.

'That's put a dampener on you,' Jacob said.

'I know you don't like us doing that, bro. It feels more serious when Freya sends it straight over. It's full of emotion and chunks of extra information I have to sift through.' Dinah said.

Jacob said nothing but his disapproval was written clearly in his arched eyebrow.

It scares him. He still sees himself as a sidekick, not a hero.

'When are we going to see the bookshop guy?' Dinah asked.

'We hadn't decided if it would be our next move,' Freya said, looking at Jacob briefly.

'It's sensible. He'll be able to tell us how to reverse the thing. I mean Hettie's dead, and he's our only other contact, right?' Dinah said.

'We can't ask Pam, and definitely can't ask Victor or Barb. They'd probably try to kill us or something.' Freya pushed her knife and fork with her fingertip. The other two looked to her for answers, to come up with plans. She didn't have any better idea than they did. She wished it would all go back to the way it was before, but the further into this new world they got the less likely that became.

'We could go now, it's probably open. We all need to go, that's what you said Freya, right?' Jacob said. His left leg was bouncing up and down as though anxious to move.

'Alright, let's go.'

*

It was after midday when the trio arrived at the occult bookstore in the Melbourne CBD. Dinah had insisted on getting a toasted ham and cheese croissant for the road on the way out of the café. Jacob drove, although parking in the city was dreadful. Traffic moved sluggishly, there was a football game on which always clogged up the roads.

Freya saw the raven perched on the back of a bench opposite the bookstore as they arrived. He flew up to the top of the building as they approached and seemed to settle in to observe. Freya inclined her head in his direction as they passed through the maroon door.

The bookstore seemed much smaller this time with the three of them inside. Two other patrons were inside, a boy and a girl who couldn't have been much older than fifteen, were both wearing all black. The boy wore huge leather boots and two large belts covered in metal accessories. The girl wore the same but had put a pair of large metal and leather goggles around her short black hair.

As Freya entered the room, the last of the three, they glanced over and whispered something. She got an impression they were stealing but told herself she was being prejudiced.

'It's so cool,' Dinah said aloud. She moved to the nearest shelf and started picking up and examining various items.

'Let's go,' the boy said to the girl. She nodded, took his hand and moved toward the door. As they passed Freya almost put her hand out to stop them. She saw both of them, face up on a dank carpeted floor, somewhere cold and unwelcoming. They had become Withered.

She shook her head and blinked her eyes to clear the image. They seemed like nuisances, but they didn't deserve that, no one did.

'I saw it too,' Dinah said, putting down a pewter unicorn figurine. 'It came on so strongly I got it from you without even trying.'

Theo stuck his head out from behind the little curtain. 'They've gone then, finally. I could feel you coming, Freya, I hoped I wouldn't have to throw them out.'

'I—' Freya started to say, but Theo put up his finger to stop her.

'I know they took one of the books. It's not expensive, and it's not dangerous. I'm sure they'll be back to spend their pocket money when they've read it…but the look on your face tells me perhaps I'm wrong.'

'I saw them, Withered, Dinah saw it too. She caught it off me.'

'Your entourage. Or should I say, circle.' The older man dipped his head in greeting. 'I'm Theodore, I have some little talent and some knowledge, but no courage. It's lovely to make your acquaintance.' He held out his hand.

'Jacob.' He shook the older man's hand, and Theo held on for slightly longer than necessary.

'Gift of the golden voice, I see. And you, my dear?'
'Dinah.'

Theo took her hand and dropped it instantly as though it were hot. 'Goodness! You're very nosy, my girl.'

Freya worried the older man was offended until a sly grin crept over his face.

'A lot of power between the three of you. And you're brother and sister then? Yes, yes, always good to have a blood kinship in a circle. Now let me close up and we can have a cup of tea and you can ask about the counter-ritual.' Theo moved quickly and silently down the stairs; his small birdlike hands clasped in front of him.

'What did you get from him?' Jacob asked Dinah in a low whisper.

'There's so much, in one little touch.' Her eyes were wide. 'It's all a bit jumbled but we can trust him, mostly. He didn't seem to be working with Victor, he's terribly afraid but I think he genuinely wants to help you, Freya.'

'What do you mean?' Freya asked, her voice slightly higher in pitch than she had intended. Dinah wriggled her eyebrows and said nothing, Jacob made a low grunting growling sound in his throat.

When Theo bobbed back into the little shop, he seemed more settled. He drew back the little velvet curtain behind the counter and tied it with a tired-looking gold tassel. He filled the kettle and set it to boil. 'We won't all fit back there, you'll excuse me if we must converse out here.'

Jacob planted his feet squarely on the threadbare dark red carpet and crossed his arms across his chest, Freya had to concentrate very hard not to giggle at how distrusting he was of this little man.

'You know why we're here?' Freya asked.

'Yes, I saw you coming in my mind, but when I shook your hands, I got all I needed to know.'

'You dropped mine so quickly,' Dinah blurted.

'I did, but you are an open book, despite whatever you might have read from me, I read enough from you to know you're the girl for the job.' Theo winked.

A sweep of emotions ran across Dinah's face; shock, hurt, concern, disgust. Freya frowned, it was a creepy thing to say and she started to second-guess her trust in the old man. She silently watched him make tea, the three of them listening as he prattled on about one thing or another. A lot of words but very little meaning, it reminded Freya of a politician.

Once they each had a steaming mug of tea in hand, she had watched carefully as he put the teabags into their cups. She sniffed hers, and it seemed safe, but her faith in Theo was running very thin.

'We need to know how to close the portal to Vanaheim and bring everyone out of their comas.'

Theo closed his mouth with a snap of teeth against teeth. He took a few short breaths through his nose before answering, his bird like fingers rubbing over one another in front of his torso. 'I was getting there. You know I'm not a brave man, Freya, it's why I can't help you, why Hettie told me to find you and never suggested I act to stop this myself.'

'Can you help us or not?' Freya asked. She was sick of his pointless talk.

He sighed. 'Yes. I'll tell you what needs to be done. You know there is a price? Not just fatigue like with the visions, you have to give it part of yourself.'

Freya thought of the raven plucking out her eye. *Haven't I sacrificed enough?*

'You might think you've given enough already, maybe you have, the price is not up to me, nor who pays it.' Theo looked at Jacob. Freya realised he was the only one of the circle who was physically whole, with her eye and Dinah's hearing. He'd lost his voice briefly, but it had returned. What if he had to give something up? Would he do it?

'I had been wondering,' Jacob said, his arms now uncrossed and dangling loosely by his side. 'We know Victor and his cronies are taking their price from others, but we can't. Once the portal is closed, we'll lose our power and maybe something more. Something we can't possibly know in advance.'

'Is that why you've been so sulky?' Freya asked, anger rising like fire from her belly.

'Would you have agreed to lose your eye if you'd been given the choice? I've watched people try to rebuild themselves after trauma, losing a hand or a leg in a car accident, and I see how much strength it takes. I don't know if I have it in me.'

Dinah stared at her brother. 'This isn't something you can opt out of, like your relationship. Or dropping out of medicine because it was eating into your social life. Dad told me. I'm surprised you had enough follow-through to be an OT.'

Freya looked from one sibling to the other, appalled at his weakness. 'If you're not committed to this, Jacob, speak now. Dinah and I will find a third to form the circle. The apocalypse isn't going to stop because you decide you're too scared.'

'I'll wait for you in the car, Dinah.' Jacob looked straight through her before shoving his hands into his pockets and stomping down the stairs. Freya didn't know how the conversation had got away from her so quickly.

'He's scared,' Dinah said.

'We're all scared.'

'He'll come around. Rhonda broke his heart this morning, he broke up with her, but it isn't a good time.'

'It never is.' Freya unclenched her hands from around the mug of tea and turned back to Theo. Her instinct was to follow Jacob out and convince him to come back, but she was so angry she couldn't.

'You're no help, needling his fear. We're trying to save the world, something you've been quite clear you won't help with, and now you're stirring up trouble. We may not have anyone else to ask, but at this point I'd rather take Dinah and do what I can without you.' Freya closed her mouth and slammed her half full mug of tea on the counter. She turned to Dinah, willing her to understand they had to leave.

'I don't think it's time to go yet. He's sorry about Jacob,' Dinah said. Her eyes held apologies for disagreeing.

Freya folded her arms and waited. She would not be the first to speak. Theodore had caused the rift between the three of them and he needed to repair it. Or at least restore her faith he knew what he was doing.

Theo stood, wringing his hands for a long time before finally he spoke. 'I didn't expect him to react that way. I'm sorry. The girl is right, I am scared. As I told you when I first met you, I haven't felt this much power in all my years. Mostly I'm scared of if you can't close the portal and defeat this person. I don't want them to find me and turn me into a vegetable.'

'You said all of that.'

There was a tapping on the window, and all three turned to see the raven knocking his beak against the glass.

'What do you want, my friend?' Freya said. Her mind was filled with a vision, Theo was sitting next to a hospital bed where a small, frail woman lay, withered. He wept over her, kissing her hand over and over. Then the vision changed; Theo was at a funeral, in the casket was an older woman, a different woman. The vision faded and Freya saw the bookshop around her once more. Dinah seemed unperturbed, but Theo was quite pale.

'It was Hettie's funeral wasn't it?' Freya asked, her tone soft. 'And who was in the hospital, your wife maybe?'

Theo's eyes widened. 'How?'

'The bird. Huginn we think. When I need a bit of help, he shows me things I need to see.'

'Why doesn't he show you the ritual then?'

'You know why. Huginn is thought. He can only show me things that are or have been, not the future. When I get visions of the future, they're not from him and they're blurry. I don't understand the rules, but he wants you to help.'

'We know who, where, and when; the beach, the portal, and the equinox. What we don't know is how,' Dinah said.

'We need you, Theo.' Freya stepped forward and took his hands in hers. With all her being she wished him well, sent him reassuring energies. 'I can get her back, I'm sure of it, but not without you.'

Chapter 16

Theo sniffed loudly and a tear ran down his wrinkled cheek. 'You can be very persuasive when you want to be, Miss Gordon.'

'We're in a bit of a hurry...'

'My apologies. I have been thinking about the ritual, I knew you would come to me for guidance. There is a rift between the worlds; a hole runs from Midgard to Vanaheim you need to close, but you must be careful.

'The first step is to bind Victor and his circle to stop them drawing any more power through the portal. This should also stop them seeing you're trying to close the portal. Secondly, break the ties between the Withered and Vanaheim, I believe this will start to reverse whatever Victor has set into motion, without the fuel to maintain it, his magics will unravel. Lastly, pull the fabric of the universe together and seal the hole. I think midnight is best for this part.'

'Sound simple enough,' Dinah said.

Freya grunted.

'Don't be fooled young one, it may sound like three tasks, but each has its own obstacles, and you cannot proceed to the next step if the one before is incomplete.

'The first step, the binding requires something of Victor's, hair, some item of sentimental value although it would probably work with an effigy or poppet. The three of you are a powerful circle, but so is Victor's circle...' Theo's eyes were dull as though he was internally debating.

'Yes, hair or an item of value is best. Then use white and purple ribbon to wrap around the hair or object and each of you recite the ritual words three times. The white ribbon is standard for binding, the purple is for Vanaheim.'

'Will he know we've bound him?' Freya asked. If each step was dependent on the others, and they each required a price, she needed to know how soon after one another they had to be done.

'He will know, perhaps not immediately, you may have a few hours before he realises. The three parts of the ritual must be performed together if you're to catch Victor unawares.

Freya frowned, her mind turning at a million miles an hour.

'The second step, severing the ties will require a reed for each person who has been withered. Each reed must be sliced in two with a runic dagger and then burned with sage. There are words that go with this section too, and you all repeat them three times. Keep the ash for part three.

'By now, Victor will know what you're up to, even with the binding and will no doubt come running to the portal. I would suggest all three parts are undertaken on the beach so you can get straight on.'

Freya's mind filled with the wild wind and storm that sprang up around Victor when he opened the portal, the elements did not take kindly to this sort of spell casting.

'At midnight, mix the ash of the burned reeds with sea water and rub it over your hands. This part requires the highest price, you will each make a cut with the dagger and draw a circle around the portal with your blood. You must stand inside the blood circle and chant to weave the fibres of reality together. Whatever agent Victor has been working with in Vanaheim won't want this, so you may be confronted with some opposing energy.'

With each step Theo described, the sinking feeling in Freya's belly increased. How was she going to convince Jacob to literally bleed to close the portal? She looked to Dinah and saw in her face she was thinking the same.

'Oh,' Dinah said. Her face had turned a shade of pale grey and she swayed a little.

'Sit down, dear,' Theo said, taking her upper arm and guiding her firmly to one of the folding chairs behind his little velvet curtain. 'It must seem like rather a difficult task, and for women who've never done a ritual at all.'

It made a kind of sense, but they needed Jacob, he had the golden voice and if they needed to chant his voice would be essential, but how could she turn him around? He had been hesitant all the way but now he seemed ready to leave them.

Freya couldn't leave until Dinah's colour returned, but they had been in the little shop for a long time and Jacob hadn't returned. Was he so stubborn he would leave them there? Or would she find him lurking around the corner. She wished she could find him—but perhaps she could.

Freya closed her eyes and tried to empty her mind. She called on the warm feeling of honey and the sound of wind rushing around her. In her mind's eye she imagined Jacob; broad shoulders, slightly salt and pepper hair, intense ice-blue eyes, the clean woody smell of his cologne and minty toothpaste. She tried to find him in the world, reaching out towards him as she had with Eva. It was much harder to keep him in her mind as she didn't know exactly where he was as she had with Eva. Thinking of him so deeply was starting to stir her attraction to him which did not help her concentration.

After several minutes Freya gave up and opened her eyes. Dinah and Theo were both watching her quietly.

'Have you done that before?' Dinah asked. 'Found someone?'

'I got into Eva's head earlier. It was a bit of an accident, I was sure it wouldn't work, but I knew where she was,' Freya said.

'I could feel you poking around looking for Jacob. It felt like, pins and needles behind my eyes.' Dinah looked up at Theo from her seat.

'I felt your energy sweeping over me looking for him. You need to practise your craft Freya, the talent is there, the power is there, but your control is sorely lacking.'

'Easy for you to say. You've had this stuff around your entire life, I only recently admitted I wasn't going crazy.'

'He's not trying to be mean. We should practise. We could probably really fuck some stuff up trying to close the portal if we're not focused and practiced,' Dinah said.

'Language.' Freya folded her arms. She wanted to be annoyed but they both made valid points. She had no control, she had very little idea how much power she had, and she hadn't pushed herself, she was afraid.

'You need to find Hettie's instructions on shielding yourself too. Throw that much magic around to practice and Victor and his crew will find you well before the equinox. Everything we do sends ripples out. Hettie was particularly skilled in hiding or minimising the mark her magic left on the world.'

At the moment there was a gentle tapping on the door, Freya first thought it must be the raven again, but she looked up and Jacob stepped back into the shop.

'I thought the door was locked,' Freya said.

'I've been waiting at the bottom of the stairs.'

Freya laughed, a great nervous outburst. 'Did you, uh, hear everything?'

'No, I couldn't hear you, but—this sounds crazy—I thought you were looking for me, so I came back.'

'I was looking for you, with my mind, but I didn't find you.'

'You thought I was further away; you were getting colder.' He smiled, apologetic.

She opened her mouth to reply but then decided against it.

'I'm glad you came back,' Dinah said. 'It seemed way more scary without you.'

'Sorry kiddo, it's been a tough day.'

Freya sniffed, today it was a good excuse, she wanted to think the best of him, but didn't want to be caught unawares by him storming off again as soon as things got serious. They all had a role to play, his was no less important than hers or Dinah's, or Theo's or Hettie's.

'We can fill you in on what you missed later. We should go do some more reading.' Freya picked up her grey overcoat and slipped it on. Theo's watchful eyes crawled over her, trying to get into her mind for some reason. 'You feel up to walking back to the car, Dee?'

'Why wouldn't she? Did something happen?' Jacob asked.

'I felt a bit weird and had to sit down. It's no biggie.'

Freya took the girl's arm and helped her to stand. 'We'll be in touch, Mr Halloway.'

Chapter 17

They were silent as they walked out of Theo's store and back to the car. Jacob turned over the engine and the radio bubbled into life.

'We need to talk—' Freya started to say.

'I'm sorry I walked out—' Jacob said at the same time. 'Sorry, go on.'

'I was going to say we should probably talk about what Halloway said the ritual involved.'

'We do. But um, are we okay? I felt a vibe when I walked back in that seemed a bit hostile.'

Freya sniffed.

'She's got the shits with Theo,' Dinah said.

'I did wonder why you weren't using his first name anymore.'

'I don't have the shits. He's a patronising arse and a coward. If he wanted to help, he'd be doing the research with us, going through Hettie's stuff scouring and telling us the best way forward. Instead he gives us cryptic bullshit, lists a fucking seventeen-part ritual and then has the gall to tell me I need to practise shielding myself.'

Jacob glanced at Dinah in the rear-view mirror. 'I've missed something.'

'Freya's freaking out because it's harder than she expected, and she worried she'd have to do it without you. Plus, Victor might be able to feel what we're doing, a problem she'd had in the back of her mind to deal with later but now it's later and it's too many problems for one person. Did I get it about right?' Dinah sounded very pleased with herself.

'I don't care for your tone, or your poking about in my brain. But that about sums it up,' Freya said, her arms still crossed tightly across her breasts.

'It was stupid of me to walk out. Occasionally it all gets a bit too real, like today, and I have to have a break.'

'We all have those moments. I need to know you won't have one when I'm relying on you to hold the circle. If I can't trust you, Jacob, Dinah and I will find another person to our third.' In the passenger seat Freya had to turn her whole upper body to look at Jacob, properly. His cheeks had turned pink and he seemed to be having trouble forming a reply.

'I won't let you down again,' he said finally.

'I hope not.' She turned back to face forward, watching the other traffic slip past, blissfully unaware of the spiritual war being waged under their noses.

Dinah spent the trip back to Freya's apartment filling Jacob in on what had happened while he was gone. He twitched a couple of times as she described the ritual but was largely silent, taking everything in.

'I suppose you should come up, we need to get on with some stuff and you won't be able to get anything done with Rhonda—is she still there?'

'I don't know. I'm putting it off as long as I can for the moment. I asked her to pack and go to a hotel or a friend's place, but she won't. She thinks she can convince me to let her stay, and I don't have anything left to give her.' Jacob dropped his hands from the steering wheel, and they landed in his lap with a forlorn slap. Freya's mood had softened, seeing him this sad reminded her of the difficult morning he'd had.

'I don't have much room but if you wanna crash on my floor you're welcome to,' she said.

'Thanks, I'll see how it goes.' Jacob stepped out of the car and the topic was closed.

Inside, Dinah and Jacob sat on Freya's bed, she took the armchair once she'd taken care of fresh cups of tea for everyone. Dinah kept looking from her to Jacob and seemed to be working up the courage to say something. Freya put the drinks onto a small coffee table that sometimes doubled as a stool between them, her green tea would need to cool a little before she drank it.

'What now?' Jacob looked to Freya for an answer. She clenched her teeth and took a breath. Why did he look to her for leadership? It was exhausting and scary.

'Can we trust Theo?' Dinah said.

'Trust is a funny thing. I don't think he's lying to us, at least not about the ritual. There's something going on though.'

'He was giving off some weird vibes the whole time. I couldn't get a proper read, maybe he was blocking me. It's hard to say whether it's because he's an agent for

Victor, unlikely but possible, or because he's done something he doesn't want us to know about but is ashamed of.'

'Or both,' Jacob said.

'He knows more about Victor than he's letting on. Maybe it's an Obi-Wan Kenobi thing—he taught Victor and feels morally responsible for the bullshit he's brought into the world,' Freya said.

'That would make sense with the vibes I got. Shame he didn't act directly,' Dinah said.

'But Victor had no power before he opened the portal. I can't imagine opening a portal could be done without power,' Jacob said.

'Pam's sister Barb, and her daughter Mia, would have done it for him. Even with hardly any power himself he could contribute to a circle if the other two were strong.' Freya picked up her tea.

'We've got until the equinox to gather the materials for the ritual. I'm more concerned about shielding and trying out some smaller rituals so it isn't the first time we try to cast a circle,' Jacob said. His jaw was rippling as he clenched and unclenched it.

Freya put down her tea and picked up Hettie's spell book. She stroked the fore-edge allowed her fingers to be guided to a place where a blocking spell could be found. She had no memory of one being in there, but last time she hadn't been looking for it. Her fingers snagged on a page close to the start, Freya flipped it open.

'Protecting your mind and magic from unwanted observation,' she read aloud.

The spell caster and clairvoyant must become adept at hiding their thoughts and their powers from minds who would not wish them well. Simple precautions can be taken to help this:

- **Burning sage to cleanse the home regularly, and to expel unwanted spirits or presences**
- **Imagining oneself enfolded in pale pink or white protective light at all times**
- **Burning black candles and drawing a circle of salt especially during a spell casting or ritual**
- **Emptying the mind with meditation**
- **Keeping a charm bag on the person, close to the skin, at all times.**

Other precautions may involve binding an enemy to do no harm or blinding an enemy to your works.

'Doesn't sound too hard,' she said, looking up at the other two.

Dinah nodded.

'Meditation and the protective light sound like they would need constant upkeep from you, you'd have to remember to do it or it wouldn't work. We need a charm bag. And maybe try to block Victor from seeing us specifically. What does it say about that?'

Freya scanned the page and flipped to the next. 'You need an item of theirs or an effigy, like Halloway said, and you put the item into an envelope and seal it with white ribbon and black wax.'

'We don't have an item of Victor's. I'm the only one of us who knows what he looks like, so I guess I have to make an effigy.' Dinah looked pale and tired.

'It's okay, kid, we'll be there to help you.' Jacob patted his sister's knee. 'What's an effigy involve?'

'I wish this had an index,' she said as she flipped through pages.

'Effigies or poppets can be wood and twine, fabric, wax or any other natural product. The characteristics of the intended subject can be added using a photo, lock of hair or item belonging to the intended subject,' Dinah read from her phone.

'Did you Google that?' Freya asked.

'Yeah, quicker than searching Hettie's book. Plus, we know a bit about magic now so we can figure out what's true and what's garbage.' She smiled. Freya wanted to be annoyed but Dinah's optimism was infectious.

'Can you draw him then? Or make the poppet look like him?'

'Yeah. Might take me a week. And I can't let Dad see, he'll think it's heaps creepy.'

'Unless you told him it was some musician he's never heard of,' Jacob said. He looked past Freya to the darkening sky. 'I should get you home for dinner.'

'I can get myself home. You and Freya can keep going with this stuff.' Dinah winked at Freya and she was sure Jacob caught it. He didn't make any sign of having seen her.

'You're only thirteen, I'm taking you home. Freya can come for a ride and we'll get dinner on the way back if you want.'

Perhaps he did see the wink after all.

*

Once they had dropped Dinah off and watched her bound into the house Jacob let out a long sigh.

'Honestly, if you don't want to risk going home, the offer of my floor is still there,' Freya said, putting her hand on his. He stared straight ahead through the windscreen for a while before answering.

'Have you got a blow-up mattress or anything? I don't know whether it's worse destroying my back on your wooden floor or facing Rhonda.' He turned to her and smiled, although his eyes remained sad.

'I take it back,' Freya joked.

They got takeaway Thai from a place not far from Freya's apartment. When they had eaten, she found the camping mattress in the cupboard and put her yoga mat under it for a little more padding. It wasn't much but she'd slept on worse. She wanted to invite him into the bed, but it was too soon, too tempting. The more she tried to push the idea from her mind the more it sprang back.

'I'm going to text her to tell her I'll be back in the morning and she better not be there. I don't want her to worry but I don't want to talk to her,' Jacob said, he sat on what would be his bed and scrunched up his face. 'If I can't sleep, can I get in with you?'

'In your dreams, buddy,' Freya heard herself reply.

*

In the morning Freya woke to find Jacob in the bed. She didn't remember him getting in, he must have been very stealthy. Perhaps all the adventure of the day before had worn her out more than she thought. He smelled good, she turned her head to look at him in the early morning light. He seemed so peaceful, so warm. His body, hard muscle, and yet just the right amount of tenderness.

Barely ten centimetres lay between them, yet she couldn't reach across the divide yet. Let him come to you, she told herself.

Jacob sighed deeply but didn't wake. Time stretched out as she watched his chest rise and fall beside her. Then her bladder protested. One side of the bed was against the wall, the other blocked by Jacob. She tried to slide her way down the bed without waking him, but he woke as she was halfway out and she froze, as though caught in an illicit act.

'What are you doing?' he asked.

'I could ask you the same. When I went to sleep you were on the floor.'

Jacob looked away. Freya took the opportunity to wriggle out of the bed and dash to the bathroom.

On her way back she grabbed her bathrobe. Jacob was in the armchair; he'd dressed and was pulling his socks on as she entered.

'There's no rush,' she said, a small tickle of guilt started in her stomach. 'Will you have a coffee? Or fruit toast before you face your apartment?' And possibly Rhonda, Freya thought but did not add.

'Are you sure?'

'I was only teasing.'

'I didn't mean to, what I mean is, it was unconscious, getting into the bed.'

'It's fine, really.' She couldn't bear to watch his serious expression and turned to make coffee with her stovetop pot. She opened the curtains and kept her back turned for several minutes, pottering about her tiny kitchenette. She told herself it was so Jacob to compose himself, but it gave her some time to get her inappropriate thoughts under control.

'Are you having fruit toast?' she asked, turning back to face him.

'Yes. Rhonda will be waiting till I get back so she can make puppy dog eyes at me.' His phone was gripped tightly in his hand.

'Did you get a message from her?'

'She couldn't let me have the last word. It makes me so angry.'

'I can imagine. It's so hurtful for her to ignore your request for her to leave.'

Jacob grunted and shoved his phone deep into his jeans pocket. The toast popped up and Freya turned back to attend to it. The tension in the room crackled, she had no idea what to say. If she offered him comfort, she worried she would try to kiss him. But wouldn't a friend give him a hug? Let him vent about his ex, commiserate with him without a hidden agenda. She wished she were a better person.

Freya finished buttering the fruit toast as the coffee pot spluttered indicating it was ready. She put Jacob's breakfast on the small stool she'd used as a table the night before, she put hers on the floor and sat facing him, leaning against the bed. The silence wasn't comfortable, but the tension had drained a little.

'I'm not a morning person at the best of times, and I can't believe I got into bed with you. You're trying to be a good friend and I made it sleazy.'

Freya nearly choked on the sip of coffee she had in her mouth. 'You didn't. I thought I made it sleazy.'

A smile came across Jacob's lips. 'If we're both thinking the same thing, then, why not go with it?' Even as he said it, the flush came back onto his cheeks.

Freya put her hand on his knee. 'Settle everything with Rhonda, then we can see if there is something here.'

'Of course.' Jacob took an enormous bite from his fruit toast, perhaps to stop himself making any further remarks.

Jacob's phone started to ring from the pocket of his pants. He sighed heavily and pulled it out. By his face, it was Rhonda.

'Hi,' he said. Freya didn't want to overhear, but in her tiny apartment there was nowhere she could go.

'Where I stayed is no concern of yours. I told you yesterday we're done. Are you still in the apartment?' He rubbed his free hand across his forehead. Freya took the breakfast dishes to the sink in an effort to make herself inconspicuous.

'I'm not changing my mind. Don't make this more difficult than it needs to be, please.' He sounded tired. There was a long pause before he spoke again. 'I'll help you take some stuff to your mum's then. See you soon.'

Freya rinsed the dishes and stacked them neatly to be washed properly later. She didn't turn around, waiting for Jacob to address her first.

'I better get going,' he said at last.

'Is everything okay?'

'She says she needs help packing up all the important stuff, so I don't accidentally throw it out while she's away. I have no idea how much she's going to make us pack, it seems like something that could have been left for another time, but she insists on doing it now. Thanks for the sanctuary overnight. Can I come hide out here in the week if things get hectic?'

Freya hesitated, she wanted him there and as a friend she wouldn't think twice, but the temptation to kiss him had been strong this morning, and she wasn't sure she would be able to resist again. And he wanted her to. 'Any time.'

'Thank you. And thanks for breakfast.' Jacob picked up his jacket and headed to the door. He turned in the doorway to blow her a kiss. 'See you soon.'

She let out her breath in one long whoosh. Her body was tingling all over in a very confusing way; aroused but also vibrating with tension. It was one thing to harbour a secret crush, but entirely another thing to have him staying the night. She flopped onto the bed face first and was greeted with his scent on her sheets.

Eva would know how to deal with this. She'd probably tell me to jump him and sort out the emotions later. Thinking of Eva reminded Freya she still had little to no idea how she had been Withered. Vanaheim was drawing power from these people, as was Victor but they had all touched someone. If Freya could figure out the circumstances leading up to the Withering, they might be able to prevent any more between now and the equinox.

Despite the unpleasantness of visiting the hospital she had to. Perhaps if she concentrated on keeping herself wrapped in white light she could stop her power being noticed, and protect herself from the terrible fatigue that often accompanied her visits to the ward.

She looked out the window, hoping to see the raven for confirmation she was doing the right thing, but she couldn't see him sitting on his usual perch in the tree.

Chapter 18

Outside the hospital Freya prepared herself; imagining herself wrapped in a warm layer of glowing white light which would protect and shield her, before stepping over the threshold.

White light, white light, she repeated to herself as she rode up in the lifts and stepped out onto the floor where all the Withered patients were. Freya felt the dread and fear in the room as though it were far away, like the sound of the sea in a shell not the roar of an angry ocean.

Eva looked thin. The drips and tubes used to keep her alive in her comatose state only kept her from dying. Her muscles were wasting away. Freya took her hand and looked into her eyes and positioned herself to be sure Eva would see her.

As soon as their skin touched Freya reminded herself of the white light, it would keep her safe from the draining influence of Vanaheim and stop Victor from knowing what she was up to.

'I've come for a visit. I know you can feel me and see me. I miss you so much.' Despite wrapping herself in light tears start to roll down Freya's cheeks. 'Everything is fucked. You have no idea. There's this boy and he's dumped his girlfriend but it's going to be messy and I shouldn't take advantage of him right now, but you would probably say go for it; if was meant to be it would be.'

Her words came out in a jumbled rush. Freya took a deep breath and tried to centre herself. *White light, white light.*

'I'm sorry,' she said, and brushed aside her tears. 'I came to find out how you got here. I'm sure if I ask the right questions then I'll be able to find it in your head. Okay?'

It seemed important to get Eva's permission before she tried to go into her mind. The raven hadn't turned up to reassure her; she was going on faith it was the right move.

Freya cleared her mind of everything except the white light and reached her mind towards Eva. Almost at once, she found herself in a dark space, the walls, floor and ceiling covered in pinpricks of light like a sky full of stars. The couch appeared in the middle and on it sat her best friend.

Freya looked into her eyes. 'I know you can't talk to me. I will do the talking and you show me what you can, okay?'

'Last time you showed me someone touching you and then you went home and lay down. I need you to show me that again,' Freya continued. Where they sat was replaced with an image of Eva talking to an older man, in a fancy looking skin-care shop. He was a customer, he touched Eva's elbow. Freya felt a tug at her belly and a sort of momentary disconnection of her arm, Eva's arm.

It reminded her of the brief moment when she met the woman at the open mic night. Her touch had sent weird sensations rushing through her.

She urged Eva to focus on the man's face, it felt like they were in a dream. Then she and Eva were back on the seat in the dark starry room. Eva looked tired and a little frightened.

'Okay, so this guy drew power from you and that made you weak. Have you seen him before that moment?' Freya asked.

The scene she saw next was in a crowded tram, it was late summer by the heat and dress of the other passengers. The same older man was sitting next to Eva and kept brushing his bare knees against the honey-dark skin of her thigh. Each time they made contact she moved away, but he deliberately invaded her space. After a moment the man stood up and made his way out of the tram, but not before putting his hand on Eva's shoulder as he went past. Fatigue and a vague feeling of nausea descended on her before the image faded and they were back on the couch.

'Okay, two times. Were there anymore?' Freya asked. Eva was tiring, her mental self was gaunt and pale, but the determined look on her face said everything.

The next image was not the older man, but Shirley, the woman Freya had met at the open mic. They were in a doctors' office, Shirley walked towards her, seemed to stumble, and Eva put out her hand to help her up, and the same tug in the belly and feeling of disconnection followed before the vision faded.

'You were touched on three occasions, once by the woman, twice by the man. Three exposures to open the channel, everything else works in threes,' she said. 'I'm going to figure this out, and I'm going to get you back.'

Freya let her mind relax its focus on Eva and she was back inside herself. Eva's face was wet with tears. Concentrating on maintaining the white light around her, Freya turned to the man in the bed beside Eva. He was an older man, perhaps in his late fifties, with wild grey hair and three or four days' worth of grey stubble across his chin. She wondered if he had anyone to care for him, keep him looking neat. He was thin, his cheeks sunken under the stubble.

'My name is Freya, I'm trying to help you. I'm going to take your hand and try to enter your mind. I want you to tell me how you got like this. I'll be there to guide you. You'll be safe. Alright?' she said aloud.

She took the man's hand gently, his skin dry and papery. It didn't take much to slip into his mind. It looked like the inside of a staticky television. There were no couches, but she saw the man, looking plumper and less deathly standing not far away.

'In here you'll be able to show me what I need to know. You are safe,' she repeated. In the mind space, she saw the woman from the open mic night touching the man's arm. It could have been flirtatious except for predatory look in her eyes. She knew what she was doing. After this touch he had succumbed, gone home to lie down and never got up again.

Freya took a step back into his mind space. 'Thank you. I've seen her before. Were there other times?'

He answered by showing her another woman, this time young, pudgy and dressed in all black lace and leather. Her heavy eye make-up didn't completely obscure her child-like features. She took the man's hand and walked with him through a busy shopping centre, as though she knew him. Then the vision was gone.

'Who is she?' Freya asked. Before she could go any further, another image took over. The same black-clad young woman was standing in a home kitchen burning toast. The man was trying to get the smoke alarm to stop by waving a tea towel under it. The woman turned to the man and mouthed something, the visions were always silent, Freya couldn't figure it out, but she hugged the man. Perhaps they were related, father, uncle; a close family tie felt right. The young woman stepped back from the hug with a strange look on her face, a mixture of surprise, pleasure and greed.

The scene faded and she was back in the static-filled inner space of the man whose hand she held. He smiled at her and she nodded before letting go of the connection and coming back to herself in the hospital ward.

'Three touches. They take a little bit each time and at the end you're so weak the connection to Vanaheim is permanent.' Freya felt tired, but nothing compared to the last time she'd tried this. She refreshed her concentration on the white light and took several calming, centring breaths.

I have one more in me. A young man occupied the bed on the other side of Eva, he seemed to have more colour on him and perhaps hadn't been there as long. She introduced herself, took his hand and guided him to show her how he'd ended up there. As with the other two, there had been three touches, all of the same person for him and in quick succession. His boyfriend had been sucking his life force. It wasn't a face she'd seen with any of the others, but the process was the same.

How many people out there are energy vampires? If each time these people touched someone then there would be patterns in the Withered, families and friendship circles who were all overcome, but the patterns hadn't been found. It must require conscious effort to sap people, which would explain why relatively few people were in the ward, despite having been several months.

Her concentration was faltering, maintaining the white light around herself was difficult, it was time to go. She had what she needed.

'I'll come back honey, I'll get you out of this, I promise, hang in there,' she said to Eva before turning to leave.

On the tram to go home Freya let the wall of light around her fall away completely. The fatigue she had held at bay with it started to come in waves, but it was not as bad as it had been the first few times.

Freya's first instinct when she got home was to call Jacob and debrief about her afternoon, then she remembered the situation he probably came home to.

How did it go when you got home? Was she still there? I'm around if you need to talk, she sent.

If he was okay, he would call her, and she would tell him what she found. Dinah's project was drawing a sketch of Victor and practising her shielding. Jacob was dealing with his home situation. The equinox was three weeks away and they needed to be ready.

Hettie's spell book was written like a journal and Freya hadn't yet worked out any system to where to find something. She'd had success with letting her fingers find the right pages, perhaps it was unconscious magic, but she wished the old lady had indexed everything.

Creating a protection pouch seemed easy enough, she looked up some suggestions online, then scanned through Hettie's spell book for something similar. If she trusted Theo, she would have phoned him to ask, or had him make them each a pouch, but something as important as a protection spell shouldn't be left to a man she had doubts about.

She needed a purple hessian pouch, basil, bay, clove, lavender, one clear quartz crystal, one black tourmaline crystal, and salt. Theo didn't have magic supplies, so Freya looked for a shop she could visit tomorrow during her lunch break, hopefully without being drawn into a long conversation with the owner. She hoped the magic shop owner would have no talent, someone else feeling her presence or finding out her mission filled her with dread. The sooner she had the protection pouch the easier it would be to keep herself hidden.

Jacob had not responded to her message, and though she wanted to tell him everything she felt for him, he was likely still trying to get rid of Rhonda.

Why she'd want to stick around when he doesn't want her there is beyond me. Time to relax and take her mind off the impending ritual, and Jacob, and everything else going on. She opened her favourite streaming site and selected a sitcom she'd seen many times over. As she settled herself on the bed to watch a few episodes, Huginn was perched on the tree outside the window. In the half-light it took her a moment to recognise him, a shiver of foreboding ran down her spine. Why was he here? And why did she seem suddenly so anxious? The visions she was bracing for never came, and the sense of dread slowly seeped away. Huginn dipped his head and flapped away.

I wish I understood the rules of the game I'm playing. She closed the curtains and tried to immerse herself in trashy comforting TV.

*

In a little arcade in the city Freya found a magic supplies shop. Only a couple of minutes' walk from her office, the windows were filled with kitsch nonsense like Theo's bookshop. Inside the walls were deep purple, a spherical stone fountain tinkled in a corner and the patchouli incense was overpowering. The shop was small, crowded with five or six people inside.

She took her time wandering through the items on display, most of what she needed was readily to hand. Herbs were together on one side, the crystals in clear Perspex buckets, it seemed odd to hold them in something so unnatural but perhaps she had an overly romantic notion of a magic supplies shop. She took enough to make a pouch for each of them to carry in a pocket or on a string around the neck. Freya's eyes roamed around the shop, she had an urge to buy something else and thought some object might call to her.

Next to the counter, a range of crystals on slim silver chains were on display. Her eye fell on a series of blue-green pendants, smooth, round turquoise stones in simple silver settings; not cheap, but not expensive either. There were three, not the same, but similar, clearly by the same craftsperson and responding to the unique shape of the stones.

The young woman behind the counter had her black hair plaited down her back, it hung to her buttocks.

'Excuse me,' Freya said. The woman turned to greet her a smile plastered on her face. The smile faltered for a moment when their eyes met, she recovered quickly.

'What can I do for you?' she asked.

'I'm getting these.' Freya put her collection of items on the counter, the crystals clunked heavily on the class top. The assistant's eyes widened slightly as she took in the array of items Freya was buying.

'It's good you're making pouches. If I had your power, I'd want to shield it.'

'Do I know you?'

'No,' the assistant dropped her voice and leaned in. 'I thought you were a myth, you know, someone to save us from this coma thing. The message boards are all going on about someone who will come to restore the balance, but I never thought I'd meet you.'

Freya's cheeks warmed with a blush. The bustle and noise of the shop around her, the smell of the incense, the burbling fountain, all faded away. They stared into each other's eyes for a moment, it stretched out for a long time before Freya remember she needed to put the white light around her.

'Sorry,' the girl stepped back and shook herself a little. 'I didn't mean to—it's so shiny. You kind of glow.'

'Uh, thanks.' Freya frowned, this was not the reaction she'd had from Theo, and hadn't come prepared for a groupie. The young woman took the items, wrapped them each in mauve tissue paper and placed them into a large brown paper bag.

'You'll need to cleanse them all before you can use them or put them into pouches, you never know who's been handling things,' she said as she held out the bag to Freya.

'Thanks.'

Fleur Blüm

Their hands touched and suddenly Freya was flooded with images of this young woman's life – childhood birthdays, twirling around until she fell over, sitting in her classes doodling pentagrams, wishing all the while she would grow up to have real power, and then in an instant she did have some power, she could see energy around people, not everyone, but some. Pulsing colours, usually one but sometimes a mix. One stuck in Freya's mind's eye, a man who had no face. His colours were deep purple and black, with veins of silver, like Vanaheim.

'You met him?' Freya asked.

The assistant blinked and took a moment to understand. 'What?'

'Victor, you've met him. Here?'

'No, I mean yes. I've met him, but not here. It was at a party. I didn't like him at all, but he's very persuasive. He wanted me to be with him, I didn't want to but he made it so I couldn't refuse. I hoped it was all a bad dream, but it wasn't, was it.'

'What happened?'

'I don't remember, but I felt like I'd been hit by a truck for days afterwards, I couldn't see auras, I thought I'd lost the gift. I think we were physically together, but it's all a blur.'

Sick fuck. He raped her and fed from her magic.

'I'm sorry.'

'Why are you sorry? It's not your fault.' She wiped her eyes.

264

'I'm going to fix it.'

The assistant nodded; her mouth pressed into a determined line. 'If there's anything I can do to help, let me know.' She wrote her name and phone number on a business card and handed it to Freya.

Walking back to her office with the brown paper bag Freya tried to shake the creeping unease the assistant had filled her with. It was like she was famous but in the worst possible way.

The danger from Victor was viscerally close and it felt as though a hand were grasping her throat, making it hard to breathe. She stopped a block away from her office and sat on a green metal bench to calm herself. She closed her eyes and tried to clear her mind.

A few long, slow breaths visualising the white light and she calmed, although the urgency of her mission hovered at the edge of her mind.

Freya looked up towards her building and a huge raven hopped along the footpath near her.

'Hello, my friend, come to check on me?' she asked.

The bird cawed and hopped closer to her, up onto the bench. Freya reached out to stroke his breast feathers and felt the honey warm feeling of euphoria slide over her. Everything that had seemed difficult and overwhelming seemed easy, and her muscles relaxed.

The bird tapped her hand with his beak, and she opened her eyes again. 'Thank you. I don't know what I'd do if I didn't have you on my side.'

*

In the evening, Freya cleansed the stones as Hettie instructed. She burned a black candle and wafted the smoke through the herbs and other items to get rid of bad energy.

The pouch seemed so small and inconsequential she almost didn't bother to put it on, but she slipped the cord over her neck and allowed the pouch to hang inside her white button up shirt, between her breasts, over her heart. For a moment nothing happened, then a little ebb of calm started to flow from the pouch.

'I am safe, I am hidden. I am safe, I am hidden. I am safe, I am hidden.' She said the words nine times in total, imagining the white light surrounding her and forming a permanent, impenetrable bubble, then she blew out the black candle and the small ritual was done. Little tingles of power zapped along her fingers for a moment.

She felt the same, and yet everything was completely different. Outside, the moonlight seemed more silver, the outlines of trees were more sharply defined, the raven sat on one of the branches.

'Thank you,' she said aloud. The bird bobbed his head and flew off into the night. Perhaps she didn't need his constant protection anymore.

Getting the pouch to Jacob and Dinah now seemed urgent, if she was protected and they weren't anything could happen to them. She hadn't heard from Jacob all day; she had assumed he was busy at work.

I've made protection pouches for you and Dinah. I think you should grab them sooner than later. She texted him, no need to ask about Rhonda, if something had happened, he would tell her in his own time.

I'll come round now. He sent back a few minutes later.

By the time she'd read his message the buzzer from her front door went off. 'That was quick,' she said into the phone linked to the front door, and pressed the button to let him in.

'Hi,' Jacob said at her apartment door.

'Hi.'

He took a seat in the armchair and looked at the floor, his shoulders were hunched.

'Everything okay?' Freya asked.

'I guess. I was sitting in my car outside your place, trying to get up the courage to buzz you.'

'Ah.' Freya leaned on the kitchen counter, looking at Jacob's profile. His hands rubbed over each other mechanically.

'I want to talk to you, but I don't know what to say. Rhonda left this morning. It was awful. I wanted to tell you about it, but we have so much other stuff going on, it didn't seem important.'

Freya bit her lower lip. The pouch would certainly make him feel more centred, it was too bad the raven had flown off, a shot of calming honey feeling would put Jacob in a better frame of mind. 'I'm your friend, you can always talk to me. Put this on first.'

The ritual was simple enough, Freya walked Jacob through what he needed to do and watched him drop the string around his neck and the pouch inside his shirt. He said the words and as he finished, she could almost see the white light surrounding and protecting him. He sat up straight and the frown etched in his brow melted away.

'Shit. That's a lot better.' He smiled, his straight white teeth bright under his cool blue eyes. She wanted to kiss him so much, but she pushed the feeling down.

'Maybe Victor was putting bad juju on us.'

'Must have been.'

They talked for a couple of hours Freya told Jacob about her discovery at the hospital, and he told her all about trying to get Rhonda out of the house.

'Do you think she'll stay away?' Freya asked.

'Dunno. I'm having the locks changed tomorrow. I'm taking the day off work to make sure it's done before she changes her mind.'

'You still have lots of her stuff though, right?'

'I'll have to get it back to her. It will be painful, but relief definitely outweighs it.' He stared blankly at the wall behind her.

It was almost ten o'clock and while she enjoyed his company, having him there was a temptation she should avoid. She should be focusing her energy on defeating Victor, not seducing a heartbroken Jacob.

He shook his head and seemed to come back to the present. 'I'd better be off.'

Despite knowing it was for the best, she was disappointed he had to leave.

*

Singular Focus

On Thursday evening, Dinah sent Freya a sketch of Victor to the group text. Younger than Freya expected, he had a strong jawline, prominent aquiline nose, and black hair worn a little long.

I thought he'd be older. She texted Dinah and Jacob in response.

That's pretty spot on, Dinah, Jacob sent back.

Maybe he has an old soul, or because you're intimidated by him. Easier to be scared of someone old, Dinah replied.

The truth of Dinah's comment seared into Freya's mind. She'd had her head in the books of an old woman, trying to learn the rituals of an ancient religion, but hadn't really thought about Victor, or who he was. Power hungry, weak minded and clearly not concerned about hurting others. Perhaps he didn't know the extent of the deal he made to gain power.

How could he be unaware? His knowledge and sensitivity to the changing magical currents were more attuned than hers were. He'd been a practitioner longer than she had, despite having had little power before he opened the portal to Vanaheim.

Knowing what Victor looked like, and his surname, allowed Freya to return to searching through the internet and social media for mentions of him. She hadn't found anything previously and didn't this time either. While waiting for the equinox to arrive it seemed like a good idea to try to get to know her enemy, so she spent time going back through the forums and reading his conversations. He was surprisingly angry and bitter for a young man, quick to insult anyone who didn't agree with him.

Hettie's spell book also had a few mentions of a new presence in the magical energies, it could only be Victor and his circle.

Don't get too comfortable, knowing he's a fragile man-baby won't stop him hurting you or the other two. She stared at the sketch trying to learn something more about him. No photos had come up of Victor, it was her only visual reference for him. His image stayed burned into her brain when she closed her eyes.

In her dreams Freya saw Victor standing on the beach, black robes whipping around his legs, thunderhead above him, bringing down lightning to open the portal to Vanaheim and create the black sludge puddle, the scar between the worlds. It didn't have the quality of a vision but of a regular dream. Freya watched from the sidelines, unable to move, while the ritual unfolded before her. She woke feeling weak, defeated before she'd even begun. The protection pouch lay on her bedside table, and she slipped it over her head. The pouch touched her skin, the anxiety swirling in her belly calmed and the sense of dread eased.

I need to wear the pouch to sleep, perhaps he's been trying to find me when I take it off.

Chapter 19

The equinox fell on a Wednesday. The day before dawned cool, but not too cold. Freya had slept fitfully the night before and woke at first light. She showered and dressed, her mind spinning, playing through the ritual over and over. Dinah's father had become suspicious of her time spent with her half-brother, and the only reason he had agreed to it was that it was school holidays. Jacob had managed to convince his father to let her stay the night as well claiming he needed the company after the break-up.

What she would wear had been a point of great concern for Freya for the last few days, it was a focus for her other anxiety about the ritual. In the end she chose a pair of slim fitted black jeans, a grey knitted top and a light black jacket. The weather had started to warm, but with Melbourne's notoriously changeable weather, and the fact they would be on the beach with wind coming off Bass Straight, she dressed in layers.

The materials for the ritual were packed into her duffel bag, she checked through them all one more time: runic dagger, purple ribbon, white ribbon, the poppet representing Victor, sage, reeds, salt, a cigarette lighter and matches as well as a large, shallow steel bowl to catch the ash and mix with seawater.

None of them had any idea how long each ritual would take to complete, nor how much rest they might need between each one. The final ritual had to start at midnight on the equinox for maximum magical flow.

Passers-by was a problem she hadn't entirely resolved, she chewed on her lip as she thought about it again. The first two parts of the ritual would be relatively easy to explain away, they were innocuous, and apart from burning the reeds and sage which could be a fire hazard, she could say what they were doing was ceremonial and of no consequence. But if someone came upon them in the deep night surrounded by blood it would be much harder to dismiss. Jacob's ability to calm and entrance people with his singing might be their only defence, but it would take time and expose them to a greater risk Victor would figure out what they were up to.

The buzzer from the doorbell brayed loudly and she jumped. She picked up the receiver and spoke into it. 'I'm coming down.'

Checking the duffel bag once more, she added the spell book and zipped it up. Freya put her handbag over her shoulder and jogged towards the stairs down to the front of her apartment building. Closing the door behind her felt incredibly final, she told herself she was being silly, but the next time she walked into her home she would be different whether they were successful or not.

'Hey.' Jacob stood at the door to the apartment building and had parked his silver four-wheel drive directly outside.

'Hey.' Freya dropped the duffel into the back seat and slid in beside him in the front. She buckled her seatbelt and exhaled heavily. Jacob reached over to take her hand and squeeze it.

'It will be alright,' he said.

'I'm glad one of us is confident.' She smiled and turned to look at him. His face had a grey undertone and his jaw was clenched, perhaps not as confident as he appeared.

They met Dinah at Richmond train station. It was hard for Freya being in the passenger seat as her field of vision on the right was diminished. She had to spend most of her time turned towards Jacob, as they drove, to see him. The drive took almost two hours, traffic was largely going the other way but was still busy.

Dinah played a podcast from her phone through the car speakers; a welcome excuse not to talk.

About five minutes before the beach turnoff a cold hard pit of nerves landed in Freya's belly. She started to feel nauseated and focused on her breathing.

'It's okay, I'm scared too. We'll be fine,' Dinah said.

Freya twisted to look at her.

'You might be wearing the pouch, but I know you, and you're really close and you're giving off waves of energy,' she added.

'Oh,' Freya replied.

'You're not the only one who's nervous though,' Dinah said. 'Jacob's as bad as you, and I admit I'm not super calm myself.' She smiled, and Freya gave her knee a reassuring squeeze.

Jacob parked the car and switched off the engine. Silence filled the cabin and for a long moment no one spoke or moved. The scrubby foreshore trees danced in the wind, the skies were grey, but glary.

'Right,' Freya said.

'Right,' Jacob replied. They both reached for their door handles at the same time.

The walk to the hollow where the black inky scar in the foreshore seemed shorter this time. The stuff they brought with them took up two large bags, at least the area was hidden from the view of people on the beach and from the foreshore path; maybe Victor had chosen the place specifically to be away from the casual prying eye.

'First binding,' Freya said. She took the ribbons, salt, and poppet out of the duffel bag and laid them on the ground next to the scar. Dinah had made a fabric doll and sewed the sketch of Victor's face onto it. With everything else going on, trying to get close enough to get hair or an item of importance was too much of a risk.

Freya faced the ocean, Hettie's spell book and what she knew of Siedhr agreed this would be the most powerful aspect. Jacob and Dinah took their places facing her, with the scar on the ground between them.

Taking the salt in her right hand and walking in a clockwise circle, Freya drew a line around the three of them.

'I cast this circle in the name of Odin, the all-father, and Freyja, the giver. I call on the spirits of the North, South, East and West to watch over us as we do our work,' she said as she closed the circle behind her. 'May the circle protect us under his watchful eye.'

Jacob and Dinah both repeated the words as she said them. Next, Freya took the poppet of Victor in her right hand and pushed the ends of the purple and white ribbons together against the poppet's chest.

'I bind you, Victor Mikkelsen. I bind you from causing harm,' Freya said, and wound the ribbons around the poppet. The other two repeated her words.

'I bind you, Victor Mikkelsen. I bind you from seeing my works.' She wound the ribbon around again.

'I bind you, Victor Mikkelsen. I bind you to draw power only from Midgard.' Another wrap of ribbons. The three of them continued to repeat these three sets of bindings until the poppet was entirely wrapped and the ribbons had run out.

'I bind you, Victor Mikkelsen in the name of Odin, the all-father, and Freyja, the giver.' They repeated this phrase three times each then Freya put down the poppet and looked up at the other two. They both nodded. It didn't feel like anything had changed, the air was salty and a little chilly, the wind whipped the tips of the scraggly branches and the skies were overcast.

'I thank the spirits of the North, South, East and West for watching over us as we did our work. I thank Odin, the all-father, and Freya, the giver, for watching over us as we did our work. The circle is now open, but never broken.'

Jacob and Dinah repeated her words and Freya used her right foot to brush away some of the salt to open the circle. As she did, two large black ravens cried out loudly and took to the sky. They circled overhead for a moment before flying off towards the east.

'I didn't notice those two before, but I guess now we've stopped they can go give a report or whatever they're doing,' Jacob said.

'I usually only see one, it must be a big day for us?' Freya wondered aloud.

Freya stepped outside of the circle of salt and felt a wave of fatigue and nausea wash over her.

'Sit down,' Dinah said, rushing to her side and grabbing her arm. 'You look terrible.'

'I thought I was okay, but it's like my body is too heavy.'

Jacob had brought a blanket and some cushions from the back of the car and laid them out in the hollow. Freya sat down heavily, resting her head on her bent knees. She inhaled slowly and deliberately through her nose and sighed out through her mouth. In her mind she wrapped herself in warm pinkish white light and thought of the restorative feeling she had had when she touched Huginn.

Jacob and Dinah were murmuring near her, but she was too tired to make out their words.

'Drink this.' Jacob held out a small cup filled with steaming liquid. She took a sip; hot, strong, sweet tea.

'Thank you,' she said.

'I don't think it took as much out of us as it did you,' Jacob said. 'I feel okay, a bit tired. Do you think you can, I dunno, draw on us more for the next one? You'll be exhausted well before we get to midnight at this rate.'

'I'll be okay in a minute,' Freya replied. The tea helped, but she wanted to close her eyes. It was a struggle to sit up.

'You're white as a sheet and your scars are all purple. Maybe we should go back to the car for a while,' Dinah said.

'I don't think we should all leave the portal unattended.'

'I'll stay here. It's not even midday, you can rest for an hour or two before we attempt the second step.' Jacob's hand laid warm on her upper back. Freya lifted her head and nodded.

Huginn was sitting in a tree overlooking the carpark as they approached. Freya nodded her head in his direction, and he bobbed back. She was reassured he was keeping watch, despite anything else that might be happening, and despite the fact he had taken her eye, she had come to see his presence as a comfort.

The back seat was not comfortable to lie in, she ended up half-curled, half-shoved in the corner, her head resting on her rolled-up jacket. She snuck a glance at Dinah who was playing on her phone. Her earlier nervousness had subsided, and she was back to being a child, instead of carrying the weight of the world on her shoulders.

Sometime later Freya opened her eyes and realised she must have been asleep.

'How are you feeling?' Dinah asked.

Freya thought for a moment, her neck was stiff and sore from the strange angle it had been resting in, but otherwise she felt much restored. 'I'm doing okay.'

'You will need draw from me and Jacob. I sort of felt the swirling energy around you, but I didn't think to add to it. I guess we're all still really new at this.'

'I'm okay, I promise.' She knew Dinah was right, if the circle was to serve its function, they had to contribute equally; only with all of them connected would their sum be greater than their parts.

In the back of the car were sandwiches Jacob had packed for their lunch. Freya reached over the backseat and grabbed the bag. 'Let's go see how your brother is doing.'

'You look much better,' Jacob said as they approached.

'I had a little nap.' Freya passed over the lunch bag.

'I nearly called Dinah to bring me food, I'm starving,' he said.

Freya checked the time on her phone it was nearly two in the afternoon. She had slept longer than she thought. They ate in contemplative silence, side by side watching the ocean. The sun was out, but not very warm. Freya put her sunglasses on but remained in her coat.

Having eaten and slept, Freya felt ready to attempt the second ritual. 'I need you to be in physical contact with me for this one. Should make it easier to complete the circle and to draw power through you.'

The second ritual would sever the ties to Vanaheim for each of the Withered patients. Freya had spent hours trying to find exactly how many people had been affected, but it had been impossible. She had brought three hundred and thirty-three reeds with her, the best estimate she had for the number of surviving Withered patients was three hundred and ten, and a few more wouldn't hurt. It seemed like a good, magical number too.

The bundle of reeds was enormous. She planned to cut and burn the reeds in nine batches, repeating the chant each time before burning them.

Freya cast the circle of salt once again, making sure the portal to Vanaheim was inside the circle, she called on the spirits of the directions, and on the protection of Odin and Freyja. She knelt in the sandy grass next to the inky-black scar, Jacob on her right side, and Dinah on her left, each with a hand on her shoulder.

'I sever the ties that join you to Vanaheim,' she said, cutting the first reed in two and placing it in the bowl. She continued to murmur these words as she cut each reed and placed it in the bowl. When she reached thirty-seven, she sprinkled them with sage and set them alight.

'With cleansing fire, I break this bond. From the ashes we shall rise once more, masters again of our own flesh and spirit.'

Jacob and Dinah repeated what she said, and as they all watched the flames rise up suddenly before dying down, Freya imagined the three of them as one being, energy circulating through all of them and out over the bowl and the flames.

When the fire died, she repeated what she'd done, over and over until there were no more reeds. As the flames of the last fire died down, she grasped the bowl and lifted it to the sky.

'In the name of Odin, the all-father, and Freyja, the giver, we release these souls from their servitude and cut the channel from this world to the other.'

A tendril of wind whipped around them, gathering the ashes into a tiny swirling vortex. Freya returned the bowl to the ground, covered it with a cloth to stop the ashes being blown away, and all three stood. Her feet were a little numb and stiff from kneeling, but she stood tall. She thanked the spirits and opened the circle as she had for the first ritual.

Once outside the circle of salt, Freya felt drained and unsteady. She looked to the other two and they were ashen-faced and bleary eyed.

'Do you think it worked?' Dinah asked, flopping down on the pile of cushions.

'My fingers are tingling where I had them on you, Freya,' Jacob said.

'Mine too,' Dinah replied with a giggle.

'You sound drunk,' he said.

'So do you.'

'At least this time I don't feel like I might be sick,' Freya said. She curled into a ball and rested her chin on her bent knees.

'It feels kinda different,' Dinah said.

'I thought there would be a more obvious change.' Freya closed her eyes and listened to the gentle rushing of the waves, the wind in the trees, the occasional buzz of passing traffic. Time seemed to slow down, and she found herself drifting in a warm black space. She wasn't asleep, but she wasn't awake either. A bed came into view to her left, it hadn't moved but resolved from the ether. Freya reached toward it and felt a sharp shock in her fingertips, as she might have from static electricity.

'Freya, wake up.' Jacob was shaking her shoulders.

'I'm not asleep.' She looked up at him, the concern on his face worried her.

'You were mumbling something, and then you went quiet and you weren't breathing.'

'That can't be right.' Freya turned to Dinah, who nodded. 'I feel alright, a bit tired.'

'I know you want to keep an eye on the portal but maybe we need to get away from it for a little while. It's not nice,' Jacob said.

'I can't feel it, but I'm not feeling much of anything at the moment,' Freya said, her words muddled together with fatigue. Jacob helped her stand, Dinah packed up all their gear into the duffle bag, shoved the cushions into the middle of the blanket, grabbed the corners with her free hand and dragged it behind her. If Freya had been in any state to argue she would have, but her mind was empty and sluggish.

*

Jacob drove, as they moved further away from the scar on the beach, Freya's thinking felt less like wading through honey.

'We can't do the last part without her, I'm freaking out,' Dinah said.

'It's okay. You were right, the portal is angry. Something in Vanaheim knows we've cut them off.'

'I hope the binding on Victor holds out long enough for us to close the portal,' Jacob said. His hands relaxed a little on the steering wheel.

'Where are we going?' Freya asked.

'There's a little pub with a log fireplace. I thought it might be cosy.'

Freya murmured in agreement. Although she felt better, she was still fatigued. They pulled into the empty car park, and Jacob helped Freya out of the car. She wanted to wave him away, but she didn't dare waste her strength on it. The feeling of his strong arms wrapped around her, holding her steadily, securely, made her tummy give a little flutter.

Inside the pub was mostly empty, a few patrons sat forlornly at the pokie machines. The fire was lit, around the hearth were battered, but comfortable looking leather couches, and a low coffee table.

'Is it too early to eat again?' Dinah asked.

'We've been saving the world, why not?' Jacob replied.

'Get me something, whatever,' Freya said from her position in the corner of one of the couches. Dinah took a couch opposite, Freya held her hands out towards the fire, fascinated by the colours and shapes of the flames between her fingers.

'I got you the steak and chips. You need something to fill you up after all the spell stuff, plus you still look pale.' Jacob sat down next to Dinah. She laid her head on his shoulder.

'I'm not anaemic.'

'I know. I've gone back to my staples; meat, veg, fire. God, I sound like a Neanderthal.' He laughed and it warmed Freya more than the fire to see some of the fear and tension melt away from him, even for a moment. On the window behind them, Huginn settled himself on the sill, the feeling of calm and confidence flowed through her.

'Thanks, buddy,' she said aloud.

'What?' Dinah asked.

'Huginn sent me a little reassuring burst. You didn't get it?'

'Nah. I think you're the one with the connection to the ravens and to Odin, maybe it was part of the deal with losing your eye.'

Freya hadn't thought about it, but it made a kind of sense. Odin had given up his eye to gain knowledge, she'd given hers to create the link with him.

They ate in comfortable silence, the pub remained largely empty, but Freya didn't want other people's energy interfering as she tried to collect herself and prepare for the next stage.

'Can you see what Victor is up to?' she asked Dinah after darkness had fallen outside.

Dinah frowned for a moment, squinting her eyes as though it helped her concentrate. 'He's muffled like he's started wearing one of these pouches, but he's confused and angry. He might be onto us.'

'If he's in the city, it will take him at least an hour to get here if he figures out we're trying to close off his source,' Jacob said.

'There's still hours till midnight.'

'Can we start earlier? I mean if he's coming to crash the party should we go now and try to get it done before he arrives,' Jacob asked.

'Doesn't seem like a good idea. Midnight on the equinox is a significant time for power and I'm not sure I'm up to going back yet.' Freya rubbed her fingers across the scars above her eyebrow.

'I don't think he's figured it out yet. It's dampened, but he seems scattered. If he knew what we were doing he'd be all laser focus, y'know?' Dinah said.

Freya was not reassured. Everything they had done relied on the third part of the ritual and closing the portal between the worlds. If they didn't get the scar repaired, Victor and all the others would be able to reopen their connections. Anyone who had been released from their coma would be at risk of being pulled back. Freya shuddered, she closed her eyes and tucked her feet up under her.

Chapter 20

Freya dozed fitfully and woke with a start. 'He's coming' she said. In her dream she had seen Victor striding towards her over the dune from the beach. She hadn't finished and the portal to Vanaheim was still open.

'You saw him,' Dinah said. It was not a question.

'We'd better get going. We'll have to start the spell as soon as we get there. We can't wait any longer.' She looked at the time, nearly eleven. It would have to do. Jacob and Dinah looked at each other, their faces pale. 'What?'

'Your scars look very raw. I noticed they were red when we were having dinner, but it's much worse now,' Jacob said.

Freya put her hand to her right eye socket and felt the delicate tissue. She inhaled sharply as her old wounds seared with pain. 'Nothing to be done about it now. Maybe the scars reflect the portal.'

Driving back to the beach, energy from Vanaheim pulsed more and more strongly through her, buffeting her as though it were a stiff wind. She clenched her jaw and focused on the task ahead.

This would be the real test of her strength, which thankfully had been largely restored. They would stand with hands joined and chant to knit the fabric of the worlds across the rip in reality.

The hollow was very dark, and the cold wind bit her flesh. A purplish light came through the inky blackness in the middle of the portal as energy from Vanaheim passed through.

She stood facing the ocean, Jacob and Dinah opposite her. They would hold their arms outstretched in order to keep the portal between them and still grasp hands. Dinah mixed the reed ashes with seawater in the silver bowl and they each covered their hands and forearms. Freya shivered.

Freya cast the circle in salt, as she had for the other two rituals. Then she used the runic dagger to cut a long, shallow incision down her right forearm. Jacob did the same, and then Dinah. Together they walked the circle again, letting their blood flow onto the ring of salt.

'My blood is my sacrifice, take it and let my will be done,' they chanted.

The air around Freya's ears tingled with electricity, she joined hands with the other two and the wind started to circle and coil around them.

'I call on Odin, the all father, I call on Freyja, the giver. I call on the elements: air, earth, water and fire. I call on these powers to restore our world.

'Let the rend between Midgard and Vanaheim be healed. Let the walls protecting us be whole.' Blood dripped from Freya's right arm through her clasped hand and onto the sandy ground.

The hole had not changed. *I guess now the chanting begins.*

'Let the rends be healed, let the walls be whole,' she started repeating. Jacob and Dinah said the words with her. As they chanted, Freya's mind disconnected from her body as it had when the raven took her eye, she floated above herself looking down.

The wind picked up, sand spiralled around them, flinging drops of their blood and sea spray in all directions. Where the blood touched the scars in the earth, or the pool of blackness between them, little puffs of red light shone for momentarily.

Floating as she was, Freya had no sense of time, sound, nor physical sensation. Their drops of blood fed the portal and the hole began to shrink.

Below, Freya's arms began to shake, as did Jacob and Dinah's. In her floating mind it seemed vaguely like this was a bad thing. As the scars closed, they became less black, charcoal then grey. The pool's centre was no longer a fathomless sink of light, but became a dark grey hole filled with silvery strings, reminding her of pulling stringy melted cheese but in reverse.

As the melding drew to completion, Freya's mind-self hovered closer and closer to her physical self. It had begun to rain, and the wounds around her eye had started to bleed. Water and blood ran down her face.

Suddenly she was back inside her body, chanting the words. Her arms felt like lead weights had replaced her hands, the right side of her face was on fire with pain, as was her right forearm, and her legs trembled beneath her.

Above her dark, billowing clouds; the oncoming storm she had foreseen. Freya didn't remember falling down, but all three of them were laid flat on the sand. Moving required an immense effort. She pushed herself up onto her elbow and looked around her. The urge to flee was so strong it almost counteracted her exhaustion.

'Are you two alright?' she said. Dinah's eyes were still closed, but Jacob had rolled onto his side, his hand over his face to protect it from the sharp, angry drops of rain.

'I hurt in places I didn't know could hurt. I guess we're not dead though,' he said.

'Not dead.' She looked at the place in the centre of the circle, the place where the rip in reality had started. The radiating stripes of blackened ground had been erased, and the pool had been reduced to a grey smudge the size of a tennis ball.

'It's not finished,' she said. The tears and fear she had been holding back burst through her fatigue and pain and she wept.

'It worked Freya, look! It worked,' Dinah said, finally raising her head.

'I won't be enough. He can reopen it.'

'You're right,' a raspy, deep male voice said from the top of the hill next to the hollow.

'Victor.' Freya and Jacob spoke as one. For a moment he stood, his long coat flapping behind him.

'Jacob, help,' Freya said. In their planning sessions when Victor and his cronies turned up it was down to Jacob. He had the voice.

He started to sing the opening of *Wonderwall*. It seemed an odd choice to start with, perhaps the first thing that popped into his mind. Victor took a few steps toward them, but they were hesitant, as though he'd walked into a room and forgotten what he'd come in for. His eyes were glazed and unfocused.

'Grab the bowl, let's go before he snaps out of it,' Freya said to Dinah. She grabbed the dagger from the sand and scrambled back towards the car. Jacob kept singing, as soon as he stopped the magic would fade, the longer he could give them the better.

As they rushed towards the car, Freya drew on the last of her energy reserves. She had to get them all out of there before she crashed. Victor trailed after them, following Jacob's voice.

'I'll drive, at least till we get away from here,' Freya said, grabbing the keys from Jacob. They all piled into the four-wheel drive. The tires squealed on the wet asphalt as they peeled out of the car park onto the deserted road. In the rear-view mirror Victor stood swaying in the car park.

Chapter 21

'Fuck. Fuck fuck!' Freya said as they sped down the freeway back towards Melbourne. Her hands were covered in ash and blood, and her face stung where the scars had bled. She needed to get them somewhere Victor couldn't follow them, far enough away he wouldn't be able to feel her presence, but her eyes kept drifting closed.

Twenty minutes after they left the beach the rain had eased, and the neon lights of a service station appeared on the side of the road. Freya pulled into it and switched off the engine.

'What do we do now?' Dinah asked.

Freya turned to face her in the back seat. 'I think we do a bit of a clean-up, get some dressings on these cuts and get back to Jacob's as quick as we can. There's no telling how long it will take Victor to come after us.'

'Jacob doesn't look so good.'

For the first time, Freya took in his pale skin and shallow breathing. He was staring straight ahead as though he wasn't really in there. 'Jacob? Come inside and we'll wash up. You want a hot chocolate or something?' She touched her hand to his and he was ice cold. They were all soaked to the skin, their clothes bloodied and dirty. No doubt, as soon as they walked into the service station, they would have the police on the phone, and they couldn't afford to be stuck answering questions.

'Actually, we should go straight home. Let's not get out.'

'I think you're right,' Dinah said.

'Pass me one of the water bottles in the back, will you? And one for Jacob. If you can get him to drink.'

They drove in silence, the late-night roads were mostly deserted, one less thing for Freya to worry about. As she came off the freeway to go through the suburbs to Fitzroy, she thought someone was following them, but they turned off and she relaxed a little.

She had never been as tired as she was right then. After guiding a largely non-responsive Jacob up the stairs and into his apartment, Freya peeled off her cold, wet clothing and pulled on some track pants and a T-shirt.

The blood and ash washed away relatively easily, Freya rinsed her wound with Betadine and managed to get it all over Jacob's bathroom sink. *I'll clean up later*.

In the mirror, the scars around her eye were already healed under the mess. The bleeding and rawness of earlier must have been magical rather than medical.

Dinah took her turn in the bathroom, and Freya tended to Jacob. He sat at the kitchen table, eyes glazed and empty, but with his wet clothes changed and out of the weather some of the colour returned to his cheeks.

'You in there, mister man?' Freya said. 'Come back, we're safe now.' She didn't believe it, but for the moment it didn't matter.

It was the early hours of the morning of the spring equinox, they had done what they vowed to do, and although hadn't completely closed the portal, she hoped they had released the Withered. If they got Eva back it would all be worth it.

Once she had finished cleaning up Jacob's cut, she put him to bed.

'You should get in too, Dinah.'

'I'm okay,' she said, yawning.

'Keep an eye on your brother, will you? I'm going to try to sleep on the couch for a while. We can decide what to do once we're all a little less like zombies.'

Dinah nodded and shuffled around the bed to climb in beside her brother. In the lounge Freya curled into a tight ball on the couch. She was sure sleep wouldn't come.

*

Freya woke to the sounds of clanging in the kitchen and realised she'd passed out as soon as she lay down. She uncurled, grumbling at the aches and stiffness in her muscles. She felt ancient.

Dinah was in the kitchen. 'Jacob said he needed coffee, but I don't know where it is.'

'He's awake then?'

'Yeah, said he couldn't get up to make it though, lazy sod.'

'I feel like I've been run over by a lawn mower,' Freya said.

'I know what you mean.' The large purple shadows under Dinah's eyes reinforced her own feeling of fatigue.

'Coffee would be amazing. I think it's up here.' She reached past the young girl into the cupboard above the fridge where she'd seen Jacob put the coffee. He stored it in a white enamel tin with the word 'coffee' in dark blue letters. He also had one for 'tea' and 'sugar'.

Dinah boiled the kettle, Jacob's coffee machine had disappeared with his ex, and a large French press had appeared in its place on the bench. Now she was awake, her belly grumbled loudly.

'You reckon there's any food?'

Dinah shrugged and rubbed her eyes. No doubt they felt as full of sand as Freya's own.

The fridge yielded only white bread, but it was better than nothing. She also found butter and vegemite. *Coffee and vegemite toast is a delicacy in some places.*

Once brewed, Freya and Dinah carried everything into Jacob's bedroom. He was sitting up against the grey fabric bedhead, his eyes closed against the sunlight streaming in the windows. '

'Coffee!' he said, his nostrils flaring. Dinah snuggled in next to her brother and Freya slid in next to her. If it hadn't been for the near-death experience of the night before, it might have been a perfect morning.

They chatted quietly and Freya started to feel more human. No one broached the topic of the ritual, but the image of the grey remnant of the portal was seared into Freya's mind.

'It's not over yet,' Jacob said, his hands cradled around the half-finished cup of coffee.

'The hole isn't repaired. Something stopped us, or we failed.' Even to her own ears Freya sounded bitter. Her throat felt scratchy and she remembered all the chanting she'd done while her mind was floating above her. 'Did anyone else have an out of body thing?'

'Floating above ourselves? Yeah, I had that,' Jacob said.

Dinah nodded.

'I don't understand why that happened. Hettie doesn't say anything about it in her book. I don't know why we fell over.'

'Victor whammied us?' Dinah said. 'He did turn up immediately after that.'

'Maybe. I'm so disappointed we didn't finish the job.' Freya pushed the heels of her hands into her eye sockets in the hope it would stop the tears she felt building. Her chest was tight and tingling. Dinah put her small hand on her shoulder, she took a breath and calmed down.

'We did everything we could. We'll figure out how to finish it off another time.' Jacob said.

'Victor knows what we're up to now. He knows our faces. He's going to try to stop us.'

'It's early, we're all overtired and emotional. Let's rest and recover a bit.'

Freya felt dismissed. Jacob's voice was cold and hostile. This wasn't the response she'd hoped for, weren't they past his moodiness? 'I guess I'll go back to my place then. Try to work out when the next good day for rituals is.' The cut on her right forearm throbbed under the dressings she'd applied last night. She sighed and slid out of the bed.

In the lounge she gathered her stuff, she hadn't realised how much of a mess they'd made the night before. He wanted her out of his space, so she was going.

Dinah followed her out the door and called to her. 'Don't be upset with Dufus in there. The singing was draining and he's still trying to get his head around everything.'

'What is there to get his head around? We have to close the rip in reality and save the world. It's dangerous, and difficult and I don't know what I'm doing and he's pouting and throwing me out.'

'Today you're angry and determined, but Jacob's afraid. As afraid as you were yesterday. Give him a day or two to pull himself together.'

'You're really grown up sometimes. I hope you know I couldn't have done any of this without you.' Freya held her arms out and Dinah hugged her.

*

Back in her apartment Freya took a long hot shower and redressed the cut on her arm. It wasn't deep, but it was long and reopened when she moved the wrong way.

It was midday when she had finished, she closed the curtains and lay in bed.

Despite being exhausted she couldn't sleep. Everything was spinning around in her mind. Were the Withered waking up? Had Victor reopened the portal? Had all their work been reversed? Or was Victor hindered by not having his circle there, and having missed the eve of the equinox? There were so many things she didn't know and of the two people she could ask, Hettie and Theo, one was dead and the other untrustworthy.

Maybe the woman from the magic supply shop could help them, but involving more people meant there were more to be hurt if things went wrong, or Victor wanted to punish them. Freya had no idea how ruthless he might be in pursuing them or in getting his power source restored.

He might set up a guard or protect the portal now.

After lying down for an hour or so, Freya gave up on sleep and got up to visit the hospital.

*

From outside the building Freya could tell at least some of the Withered patients had recovered. The cacophony of emotions flooding into the atmosphere around them was so strong it felt like a physical force.

The nurses' station was empty, no doubt they were all run off their feet dealing with patients. She knew the way to Eva's bed without having to ask.

The room, which held six patients, was noisy with hospital staff and visitors. She made her way to Eva's bed and saw her friend was sitting up in bed a little, she looked gaunt and tired, but more alive than she had for months.

'Freya,' Eva croaked.

'Eva. My God. It's good to see you.'

'You look awful.'

'So do you.' Freya laughed, tears leaking down her face. 'I thought you might have slipped away from me again.'

'You did good, babe.' When Eva flicked her eyes towards the glass of water nearby, she picked it up and held the straw to Eva's lips as she took a couple of small sips.

'Do you remember anything about what happened?'

'Not really. I just woke up. I'm pretty weak though, I think I used up all the energy I had earlier.' She trailed off.

'You don't have to talk. I'm so glad you're back.' Freya sat in the chair next to the bed and took Eva's hand. Her skin was cold and clammy, nothing but skin and bones, but her best friend was back.

Eva closed her eyes and rested her head back against the pillow. For a long time Freya sat staring in wonder. All her doubts and worries were quiet while she looked at her best friend; she would do anything to make sure she stayed safe.

Of the six beds in the ward, only one appeared to still be in the coma-like state. Eva was sleeping, so she got up and went over to them. A fellow in his thirties, dark brown hair, olive skin and not as wasted as some of the others. She took his hand and gentle probed his mind with hers.

Inside the room of his mind was a black empty space, he stood in the middle and looked confused.

'It's okay, my name is Freya. I'm here to help. I wanted to ask if you remember waking up last night at all.'

He frowned, suspicious perhaps of this foreign presence in his coma, then nodded his head.

'I know you can't talk here, so I'll try to keep the questions yes or no. Did you fall back into this place quickly?'

He nodded. He must have been unlucky and had his tether to Vanaheim restored. All the Withered were vulnerable to being sucked back into their terrifying, lonely inner selves.

'Thank you,' she said, and released him. Those who were previously Withered were more susceptible to being sucked back in. The threads from Vanaheim knew them and sought them out.

I have to make a protection pouch for Eva.

Despite the ward being now filled with mostly recovering patients, the energies swirling in the space were still stressful.

'I have to go, hun, but I'll be back to see you soon. I promise,' Freya said, taking Eva's hand once more.

Eva smiled weakly; she would have a long recovery with all of the muscle wastage from being stuck in a hospital bed for months.

'I'll bring you something to help. It's so good to have you back, I have so much to tell you.'

'Next time.' Eva's eyes slid closed and Freya took her cue to leave.

*

The next day, Friday, Freya would have to work. During her lunchbreak she would go down to the magic supplies shop and get more ingredients for a pouch for Eva. If she went past the hospital on the way home, she hoped that would be soon enough to protect her. She considered giving Eva her own pouch but the risk of Victor sensing her when she took it off was serious for not only herself. At least if Eva relapsed it could be reversed.

The magic shop was crowded, as it had been last time she was there, full of morose brooding types. Freya doubted any of them knew it was real, or the deadly consequences if misused.

The woman working there recognised her and came straight over. 'Did it work?'

'Hi. Yeah, mostly. I have to go back and finish it off, but we took a few steps toward fixing the problems.' She was hesitant to be too straightforward in her terms, in case a spy of Victor's was lurking.

'I felt it, you know. It was epic. But, like, I thought it probably hadn't totally worked coz I still have my new talents.'

Freya nodded. This young woman seemed to know things, and Freya had a good feeling about her, but she couldn't trust anyone outside her circle, at least not totally.

'I need some more stuff for another pouch.'

'Did one of them not work?' the woman asked.

'It's for a friend.'

The young woman smiled, and a little bit of light came back into her eyes. 'They're great, aren't they?' She started to chatter, discussing the relative strengths and weaknesses of various components of a protection pouch, and of the spell that went with it. Freya only half-listened, instead she let the words wash over her and tried to gently probe the young woman's mind for clues about her trustworthiness.

The string of chatter faltered for a moment and the woman turned to frown at her. 'You've gotten much better you know.'

'Sorry.' Freya's cheeks started to burn. She had hoped to get away without being caught snooping in this young woman's mind.

'I don't mind, I mean, you're saving the world right, and if you take my advice you need to know you can trust me. You can by the way. It's such an honour to help. I was dying to tell everyone I've ever met about the last time you came in—'

'You didn't, did you?' Freya interrupted.

'No, obviously. I didn't want someone to pass it back to the bad guys. But when it's all over you can bet I'm gonna be bragging about it on Facebook.' She giggled. It was sweet really, this woman's belief in the power of good to restore the world. She swallowed, what if they couldn't?

'One more thing, when's the next powerful day to do a spell?' She'd blurted it out before having time to think about the implications of her knowing their schedule.

'Oh, uh.' She thought for a moment. 'Full moons are good, otherwise you'd have to wait till the thirty-first of October for Beltane probably.'

Freya thanked her and paid for her items. Walking back to the office she was tempted to drop in on Theo, but she remembered the mountain of work on her desk and decided against it.

Hettie trusted him, but I can't shake this bad feeling. She shook her head; it was a question for another day now.

The full moon was nearly two weeks away, but the end of October was over a month. Freya didn't believe Victor would take long to find them.

Not for the first time, she wished she had clearer instructions on what to do. The ravens reassured her she was on the right track, but it wasn't the same as having someone tell you. For months she'd been blundering around in the dark, using cryptic information to piece it together and hope. The only thing she'd had proper instructions for was the ritual and that hadn't worked properly.

Could Theo have given us faulty information on purpose? Perhaps that was why it hadn't worked; some element of what Theo had told them was off. It could have been Victor blocking them, but it could easily have been Theo.

*

Freya dropped the pouch to Eva on her way home but didn't linger in the ward. After dinner Freya had a call from her brother Axel. She hadn't heard from him for a long time, the last she'd heard he was living with their mother.

'Hi,' she said.

'Hi.' The silence between them. She should have called him; he'd been dumped and was hurting. It couldn't feel good to be living with his mother again.

'How's things?' she said eventually.

'They're alright.'

'How's my car?'

'Fine. No problems there.' The speed with which he replied made her suspicious.

'Still at Mum's?'

'Yeah.' He laughed but it sounded hollow.

'You okay, bro?'

'I miss my ex. He's been texting me lately. Saying how sorry he is, how much he misses me. How he'll be better. I—' his voice cracked. 'I'm tempted to go back.'

Freya took a moment before she answered, she didn't want to seem insensitive. 'You know going back to him will make you miserable. People don't fundamentally change. He hasn't got his shit together and you don't want to be carrying him forever. You're only considering it because you're living with Mum. Sometimes I think it's lonelier to be in her presence than to be alone.'

Axel sighed. 'Maybe you're right.'

'When am I not right?'

He laughed softly. 'I knew you'd talk sense into me.'

'You called me because you knew it was a bad idea and I'd tell you that.'

'Yeah.'

They talked for a while longer, it was nice to catch up with her brother although when he asked her how she had been doing she found it hard to talk about anything. She didn't want to mention the *Seidhr* stuff, and she and Jacob weren't a thing yet, which only really left work, which was boring.

'You've been quiet today, you okay?' Axel asked after a long, empty pause between them had stretched on for some time.

'Yeah. Just been busy with stuff.'

'What sort of stuff? You can tell me.'

If only I could. 'I saw Eva this morning, in the hospital.'

'What? She's in hospital?'

'Didn't I tell you? She was in one of those weird comas.'

'Was? No one recovers from those do they?'

'That's the thing, most of them woke up, a day or two ago. No one's sure why, but hopefully they don't relapse.'

'Shit. If they don't know what caused it, or why they all woke up I'm worried. But good news she's better.' A tinge of disbelief and hesitation lingered in his voice. It would take too long to explain so she made her excuses and hung up.

Tomorrow would be the first Saturday in a long time when she didn't already have plans to see Jacob. They had all been there for the ritual, they had all sacrificed the same things, Freya perhaps having paid the highest price, but after she left her hadn't even texted to check up on her.

She pulled out her laptop and searched through his social media pages, his last Facebook activity was before the ritual. *Maybe Rhonda had said something,* but why the coldness?

You feeling alright after Wednesday? Did you miss much at school? She texted to Dinah, if one of the Olsen's wasn't speaking to her, it didn't mean they both weren't. She didn't expect an immediate answer, the teen would sometimes take hours to respond and Freya wanted to take her mind off things. She found a podcast on an obscure woman from history and settled in to listen and learn about something with nothing to do with magic or comas or mythological Norse beings.

*

In the morning Freya realised she'd fallen asleep listening to the podcast without cleaning her teeth. Her mouth was furry and her tongue dry and unresponsive. The glass of water she kept beside the bed when she slept wasn't there because she had skipped her normal night-time routine and she weighed up the effort of getting out of bed and the halitosis she definitely had.

Dinah and texted back a little before midnight. **So tired. OMG. Didn't no I could be so wrecked. Jacob has shits with you btw. Dunno why.**

I'd figured that much out myself.

Do I give him space or what? I need him to finish the job.

She stood up to get a drink. Her apartment was cold, but it was almost invigorating to feel the chilly air against the bare flesh of her legs. She opened the curtains and stared out onto the world. The sun was shining, the trees were budding with new growth. Spring was showing itself in myriad ways, but the promise of summer didn't lift her spirits. She had failed to close the portal, and now she had confirmation Jacob wasn't speaking to her.

It was down to her, again. She pulled on a pair of deep grey slacks, a black cashmere sweater and a black and white checked scarf and headed out of the apartment. It would do her some good to get some fresh air and enjoy brunch at the local café. Research and agonising over Jacob would wait until she got back.

She left her phone at home so she wouldn't be tempted to call him, or to obsessively check if he'd been in contact.

*

By the time she had walked to the café she was warm despite the cool morning. Freya took a seat at a communal table in the front room and perused the menu.

The newspaper lay in the centre of the large, battered, wooden table.

'Are you reading this?' she asked a young trendy looking fellow sitting opposite.

'No, go for it,' he replied.

The front page of the paper was about the football, the grand final for the AFL was today, a fact she had forgotten in trying to save the world. She skimmed the article; a key player had been injured and the favourites to win were no longer a guaranteed victor. It was all frivolous after the stuff Freya, and her circle, had been dealing with, but most people were oblivious and things like football were important to them.

She ordered pesto scrambled eggs and a latte and flicked through the paper. Without intending to, she found herself looking for mentions of the coma patients. There was only one mention of the Withered in a brief note on page fifteen.

Several victims of the mysterious comatose condition being housed in Royal Melbourne Hospital have spontaneously regained consciousness. Doctors are tight-lipped about the recovery, citing privacy

concerns. The patients remain in hospital with their conditions being monitored, and treatment being upgraded to rehabilitation. Sources have not indicated any of these patients have been released as yet.

For something that had taken up most of her waking thoughts, and a good portion of her sleeping thoughts too, it only got a couple of paragraphs. She read the rest of the paper with moderate interest. Her breakfast was good, but she'd had better.

She was unsatisfied and restless, and despite distracting herself from Jacob and his mood swings she was seething. What right did he have to drop everything and send her away? Freya didn't believe she could do it without him and didn't fancy trying to persuade him to come back.

All that was left of the newspaper were the sports pages, and her meal was finished. She was about to order another latte when Jacob came through the front door of the café.

'I thought I might find you here,' he said.

'Oh?' She wouldn't be the one to smooth things between them.

'I was calling you, and I went around to your house, but you didn't answer. I worried Victor had got to you, but then I thought maybe you were here.'

'I am here.'

'I wanted to apologise. I was shitty to you the other day. I'm sorry.'

'Thank you for saying so.'

'Can I sit?'

'I can't stop you.' Freya was determined to remain frosty.

'I was freaking out. Again. We'd done powerful magic, not only that but we'd failed. And you were there in my bedroom, and I wanted to kiss you so badly. If the world is really ending, I want to kiss whoever I like, y'know?'

'So, you threw me out?'

'I panicked. I ended things with Rhonda, we're trying to fix interdimensional portals, my thirteen-year-old sister was right there. I felt pervy wanting you the morning after, well, everything.'

Freya crossed her arms. In the scheme of things, it was a reasonable excuse, but he hadn't responded to her since. A waitress approached them.

'Are you having anything?' she asked Jacob.

'Oh…' He looked askance at Freya.

'No, we're just going.' She wanted to continue their conversation somewhere with less people to overhear them. 'Come to my place, I'll make another coffee.'

*

Back in her tiny apartment, Jacob's proximity was much more difficult to deny. She could smell his cologne, woody, and his nervousness, a hint of sweat. It was intoxicating. After so long trying to keep her hands off him, and days thinking he'd turned his back on the mission to find out it was to stop from kissing her. Jacob stood awkwardly in the middle her bedroom cum kitchen cum lounge with his hands buried in the pockets of his jacket. She grasped his upper arms and placed her lips on his.

For a moment she was still, waiting for a response. Initially stiff, he softened and started to kiss her back. She released his arms and pulled away, her lips were tingling where they were in contact.

He stepped forward, closing the gap between them and wrapped his arms around her waist. He held her close to his body, the warm, hard planes of him against her, and kissed her. The chasteness of her initial kiss was forgotten as they began stripping off layers of clothing, heedless of the chill in the room. Freya pulled him onto the bed, his naked body lying atop of hers. The sheer volume of skin on skin contact caused her mind to swim with overlapping images, she pushed them away. The only thing they both still wore were the protection pouches, each on a leather strap around their necks.

'Do you want this?' he asked, trailing a line of kisses along her clavicle.

'I've always wanted this.' Admitting it aloud was freeing. She tried to keep her mind in the present, Jacob's stubble tickling her pale skin, the cold air against her hot flesh.

He reached up and took off the pouch of herbs and crystals keeping them hidden from Victor.

'Are you sure that's a good idea?' she asked.

'I don't want to undersell myself, but it won't be for long. I don't want it to intrude on this.' He threw the pouch onto the floor next to the bed and took hers in his hand. He raised his eyebrows at her, as though asking her to remove hers too. She hesitated, then removed it. It wouldn't be for long.

Once the pouch was gone the images flashing through her mind spiked for a moment, she pushed them away firmly and focused once more of the lines of Jacob's flesh in front of her. *Stay in this moment, nothing else exists but you and me.*

She reached into her bedside table and rummaged around for a condom. 'I'll ditch that protection, but not this one.' She smiled.

He laughed. 'Of course.'

As soon as he entered her, she was overwhelmed with feelings, not merely physical but almost electrical. She'd never felt anything like it, her whole body was sparking with energy. Jacob shuddered, she flicked her eyes open and they caught each other's gaze.

'That's new,' he said.

'Shush,' she replied, using her legs to pull him closer onto her.

How long they were connected she couldn't have said, time distorted, her mind, her vision, her skin, were all ablaze with Jacob. She felt waves of an orgasm coming and when it broke over her, she cried out. A whitish purple light poured from her heart into the Jacob's chest and from his chest into hers. They lit up the sky with their pleasure for what seemed like forever before the light faded and the world started to reconstitute itself around them.

Jacob lay his head next to hers, still inside her. As their breathing started to return to normal, something started buzzing on the floor near Jacob's jacket.

'Is that your phone?' she asked.

'Dunno.' He made no effort to move, and the vibrating stopped. Almost immediately it started up again.

'Might be important.'

Jacob pushed himself off the bed and fumbled in the pockets of his jacket. 'Dinah?' He was silent for a moment to listen. 'I'm with Freya now, I'll put you on speaker.'

'What the fuck are you two doing?' Dinah's voice came through the phone, she sounded panicked.

'What do you mean?' Freya asked.

'Are you doing magic without me? What's going on?'

A cold stone dropped into her belly. The light she saw in her mind was not a vision. 'What do you mean?'

'A massive blast of something. Two, like, cones of light. It felt like you. What were you doing?'

Jacob turned to her, his face pale. 'The pouches.'

They both scrabbled to put the protection pouches back over their heads. She felt exposed, not only physically naked, but magically.

'Victor knows exactly where we are. How could I be so stupid?' Freya asked aloud to no one in particular.

'Oh. My. God. You guys did it, didn't you?' Dinah asked, a hint of childlike glee in her voice.

'We didn't do anything,' Jacob said. His attempt to sound authoritative wasn't fooling anyone.

'That was the biggest light show I've ever felt. Victor is definitely gonna know where you are.'

'We'll go to mine.'

'To start with sure, but he'll find your apartment too.' Freya curled herself into a ball and a shiver ran down her spine.

'Gotta go, Dee. Talk later.'

'Don't take the pouches off next time.' Dinah giggled and hung up. Freya couldn't see the funny side. She had endangered all of them all on a whim. Despite not knowing the effect sex would have on her powers she had gone ahead without any protection at all.

'I'm an idiot.' Jacob thrust his feet into his pants with more force than necessary.

'I should have thought, I was distracted.' The warm glow of their union had fled and had been replaced with a creeping, cold dread.

She dressed hurriedly and shoved some things into an overnight bag. It would be unsafe to come back to her apartment until they'd defeated Victor and closed the portal. Jacob collected the books Hettie had given them, and the notebooks Freya had been working on. Toiletries and her laptop and she was gone.

*

They sat on the couch in Jacob's apartment, nursing cups of tea in silence. He'd retreated into himself again, Freya could guess what he was thinking; guilty for putting her in danger, removing the pouches was his idea, or he regretted the whole thing and didn't know how to get out of it now she couldn't go home.

'I can go stay in a hotel. Or go to Eva's apartment, now she's awake and I can ask her. Although maybe she fell behind on the rent and they evicted her. Imagine waking up from a coma and being evicted.' She was rambling to fill the silence.

'What? Don't be silly, you can stay here,' he said. 'There's no bed in the study, so um, I thought I'd make up the couch.'

'Right.' No discussion then, she thought. She clenched her teeth; they'd given in to the attraction they'd been fighting for months and already he had closed her out. 'Do you regret what we did?'

Jacob looked at her for the first time since they'd arrived. 'There is a target on our backs because of one silly decision. It was my idea to ... I didn't think…'

'I should have known, I had read some stuff about *Seidhr* and sex magic, but I wasn't thinking straight. I'll go.'

'Don't go.' Jacob reached for her hand. 'I'm sorry I'm so shaken. Everything we've been through has been such a rollercoaster, and now this. After being with you, I know what it's supposed to be like—not the light show part—but I never had the kind of connection with

Rhonda I have with you. We fit together. If we could figure out how to not send up a beacon of terrifying magical energy that could be seen across Melbourne, I'd want it every day for the rest of my life, but it's too dangerous. To be in the same bed, I mean.'

Freya's cheeks heated. It hadn't occurred to her. 'I don't think I could keep my hands off you if we shared a bed again. It was hard enough last time.'

'Yeah.' Jacob blushed and cleared his throat.

'Have you still got all the stuff from the rituals down at the beach? We should do another protection spell. It can't hurt.'

'Yep.' Jacob let go of her hand and went into the study. He came back with the duffel bag, looking a bit worse for wear, covered in salt residue and sand. At least all the materials for the binding were in there.

She took out the poppet of Victor and another strand of white ribbon. 'Where's north?' she asked.

'That way.' Jacob pointed toward the back wall of the kitchen.

Freya took the salt, poppet, and new ribbons into the kitchen. 'You need to come with me, it will be better to hide you with the spell if you're inside the circle.'

His face went a little pale, but he pressed his lips together and joined her. As she had before she cast the circle, then chanted as she bound the poppet in new ribbon. They were both wearing their pouches and Freya took Jacob's hands, and wrapped them around both pouches, invoking the protection of Odin and Freyja to keep them hidden from their enemies. Her mind's eye was filled with the image of a vortex of white light surrounding them and disappearing up through the ceiling.

To end the ritual, she thanked the powers for their guidance and opened the circle, breaking the line of salt with her foot. This time when she stepped out the fatigue and nausea were much reduced. She still needed to sit down for a moment, but the world still seemed real, and she didn't think she might die, as she had when she was trying to get away from Victor; tall, lank dark hair, broad shouldered and clearly strong. Not as tall, or as solid as Jacob, but younger and willing to fight dirty. Victor would probably gouge Jacob's eye or bite his nose to win. Jacob would want a fair and gentlemanly fight, even if he lost.

'It felt easier,' she said eventually.

'Yeah.'

'Are you just saying that? You look terrible.'

He smiled. 'I'm wiped out, but different to last time. Smoother isn't the right word, a bit less raw.'

Freya nodded. Perhaps it had not been less taxing in terms of the amount of energy but in the way it had been extracted from them.

'We should ask Dinah if she felt the last one,' Freya said.

'Good idea.' Jacob had slumped down into the corner of the couch. She might have used his energy more than her own. It was almost seven o'clock, the afternoon had disappeared into night without her noticing.

Jacob and I did another protection spell. Did you feel it? She sent to Dinah.

'Is there anything to eat? Or shall I order something?' she asked, gently nudging him with her sock-clad foot.

'Get takeaway. There's a menu for the Thai place on the fridge.'

She wished she could restore some of Jacob's energy, it was hard to see him like that. He'd been the same after the beach. It might have been the singing or because *Seidhr* was a feminine power, she recovered more quickly. Regardless, her caring instinct was coming to the fore. She stroked his forehead, her hand tingled as she ran it over his skin.

*

Dinah replied early the next morning. **I didn't notice anything in particular, the pouches must've worked.**

They ate and retired for the night. Jacob insisted on taking the couch, Freya took his bed. It smelled like him, and it had taken her a long time to fall asleep wrapped in his scent. She thought Dinah was annoyed with her, the tone of the message could be snarky, but teenagers could seem prickly at the best of times.

She showed Jacob. 'What do you think?'

'She's mad about being left out. You made her part of the circle and then didn't include her.'

'How could I? We needed to do it quickly and we can't go to your father and say, "can we borrow you daughter and your kitchen to do some pagan shit?"'

'I'm not having a go.' He held up his hands in mock surrender. 'I'm suggesting that's what the tone is about.'

Freya harrumphed. He had a point. It was hard to remember Dinah was only thirteen. 'What do we do then?'

'Dinah is the least of our worries. Let's leave her for a while, she's not the type to hold a grudge. As soon as we invite her to do anything interesting, she'll be on it in a flash.' Jacob rested his bottom on the kitchen sink and sipped his morning coffee. She looked away, they had to stay away from each other. She knew what his skin felt like against hers, the scent of him still in her nostrils, it was much harder to push aside her attraction now she'd had a taste.

'The full moon is Saturday night. We'll need to repeat the rituals and make sure we close the portal. I think we can do it in closer succession, I felt okay after what we did last night. And hopefully get it all done before Victor shows up.'

'What do we do until Saturday? He knows where you live. We have to assume he's found your apartment. Do we wait for him to track us down here?'

'We could stay with a friend or relative?' Freya thought about staying with her mother and shuddered.

'He'd be able to find our friends. What about someone more peripheral—Theo? Maybe one of Hettie's friends is still around.'

'Hettie's two friends, Sylvie and Ingrid, they were Withered. I never followed them up because we didn't know how to get people out before, but we could try to find them.' Then she remembered Eva and how fragile she was. Freya would never forgive herself if anything else happened to her best friend, despite having a pouch.

'I could ask Eva if her Dad has a place. He runs serviced apartments, maybe one is vacant, and we can hide out there for a while. We might have to pay, but hopefully not full price.'

'Yeah. Can we call her at the hospital?'

'I've never tried.' Freya took out her phone and looked up the number for the Royal Melbourne.

'Hello, I'd like to speak to a patient, Eva Chowdhury, in Ward 5H.'

'I'll put you through to the nurse's station,' the woman on the other end replied.

'Ward 5H.' A man answered after a few rings.

'Hi, I'm trying to call Eva Chowdhury.'

'Ah.' There was a pause on the line. 'Her condition has deteriorated, and she's not able to come to the phone.'

Freya's throat felt as though it dried instantly. 'I was there on Friday. What happened?'

'I can't discuss it.'

'Of course. Thanks anyway.' Freya ended the call and stared down at the dull grey linoleum floor of Jacob's kitchen.

'What did they say?' he asked.

'She's back in the coma. I don't understand.' She wanted to cry. Everything she'd done, the speck of success she felt having brought Eva back from whatever hell she'd endured for months, and now it had all been taken away again.

Jacob rubbed her upper back, and the tears she'd been holding in spilled out in great heaving sobs. Everything she'd been carrying since they failed on Wednesday.

Chapter 22

Freya cried on and off for about an hour. Jacob had gently guided her to the bedroom. He held her from behind as she wept. She had been angry with him for keeping his distance, but he was right, their impulse control couldn't be relied upon and if they screwed up it was the fate of Midgard.

Jacob handed her a fresh tissue and she realised she'd been sniffling and wiping her eyes on a disgusting wet wad.

'Thanks,' she said, although it came out muddied by her swollen nose and eyes. She dreaded looking in the mirror, sure her eye would be puffy and red.

Inhaling and exhaling slowly helped her feel calm, and Jacob's strong, reassuring embrace helped. *If only we could stay like this forever.*

'It's too bad we can't stay here forever,' he said. She stiffened. 'What?'

'Are you in my brain?'

'I don't think so. It's nice. I never felt this close to Rhonda. She wouldn't let me near her when she was upset.' Jacob's stomach growled loudly from behind her.

'We didn't eat breakfast. I was so wrapped up in everything with Dinah and Eva and then I turned into a blubbering mess. You must be starving.'

'I am a bit hungry, yes. I don't mind holding you while you cry. It's been a really intense few months, and I'm useful at this.'

Freya turned to look at him, frowning. 'Do you really feel you're not useful?'

'Sometimes.'

'Without you we wouldn't ever have gotten away from Victor. It might seem like I'm the chosen one because of the eye and everything but your power is as important. I can't do it without you, and Dinah.'

Jacob's cheeks reddened. 'I'm going to go out and grab us something, maybe souvlaki? I'll let you recover a bit.'

'Gee, way to make a girl feel hot.' She smiled.

'I didn't say anything.'

'I read between the lines. Thank you.' She put her hand on his cheek, the stubble there was deliciously prickly. All of her being wanted to kiss him, to press herself against him and make love again but they couldn't risk it. She pulled away and jumped off the bed. 'I'd better wash my face.'

'Yep. I'll be back soon.'

*

When Jacob returned about twenty minutes later, he seemed much brighter.

'I've had a brainwave.'

'Oh yes?'

'We can go down to my mate, George's place, in Flinders. It's a beach shack, but he said we could stay

322

there for a while, and only half an hour from Rye. I told him my place had to be fumigated and I wanted to take a little break while it was happening.'

'Sounds great. How do you know George?'

'He used to work at the hospital, he's a nurse and we got to hanging out. He's vain and obsessed with sport, but a good guy. The beach place is his family's, but he said no one was down there.' He handed her a huge souvlaki wrapped in several layers of greaseproof paper.

'Perfect. When do we leave? What about Dinah?'

'He's out coaching under seventeens soccer, but he'll be home tonight. We can grab the keys from him on the way there.'

Freya nodded. It gave them the rest of Sunday to figure out a plan and get away. 'If Victor knows where I live then he'll figure out where I work.'

'I hadn't thought of that.' Jacob took a huge bite and chewed thoughtfully. 'We'll have to call in sick.'

*

The beach shack was exactly what she should have expected from Jacob's description, but Freya thought he must have been exaggerating. The outside was greying fibro, modernist in style and boxy—all straight lines and no character. The paint was peeling around a couple of the windows and the wooden deck had faded to the same grey as the walls. Inside was gloomy but smelled fresh. There were three bedrooms; the first had two double beds, the second had three sets of bunk beds, and the third, much smaller, had a double bed. It could sleep twelve, plus camping on the floor in the lounge, perfect for family holidays when most of your time would be spent outside.

'The beach is ten minutes' walk down the road, and the corner shop is five minutes further on.' Jacob put the keys down on the bench. Sunset came through the thick tea-tree scrub surrounding the shack, it was almost romantic. She must get her head out of the clouds. They were hiding out because the bad guy was trying to kill them.

The major drawback of this plan was the shack had no Wi-Fi. Her phone could hotspot for internet, but the reception was bad. They'd need to do their research in a café or library.

Freya dreaded the conversation with her boss tomorrow morning. She needed to think of something serious enough she couldn't come in to work for a week, but not so serious they would be suspicious. Of course, her boss couldn't ask her outright what was wrong, she'd need to imply it. A gastro-intestinal upset; highly contagious and she would be stuck in the house for a few days without raising the alarm.

'You've been here before?' Freya asked.

'A couple of times. We've had a few little birthday things and a New Year or two down here. It's not a bad spot. Gets messy when everyone's drinking though.'

If only getting drunk was their biggest problem.

'You think Dinah can get down her on Saturday to finish the ritual?'

'Yeah, no trouble.'

Freya nodded. She sat on the brown wool-upholstered couch, a relic from the seventies. She closed her eyes and rested her head back. A little while later, she opened her eyes to at the sound of tapping on the large windows facing the driveway. One of the ravens had started knocking his beak against the glass, hopping excitedly.

'You found us then,' she said. Jacob stirred in the armchair to her left, looking over his shoulder to see the bird.

'What's he doing here?'

'Dunno, I'll go ask, shall I?' Freya went out to the deck and approached the bird she assumed was Huginn. She had become much more used to his presence in her life, but occasionally she would flashback to February when she'd lost her eye.

Huginn hopped towards her. She sat on the deck, her feet stretched out in front of her, and waited for the bird to come to her.

Freya held out her hand to stroke the silky black feathers on Huginn's chest. As soon as she touched him her mind was filled with the beach. The hole had grown since their attempt to repair it last week. The black inky portal was not as large as it had been, but she felt the power being sucked through it to Vanaheim.

'I know we have to close it. Anything else?' Her mind filled with Victor pacing. He was inside his house, she assumed, dressed all in black. Shoulders hunched and hands clasped behind his back; angry. She couldn't get a good look at what he was up to, Huginn had only watched from outside.

'Good thing he hasn't figured out who you are?' she said aloud. Victor's lips were moving, he was talking to someone. She couldn't see who it was but would have bet it was Barb or possibly more likely, her daughter Mia. As acolytes they didn't seem very helpful, but perhaps he could drain them for rituals and their own talents weren't important. The negativity he carried with him flowed from him in waves.

'He's worried. And more dangerous now because he's desperate to stop us.'

'For all we know he didn't know he could be stopped,' Jacob said.

Freya swung her head around to him; she hadn't heard him approach. 'He was showing me Victor.'

'You were talking to yourself. You okay?'

'I'm okay.' She held her hand out and let Jacob pull her to her feet. 'Have you tried stroking Huginn? I get visions from him sometimes when I touch his feathers.'

Jacob hesitated.

'He won't mind, will you?' she addressed the bird, who bobbed his head in reply, before flapping up to perch on the handrail around the deck.

'I hope this isn't too much of a bother.' He moved the back of his right hand towards the silky black bird. He clearly didn't trust it and was ready to pull away at the slightest hint of a peck, but none came. Huginn cocked his head to the side as Jacob's hand ran down his breast.

Jacob's eyes became glazed and he swayed a little on his feet, much like the trance he would put people in when he sang. His hand dropped by his side and he stared blankly for a few minutes before blinking as though waking up.

'What happened?' she asked.

'It's hard to describe. Mostly stuff to give me confidence to help you. Not images—you know how in a dream sometimes you just know stuff? I knew we'd done it, closed the portal and it was all okay. I knew we'd do it because we already had.'

'Right.' Freya thought for a moment. 'Did he tell you anything about how the ritual needs to go? About what went wrong?'

'No, it was all very vague.'

She grunted. *It's always vague.* As though Odin refused to give her proper instruction. However, they were on the right track, all they had to do was evade Victor for a week and they'd be able to close the wound and bring everything back to normal.

'Sorry, I know you were hoping for something more,' Jacob said.

'We get what we get. We'll probably never know the full story. Some of the stuff I've read about Odin says he's not a straight-forward character, so why would saving the world in his name be anything else.' She shook her head and turned to go inside. Huginn squawked indignantly.

'I didn't mean to offend you,' she said over her shoulder.

Freya went inside to sit on the kitsch couch and flicked through the channels. Jacob didn't come in for a long time, she couldn't see him and wondered if he was communing with the bird or thinking or had gone off for a walk. Her soul felt heavy. She tried to focus on less distressing topics, like whether the woman on the cooking show's soufflé would rise.

It was getting dark when Jacob walked back into the shack, cheeks flushed. Freya raised an eyebrow and looked at him but didn't to ask where he'd been.

'I went for a walk.'

Freya grunted.

'I wanted to think about the stuff the bird showed me. It doesn't really make sense. I think he wanted me to do something in the ritual, like, I wasn't entirely present for the last one and contributed to Victor finding us and breaking the circle.' He flicked the kettle on and pulled down two mugs from the shelf. He looked inside and gave them a rinse.

Jacob sat beside her on the couch, setting her tea down on the coffee table next to his. 'I'm sorry I've been such a reluctant partner. You had the eye thing, a definitive marker where the world changed. I didn't have that, not properly, until the ritual worked last week. Part of me didn't really believe it would work, and of course it didn't, not entirely.' He sighed. She continued to stare at the show on the TV without really seeing it. 'Freya, will you look at me?'

She turned to him.

'I'm trying to apologise. I know you don't want to hear excuses. Huginn helped me to see why I was important. Showed me you can't do this on your own, and I guess I understand now what's at stake. You told me about your visions, but I never saw them.' He took her hand and goose bumps rose up her arms at his touch, she squashed the arousal building in her belly. 'I'm here now, one hundred and ten percent. I believe in you. More importantly I believe in me.'

Freya pulled her hand away and took her mug of tea. She cradled the hot cup for a moment before answering. 'I knew the ritual changed something for you. I need to practice my power before the full moon, to get my stamina up. We won't be able to have long breaks like last time. Victor will come at us as soon as we start. And we'll need defensive magic. I've been avoiding it, but there will be a fight and we have to win.' She sipped her tea, just the way she liked it, and she was grateful he now remembered without prompting.

'Victor draws most of his energy from Vanaheim, that's part of the deal he struck with the powers there, they get the Withered to feed on, and he gets their magic. I don't think he uses the two women in his circle properly. Once the portal is closed, Victor will be basically useless, but until then he's dangerous.'

'What will happen to us when the portal is closed?' he asked.

'We'll go back the way we were before, I guess. Our power is borrowed. I won't miss it.' She ached for the day she could touch Jacob without worrying everyone in the state would feel the ripples of their sex magic.

'If it means it's all over, I'll gladly give up all this magic stuff.'

*

They practised casting a circle, doing basic binding and astral projection rituals every day. Freya took to walking along the beach for about an hour in the morning, Jacob would go later in the afternoon. An unspoken agreement to give each other space. The rituals were tiring, but she became more confident of her abilities with each day. By Friday she was hardly depleted by short spells.

Dinah came down on the train to Frankston on Saturday morning. Jacob had gone to collect her first thing and Freya was alone in the shack reading over everything she could find in the *Seidhr* about defending the self.

The *Edda* had lots of stories about Odin going on spiritual journeys, shamanistic quests, all as vague as she had come to expect of a story about the All-father. Perhaps after a mortal had an interaction with him, they came away with only a dreamlike sense of what had occurred. An ethereal 'knowing' and had to try to reconstruct the story around what they thought happened.

Singular Focus

Odin's powers were similarly hard to pin down. Given she was channelling his will, acting as his emissary on Midgard it made sense her power would be tied to his. Freya hoped she might be able to channel lightning the way Thor had in *Marvel* movies, but Odin wasn't known for doing that.

It would have been fun to smite Victor with righteous lightning. She looked up from the books as she heard Jacob's four-wheel drive pull into the driveway. Dinah jumped out of the passenger seat and ran up to the house.

'Hi Freya. I've been so excited about today. I've been telling Jacob all about it in the car on the way here.' Dinah was talking so quickly Freya wondered if she'd had too much caffeine.

'Hi. It's good to have the team all here,' she managed to say before Dinah steamed ahead with her barrage. She couldn't be annoyed, she and Jacob had had all week to discuss, plan, debrief and practice, but on her own in her parents' house Dinah probably hadn't been able to tell anyone.

Freya had started to get nervous that morning. There wouldn't be another chance to close the portal and no way to avoid a confrontation with Victor. His face was burned into her mind. Jacob showed Dinah to her bedroom, she would sleep in one of the bunks, and let her settle in.

'I'm sorry she's so hyper, I can see you're trying to psyche yourself up,' he said, resting one hand on the back of the couch as he leaned over to address her.

'I'm okay.' Freya put her fingers to her temples and massaged them in small circles. 'We need to conserve our energy, stay settled and centred, I don't know how to get her to understand that.'

'I know.' Dinah stood in the doorway. *I should have known she'd hear.*

'I'm sorry.'

'You want it to go well. You're worried about fighting Victor. Last time you got away without having to do it, but this time he knows we're coming he knows your magic. He'll be on us quickly.'

'Of course you know all of that,' Jacob said.

'It doesn't change the fact I'm terrified *I* can't do it. *We* can't do it.' Freya sighed.

'I've been practising influencing people at school, little things like what they buy from the canteen, but it's been pretty effective. I know you two have been dabbling, Jacob told me in the car. I could kind of feel it, he was more, like, calm about everything than the first time.'

'I'm better at channelling stuff now, we both are,' Jacob said.

'We have a few hours to kill before going down to the beach. We'll need to wait until after dark, when the moon is high, to tap into the powers. I'm going to try to meditate for a while, try to get my brain and blood to stop racing.'

'Great! I love meditating. We can make a circle and like, unite our minds. It'll be good practice for later and

might help get us on the same wavelength, you know?'
Dinah stepped forward to take her hand and pulled her to
her feet. She took Jacob's hand and they formed a circle.

Once their hands were all joined Freya felt the
thoughts flowing through the other two.

*Breathe in through the nose 2... 3... 4.... Hold 2... 3...
4... Exhale through the mouth 2... 3... 4.* Dinah's voice
inside Freya's mind, the muddy quality of her speech
from her hearing impairment didn't come through in her
mind-voice. It sounded as though she was reciting
something she'd heard before, but the effect was instant.

Freya's eyes drifted closed, she focused on the breath
coming into and going out of her body. Imagining the
soft pinkish white light surrounding the three of them. A
cocoon of safety and warmth. She was surprised how
calming Dinah's voice was, waves lapping at the
seashore.

All the tension in Freya's body released, her worries
were draining out of her through the soles of her feet.
She wasn't sure how long they stood there, hands
clasped, but it felt both infinite and over in a moment.

'I've never felt like that,' Jacob said, a few moments
after Dinah let go of both their hands and they blinked
their eyes open.

'Where did you learn to do that?' Freya asked.

'Dunno. It came to me last week, we should, you
know, unite our energies. It seemed like a good idea, so I
did it.'

Freya took a step back and felt light for the first time in months. 'Wherever the idea came from, it was genius.' Perhaps Huginn had planted it, but maybe she didn't need to be told.

Their different talents complemented each other to complete the circle. Freya had forgotten the power of having a team she trusted. Her faith in humanity had been sorely tested in the months since her birthday, all the way back in February.

*

The half-hour car trip from Flinders to Rye was silent. The calming union of the meditation practice earlier in the afternoon had waned a little but Freya was content to be in quiet contemplation as Jacob drove. Dinah hadn't requested music this time. She knew how focussed they needed to be.

The cuts on their forearms had healed a little, and they would need to reopen them. The supplies were the same; the rituals would be the same. Freya expected the binding and untethering to be less arduous than last time, with only a short time to re-establish his hold Victor's impact on Midgard would be much less pronounced. Closing the portal, the third step, would be the difficult part.

Victor may have put something in place to make it difficult for them. Something she hadn't foreseen, but they were much stronger this time, and she had a kernel of confidence deep in her belly she hadn't had last time.

The beach was awash with silvery grey light cast by the low hanging full moon. The sand, sea, scrub all seemed tinted like an old movie. Breezes rippled the spikey grasses. When she got out of the car, Freya felt the pulse coming from the portal: sickly and unnatural.

Jacob took the larger bag; she took the smaller and Dinah ran out ahead of them. Excitement bubbled in the young girl, and Jacob was determined.

The hollow behind the dune where the portal was seemed clear. She saw no signs of Victor or his cronies in the car park, or on the beach but she knew better than to think they were alone.

'I'm going to go through each of the rituals one after the other. We can't open the circle. We know Victor will come as soon as we start, the pouches offer some dampening, but he'll feel it,' Freya said, clearing away the sticks and scrubby debris from around the scar. It was the same shape as last time but smaller and less imposing. The flesh around her right eye-socket tingled.

Jacob and Dinah took their positions around the inky black portal, Jacob placed all the supplies inside where the circle would be cast and squared himself. He looked ready for anything, and he might have to be.

'If Victor shows up, keep chanting. I have a plan to deal with him, but you have to keep the energy flow directed at the portal,' she said. The other two nodded, they'd been over it before, but she reassured herself by saying it. With a final exhalation, Freya started pouring the salt to cast the circle.

'I cast this circle in the name of Odin, the all-father and Freyja, the giver. I call on the spirits of the North,

South, East and West to watch over us as we do our work,' she said as she closed the circle behind her. A cold shiver ran up her spine. 'May the circle protect us under his watchful eye.'

She started with the binding spell, taking the poppet of Victor with the battered sketch of his face, she wound it with purple and white ribbon, the three of them chanting the words of binding.

'I bind you, Victor Mikkelsen in the name of Odin, the all-father, and Freyja, the giver.'

Once the words were repeated nine times Freya place the poppet on the ground and knelt next to the steel dish. The next step severed the ties between Vanaheim and the Withered. Freya cut each reed in two with the runic dagger, repeating the ritual words over each one.

'I sever the ties that join you to Vanaheim.' When she reached thirty-seven, she sprinkled them with sage and set them alight.

'With cleansing fire, I break this bond. From the ashes we shall rise once more, masters of your own flesh and spirit.' They watched the fire blaze brightly for a few moments before dying down, leaving smouldering ashes in the steel bowl.

'In the name of Odin, the all-father, and Freyja, the giver, we release these souls from their servitude and cut the channel from this world to the other.'

Jacob had brought a glass bottle, which he had filled with sea water earlier. She took the seawater and mixed it with the ashes, rubbing the mixture over her forearms, then over Dinah and Jacob's.

Freya stood and pulled the blade of the runic dagger down her arm along the cut she had made the last time. 'My blood is my sacrifice, take it and let my will be done,' she chanted as she redrew the circle in her blood.

The portal, and flesh around her eye, had become steadily angrier as they had been there, the surface once a black, glassy abyss now looked almost boiling. Electricity filled the air; a wind had come up whipping Freya's clothing around her and the previously cloudless night had become overcast. She had no idea how long they had been there, her sense of time was distorted inside the circle, but now they were entering the difficult part. The part when Victor would likely stride back over the dune and try to stop them.

The three on the beach joined hands and started their chanting. 'Let the rend between Midgard and Vanaheim be healed. Let the walls protecting us be whole.'

Freya's mind did not leave her body this time, her legs were tired, her arm stung where the cut had been re-opened. The socket where her right eye used to be throbbed and a warm sticky trail of blood flowed over her cheek. It felt as though it might rain, but no drops had fallen.

Freya fixed her eye on the portal, the roiling, bubbling scar resisted her will to close it. Dinah and Jacob, one on each side, put all their intentions into the portal, their combined magical intent pouring out of their bodies and drawing the sides of the wound together. Jacob's voice had taken on a sing-song lilt as he used his voice-power.

The sides started to knit, tendrils of silvery land-flesh reaching towards each other, reconstituting the ground beneath the portal. The blackness faded towards charcoal then to grey, but Freya's neck prickled. She continued chanting, her mouth moving by rote, and looked towards the hill that hid the sea from view.

Victor crested the hill and Freya saw he had not come alone; behind him were Barb and her daughter, both wild-eyed and frightened by the raw power in front of them. Victor's anger crackled around him, inside her circle Freya could see the lines of energy flowing around him, pulsing in time with the portal to Vanaheim, purplish grey and swirling.

Freya took the hands of Jacob and Dinah she had been holding and drew them together, they would have to hold the circle now while she dealt with Victor. A quick scan of the skies showed two black bird silhouettes of Huginn and Muninn high above them.

'The circle is complete, I am protected, no being can enter my circle without my consent,' she said, picking up the runic blade in her right hand, the blood on her hand flowing over the hilt, and the dagger felt alive.

'You have no idea what you're doing, a dumb little girl and her sidekicks trying to best the greatest practitioner in the world.' Victor's smile held no warmth, he held his arms beside him, palms towards her.

'My power is drawn from Odin, the all-father, and Freyja, the giver. I am their instrument in Midgard. Your magic is unnatural. You cannot win.' As she said it, she knew she was right, this was her purpose, had always been her purpose.

'I will break your circle and I will break you,' he said. Victor moved his hands in front of him, palms facing towards each other circling as though he was rolling a watermelon between them. The energy flow around him coalesced in his hands and started to form a ball between them.

Her mind filled with the image of him throwing the ball of energy towards her, and of a pinkish white barrier being thrown up where the line of salt was, her shield, all she had to do was will it to block his spell and her circle would hold.

The vision faded, and Victor threw his hands forward, casting the ball towards her. Freya crossed her hands across her body, sweeping upwards. As in her vision, a wall of bright energy sprang up where the salt circle lay, and the purple grey ball of energy slid around the barrier. She had held it.

As the wall of light faded, she saw Victor quickly school his face from shock and anger back to grim determination. He had believed her unskilled, and she was, without the flash of foresight of what she had to do, she would not have known she could. He reached back to his two assistants, grabbing one hand each. He swirled a ball of energy in front of him, a larger, less cohesive ball of purple grey swirls. When he cast the ball towards her, Freya repeated her block, only this time it was not so effective.

Instead of flowing around the barrier harmlessly, it stained the white light and punctured holes in it. A few strands of Victors attack got through hitting Jacob in the side, searing his clothes and causing his chanting to falter.

I can't let him attack again; the circle won't hold. She held her hands up to the skies and called the winds. 'I call on you, spirits of the wind to force my enemy away.' She swept her hands down and then thrust them forwards, the dagger in her right hand pointing at Victor.

He had drawn a lot of power to cast his second ball, and perhaps had not fully recovered from it when she buffeted him with the wind. He was pushed back a couple of steps, and the two women fell backwards onto the tussocky sand. Seeing their weakness, Freya spread her hands apart and the winds pushed the two women over the top of the hill out of sight. Victor had drained their power and now he was alone.

Freya hoped her own strength would hold out, she drew from the earth, up through her feet, and from the air around her, but it couldn't last indefinitely. She risked a glance behind her to the portal. The scar was entirely grey, the blackness had gone, and the land had almost knitted back together, Jacob and Dinah only needed a moment or two longer to seal it for good.

Singular Focus

As she turned back to Victor, he had gathered a different kind of energy around him, this time it was more grey than purple, his ability to draw from Vanaheim was diminishing with the portal closing, a smoky flame held between his two palms. The smoke billowed towards her, stretching and reaching for her.

She remembered Odin's defensive technique of turning a curse back on the person casting it. 'In the name of the all-father, I redouble your efforts towards you.' Freya pressed the heels of her hands together, fingers held apart like a flower opening and willed the smoke back towards Victor.

The smoke flowed backwards, curving to follow the shape of her hands. When the smoke reached Victor it crawled over his skin, he was obscured and covering in a dense grey cloud. For a long moment, the cloud swirled around him, angry and writhing, but untouched be the wild wind.

Instead of clearing it was absorbed, sucked inwards. Victor's muscular frame stood on the hillside, as though he was empty. He crumpled onto the sand, vacant eyes staring straight ahead. He had trapped his essence inside himself.

For a moment all Freya could do was stare at her once vital enemy in amazement. Then she heard the hoarse chanting of Jacob and Dinah, valiantly trying to finish the ritual behind her. She turned back to them, took their hands and reformed the circle of three.

There was a great thunderous clap overhead and a blinding white light. All three fell silent. Everything felt different. The air no longer crackled with electricity, the wind died down, and the clouds parted to reveal the moon's impassive face. In the silvery moonlight everything looked eerily normal.

'I thank the spirits of the North, South, East and West for watching over us as we did our work. I thank Odin, the all-father, and Freyja, the giver, for watching over us as we did our work. The circle is now open, but never broken.' Freya used the toe of her shoe to break the line of salt and blood and open the circle. It felt though someone had turned off a noise she had forgotten was on. Her ears felt woolly with the quiet.

'It's done,' Jacob said, his voice hoarse and raspy.

'I think it is.'

The ground between them showed no signs of the scar that had been there moments before. Grass grew out of the sand as it always had. Apart from the salt and blood they had sprinkled there, it looked the same as the rest of the foreshore.

'What did you do to him?' Dinah said, looking at Victor's crumbled shape.

'I cast whatever he was using back at him. It looks like he got Withered.'

'Ironic in a way, to end up trapped like so many others,' Jacob said

'I guess. A bit of a cop out really, he can't be punished like that.'

'The law doesn't recognise magical illnesses caused by portals to other dimensions,' Dinah said.

'Even if we did tell anyone, we'd sound mad—there is no scar on the ground, and there is no way to show what Victor did caused the Withering.' Freya looked up and saw the two ravens flying off over the sea. She walked up the small hill to look for Barbara and her daughter. 'Looks like his two cronies have left him here. We'll have to do something with him.'

'Oi.' Jacob prodded him with his shoe, with no response. He bent to pull Victor into a more upright position, he seemed moveable if not present in any way. 'Here, take his other arm,' Jacob said to Freya. She grabbed his hand and where there would usually have been a barrage of images with skin to skin contact, she felt nothing other than his clammy skin.

Chapter 23

They walked back to the car, half-dragging, half-carrying Victor between them. Freya was surprised how much energy she still seemed to have. After the first rituals she had been incoherent with exhaustion, her arms and legs had felt heavy as though she had stepped out of a swimming pool after too long in the water.

Jacob bundled Victor into the left-hand side back passenger seat and buckled him in. 'His eyes creep me out.'

It was true, his eyes were black and empty, Freya shuddered and looked away. She got into the front passenger seat as the siblings settled themselves in.

'You two okay?' she asked.

'I'm not really sure,' Jacob replied. His hand rested on the key in the ignition, but he hadn't turned on the engine.

'Last time I thought I might die I was so tired, but now I'm a normal amount of tired for this time of night.'

'I'm tired, but okay.' Dinah was frowning at Victor as though he might spring to life at any moment.

'I think the magic is gone.' Saying it out aloud made it feel real. Freya took Jacob's hand and tried to get into his mind, but nothing happened.

'I don't feel people's thoughts anymore. It's like I'm deaf again, there's no noise,' Dinah said.

'You're very quiet, Jacob,' Freya said.

Jacob swallowed and cleared his throat. 'I feel hollow.'

He turned on the car and pulled out of the carpark onto the deserted road. They drove in silence. Freya thought about everything that had happened since February. It seemed like a lifetime ago, her whole world had been turned upside down with hallucinations and magical quests she wouldn't have believed were real before then. She touched the skin around her right eye, it was tender, and her hand came away covered in old blood. The mirror in the back of the car's sun visor showed her scars were faded to almost the same shade as the rest of her face.

They arrived back at the beach shack without any sense of time having passed. Freya was woken from her reverie when the four-wheel drive stopped, and Jacob turned off the engine.

'I'm not sleeping in the same room as him,' Dinah said.

'I hadn't even thought about that. Of course not. You can take the other double in my room if you want,' Jacob said. His voice was hoarse and raspy, some of the velvety smoothness had disappeared, whether because of the chanting or the magic was unclear. Freya had never heard his voice before everything had happened, perhaps this is what he sounded like under normal circumstances.

It didn't make him less attractive, but she wondered if she'd fallen in love with a man she was tied to by fate, and now they'd served their purpose the spark might be gone.

Getting Victor into the house and onto the bunk bed proved more difficult than getting him into the car. He was more like a marionette, floppy and dead weight, than an automaton that could be pointed in a direction and guided forward.

'How will we get him back in the car?' Freya asked, looking down on his prone form. His legs were too long for the bed and he had fallen in an awkward position. She tried to arrange him into a more comfortable pose.

'We can't leave him here,' Jacob said.

'Ambulance?'

'When Eva was Withered we had to take her to hospital ourselves.'

'I thought that was urgent. There's no such rush for him.'

'Maybe we call someone in the morning and see if they'll come. If we rolled him in a sheet like Eva, we might be able to get him back in the car. Dinah, you might have to help.'

Dinah sniffed loudly and walked out of the room, taking her bag with her.

'He seems so helpless now,' Jacob said.

'I was worried for a minute, on the beach. It looked like he got you in the ribs.'

Jacob turned and lifted his right arm. 'He did.'

'Let's clean up.' Freya's hands were still covered in ash and dried blood, though the cut on her forearm seemed to have sealed.

In the bathroom, Jacob took off his T-shirt and revealed a spray pattern of what looked like burns. Some were large, the size of a fifty-cent coin, others were pinpricks, and some in between as though a cigarette had been put out on his skin.

'Do they hurt?' she asked.

'Not really. Like the sensation is far away.'

Freya wet a washcloth under the cold tap and gently cleaned the salt, ash and sand from the wounds. In her first aid kit she had Betadine which she liberally applied to a clean cotton ball. 'This might sting.'

Jacob's belly tensed as she dabbed the burns with the yellow-brown liquid.

'Remember to breathe,' she said. He exhaled.

'It's not too bad.'

'I'm glad. Your shirt is a goner though.'

Jacob looked down at it; the right side was perforated with holes where whatever energy Victor had thrown at them had burned through the fabric.

'Have you got a dark-coloured shirt to put on? That stuff stains.'

'Yeah, but if it gets ruined it's not the end of the world. We stopped it earlier.' Jacob laughed.

'Are you alright?'

'I don't know. I feel a bit, hysterical, like is that it? I'm waiting for something else.'

'I know the feeling.' Despite her gut telling her the portal was closed, the ravens had gone, her visions had left her, there was a lingering fear something else would try to kill them. She sat on the edge of the bath looking at Jacob's naked torso and the desire she'd tried to push down for the last week rose in her. He caught her staring at him and lifted the corner of his mouth in a half-smile.

'Even though I don't think we would send out a magic solar flare this time, my sister is here.'

'I wasn't—you're right.' Freya's cheeks burned. 'Now get out so I can clean myself up.'

Jacob scooped up his ruined T-shirt and walked out, still smirking.

The blood and ash washed off her forearms leaving only a red line where the dagger had opened her arm. Her face was bloody but most of it wiped away to show her scars, healed as they had been the day before. *Too bad I didn't get the eye back.*

She pulled the door shut on the bedroom where Victor lay, trapped inside himself, and the light under Jacob and Dinah's door was still shining. They were talking in low tones, perhaps debriefing. Her own room, the smallest in the house seemed empty without Jacob in it. She'd only shared a bed with him twice but tonight she wondered how she had ever slept without his warm body beside hers. She drew back the curtains a little so she could see the moonlight over the tea tree bushes outside the window. The silvery landscape seemed magical, even without her visions.

Singular Focus

*

Morning sun streamed into the bedroom and warmed her face the next morning. It had been a dreamless night for Freya. She rolled over and realised Jacob had snuck into her bed. He was lying flat on his back and she snuggled herself up to his side.

'When did you come in?' she asked.

'Mmm? I woke up in the middle of the night and wanted to be near you, but you looked so cute sleeping I couldn't wake you. I hope you don't mind.'

'It's a nice surprise to wake up to.' She could smell him; a specific blend of musky cologne and his own smell went straight to her groin. She reminded herself they had promised no funny business with Dinah in the house, and she wasn't going to test her resolve now. She kissed his shoulder and slid out of the bed.

'You're going?' he asked, his frown looked silly on such a sleepy face.

'Too dangerous to stay.' Freya pulled on a hoodie and padded softly to the kitchen. Coffee and fresh air were what she needed. If it were a normal Saturday morning, with her boyfriend, down at a beach house, she would have suggested a walk along the shore and breakfast at the café down the road, but there was a comatose man in one of the bedrooms they still had to deal with.

Several minutes later Jacob followed her out. His cheeks were flushed and was adjusting his jeans. She smiled.

'I've put the kettle on,' she said. The shack didn't have an electric kettle, but one boiled on the stove. They did have a French press and ground coffee beans, so it wasn't entirely primitive.

They drank their coffee sitting on the deck at the front of the house. Freya dangled her legs over the edge and rested her head and arms on the middle railing.

'Do we go back to life the way it was before?' he said.

'The world didn't end. We stopped the bad guy. I don't think Pam or Barbara or Mia are a threat on their own. I guess it's possible someone else will try to do what Victor did in the future but unless the gods step in again we won't be able to do anything about it. My power is gone.' She was sad to have lost her channel into the world beyond herself. The quiet in her head was almost as disturbing as the noise and visions had been.

Jacob murmured agreement. The front door slid open and Freya turned to see Dinah coming to find them.

'Morning.'

'Did you sleep okay?' Jacob asked.

'Not bad.' Dinah looked like she might say more but decided against it. 'What are you doing?'

'Just sitting here,' Jacob said. Dinah sat next to her brother and was quiet for a while.

'It's done isn't it?'

'Yes.' Freya smiled at her, the weight of worry she had been carrying seemed to have lifted and she looked her age again. Jacob took her hand a squeezed it.

Epilogue

Jacob, Dinah and Freya dropped Victor off at the Royal Melbourne hospital. The nurses were surprised he was being admitted as every other patient who had been in the strange comas had woken up the night before. Everyone who had survived.

No official death toll was ever published. Several of the Withered sold their stories to tabloid magazines, 'How I was trapped inside my own head for six months' and the like.

It took Eva six months to regain her strength after being inactive for so long. Her muscles had wasted, and she'd lost a lot of weight. The first three weeks she stayed in the hospital having rehab twice a day, then she was allowed back into the care of her family.

Once Dinah was returned to her father safe and sound after a night at the beach, a story her father never questioned, Freya and Jacob went back to his apartment. They did all the things they had wanted to do for weeks but couldn't because it would have brought on the end of the world. Freya never left his place. Eventually she moved all her stuff over and let go of the rental she had around the corner, it had been broken into and all her papers and belongings strewn around but most things seemed undamaged. Jacob's apartment became a tasteful if slightly cluttered space where they each had elements of their own style. He discovered a liking for flamingos but agreed to keep them to a small number.

Occasionally Freya felt a prickle in the skin around her empty right eye socket, or strong déjà vu but her visions didn't return. She kept Hettie's books, carefully storing them with her novels, ready at hand in case they were needed.

The end.